Jessica
Follow
Share it ...
sharing this
evening with
Becky
apr. 26/13

The Controlled

Becky Komant

BK
PRESS

*Publisher's Note: This book is a work of fiction. References to real
people, events, establishments, organizations, or locales are intended
only to provide a sense of authenticity, and are used fictitiously. All
other characters, and all incidents and dialogue, are drawn from the
author's imagination and are not to be construed as real.*

Published by BK Press

THE CONTROLLED
www.thecontrolledbook.com

ISBN: 978-0-9918115-0-2

Author photo by Sonia Nicholson, Kelowna British Columbia

Printed in the United States of America

Special Thanks

When I decided to take this journey into the world of writing, I wanted to keep it very private until this book was complete. However, I am blessed to have some very wonderful friends who I did share this time with. Thank you and hugs to you for your support and silence through this adventure ... You know who you are!

My wonderful family ... Now you know why I was extra busy. Thank you guys for always supporting me in everything I do. And Mom, you are such an amazing woman. Thank you for always being there and picking up the slack.

Special thank you to Craig Lancaster and Jim Thomsen for ironing out the wrinkles.

And finally, to my dearest friend and amazing writing coach Kimberly Thrasher, this journey and book would not be the same without you. Thank you for all the laughs and helping me bring this to life. I truly appreciate you.

Love you all! XO
B.

P.S. Mr. Gary Fong, it was that breakfast that started this adventure. Thanks!

I pierced the Moon, corralled the stars
To tame the passion of who we were
And are and could have been;
The spilt wine on the coffee table
Tells a tale of blood;
   - John Wayne Wall

ONE

Beginnings

Sarah bit her lip to keep from moaning. As the elevator rose, the motion of Alex's hand got faster and faster. As soon as the doors had closed, Sarah felt his hand slide underneath her skirt. The bellhop's back was to them, and he didn't notice as Alex cupped her from behind and let the tips of his fingers stroke her.

As soon as she saw The James Hotel, Sarah was overwhelmed with excitement of not only a fabulous New York holiday but also a lifetime of taking trips like this with her dashing husband. People treated him like royalty. Whether it was his striking Cuban good looks or the aura that surrounded him, he commanded attention, without having to say a word. Now, as he worked magic between her legs, she knew he had command over her, too.

When the elevator came to a halt at the top floor where The Presidential Suite awaited them, he removed his hand as quickly as he had inserted it, leaving her wet and ready to do anything and everything he wanted.

The bellhop left the luggage cart outside the door and tipped his cap to Alex, who handed him a folded bill. The door had a numbered lock, and Alex quickly punched in the code. Sarah was dying to have a peek inside.

"Wow!" she said softly as she looked around. In the center of the room, a large leather sofa faced a lit fireplace. A white shag throw rug sprawled on the floor in front of it.

Large, red floor pillows beckoned her to come and stretch out in front of the flame.

A door to the left was slightly open, and Sarah guessed that was the way to the bedroom. To the right was a bar and kitchenette. She lay down in front of the fireplace on one of the pillows while Alex brought in the bags. He peeked briefly into the bedroom and then came and stood over her.

"Oh no you don't. Come with me this way," he said. He reached down, grabbed her hand and brought her to her feet.

"Can't we lay in front of the fire?" Sarah asked. Despite her attraction to the plush carpet and warm blaze, she allowed him to lead her into the bedroom.

Sitting on top of the thick satin comforter was a woman in a see-through purple and black negligee. The lace didn't quite cover the tops of her thighs, and her long, dark hair fell behind her on a pillow. Her legs were quite long. She had them extended and crossed at the ankle. She sat with her back against the headboard and casually sipped a glass of champagne.

A tray perched next to the bed held two more champagne glasses, a large bowl of raspberries, a dish of fresh whipped cream, and the most luscious chocolate mousse Sarah had ever seen.

Sarah glanced at it all, then looked back at the woman in their bed. Her bed. *Shit!* Sarah could see her pussy. *What the hell is this?* she wondered.

"Hello, Victoria," Alex said.

Victoria smiled and raised her champagne glass in a toast. "Hi, Alex. Hi, Sarah," she said.

"Who is this?" Sarah looked at Alex. Her confusion turned into a scowl on her beautiful face.

"This is your surprise," Alex said with a Cheshire Cat grin.

"I'm not sure I understand."

Alex turned to Sarah. He grabbed the front of her blouse and ripped it open. He put one hand behind her head and pulled her face to his. He kissed her hard.

Sarah, her desire for him already hot from the elevator ride, kissed him back. Then she pulled away.

"Wait. What *is* this?" she asked again.

"This," Alex said eagerly as he removed his pants, "is going to be amazing."

His cock was sticking straight up already. He reached again for Sarah. "Baby, make love to me with Victoria here. Let her help us have a great time."

He kissed Sarah's neck and shoulders. She tried to process this. He wanted them all to make love?

"I thought we already had a great time together," Sarah said.

Alex lifted his face to her and looked her in the eye. He cradled her face between his hands and kissed the tip of her nose.

"Of course we do, baby, but this is an experience that will take our fucking to the next level. I promise, you'll love it. We'll be gentle with you, won't we, Vic?"

Sarah let her eyes wander to the bed, where Victoria still sipped her champagne. *What were they going to do?* She wondered if anyone she knew had done this kind of thing before. *Is this how rich people live?*

Sarah looked back at Alex. "Is this what you want?"

Alex laughed softly. "Oh, baby, you have no idea. Do this with me. You're so sexy."

Sarah's head was a little fuzzy from the wine she had enjoyed on the plane. She said, "I'll be right back," and went back into the living room of the suite. She walked over to the bar and grabbed a bottle of Jack from the shelf. She twisted off the plastic cap and took a long swig. It burned her throat as she swallowed. She caught her reflection in a mirror above the bar.

"You can do this," she said to herself. "He is your husband. This is what he wants, so it must be OK." She wasn't convinced that it *was* OK, but her pep talk and the booze gave her the strength to see what awaited her in the bedroom.

Alex was lying naked on the bed next to Victoria. They were close, but not touching one another. Sarah still wore her ripped-open blouse and skirt.

"Strip for me, baby," Alex said.

Sarah slowly removed her blouse and freed her breasts from the constraint of her bra. She slid her skirt and panties down together. She had no self-consciousness about her body—but she could feel Alex's eyes burning with passion as he looked at her fresh Brazilian wax.

"You're beautiful," he said. "Come here."

She crawled onto the bed from the foot and slowly made her way toward him, avoiding Victoria's legs. Victoria got up from the bed and picked up the bowl of raspberries.

"You're going to let me have my way with you, right?" Alex said. It wasn't really a question.

Sarah nodded. She had a lump in her throat and was quite sure she couldn't speak.

Alex flipped her over so she was on her back, lying sideways across the bed. Her head was near where Victoria stood.

Victoria picked up one of the raspberries and dipped it in the whipped cream. She placed it lightly on one of Sarah's nipples and gently traced the dark circle, leaving a trail of white. The raspberry was cold, and Sarah sucked in her breath. The feeling was amazingly sensual. Victoria dipped the raspberry again and repeated the process on the other breast. She looked Sarah in the eye and licked the raspberry before putting it into her own mouth.

Then she took another raspberry between her fingers and, with the touch of a feather, traced Sarah's lips. She pushed the berry into Sarah's mouth and let her finger slip briefly inside, too. Almost involuntarily, Sarah sucked on the woman's finger.

Am I really doing this? she wondered.

Alex held his cock and began to stroke himself. Victoria leaned over and began to lick the whipped cream from Sarah's nipples. Sarah lay there, not sure what to do next.

As if reading her mind, Alex said, "Put your hands on Victoria's back."

Sarah raised her arms and placed them onto Victoria's back, and ever so softly moved her hands across the material.

They stayed like that for a minute, with Victoria licking and sucking Sarah's nipples—until Alex said, "My turn, ladies," and climbed onto the bed. Victoria stood up and poured herself more champagne.

Alex placed his hands on Sarah's hips and lifted her on top of his cock, which was harder and longer than Sarah ever remembered it being. Sarah straddled him and slowly slid down.

"Stay right there, baby," he said to Sarah. Victoria was waiting patiently, having removed her lingerie. He reached up and took Victoria's hand, inviting her to join them. Without hesitation she placed her legs on either side of Alex's head and lowered herself onto his hungry tongue.

Sarah and Victoria were now eye to eye, facing each other atop Sarah's husband.

This is fucked up, Sarah thought.

She arched a suspicious eyebrow at Victoria, who simply smiled back at her. It wasn't a challenge—she actually looked like a kind woman. That thought made Sarah give her head a shake, and she closed her eyes. She began to rotate her hips in large, leisurely circles on top of Alex, pressing herself hard onto him as she moved. Gyrating like this always brought her to orgasm, and there was no way she was going to go through this night and not allow herself that pleasure.

At some point they shifted positions and Sarah once again found herself supine. Alex was on top of her, driving his hard cock into her with the force of a jackhammer. Victoria went back to playing with Sarah's breasts, taking breaks to pour champagne into Sarah's mouth from time to time. Sarah appreciated the fact that Victoria did not try to climb on top of her face the way she had done to Alex. Sarah had no desire to go *there*.

Victoria delicately placed two raspberries into Sarah's mouth and whispered, "Don't eat them."

She then covered Sarah's mouth with her own. Using her tongue, she tried to take the raspberries back. They began a wet, slurpy game and, as the champagne and Jack Daniel's kicked in, Sarah soon found herself in a tantalizing blur of sex and lips and breasts and bodies.

They continued for what seemed like hours. Sarah fought to keep her eyes open as exhaustion overtook her. She vaguely recalled Victoria getting out of the bed and retrieving clothes from a small duffel bag. The last thing Sarah remembered before drifting off to sleep was seeing Victoria pick up a wad of cash from the dresser as she exited the room.

The next morning, Sarah's head ached with the throb of a hangover—the kind of hangover in which you wonder if the memories flashing through your mind are really of yourself or from a movie you once saw.

Alex was still asleep. She lay there for a full twenty minutes after waking, not wanting to move so he didn't stir. She slowly got out of bed and tiptoed to the bathroom. She felt sticky and dirty. The showerhead was strong, and as she lathered the soap over her body her head began to clear and questions flooded her mind.

How many times had Alex and Victoria been together?

Was she a... prostitute?

Most frightening to her was, *Is this what married couples do?*

She didn't like the sadness that permeated her insides or the idea that her love wasn't enough for him. He said it himself: "Let her help us have a great time."

She brushed her teeth and studied herself in the mirror. Did she look different now that she was experienced in threesome sex? She didn't think so. If anything, she looked too young and innocent to know so much about what happens behind the closed doors of The Presidential Suite in New York.

She could hear Alex talking to someone and prayed to God that Victoria wasn't back. She strained her ears and mercifully heard the hotel room door close and the voices stop. She left the bathroom.

"So did you have fun?" Alex asked her. He offered her a cup of coffee from the food cart brought up by room service.

"Um, did *you* have fun?" she asked right back.

"Oh, yes. I love you so much. Thank you for being open. I hope it was good for you," Alex said. He untied his robe and she could see his manhood sticking up again, ready for another round. She felt awful. Yet she wanted to make him happy.

"Alex, why did you marry me?" Sarah asked.

"Why would you ask that?" he said. He took her coffee from her and guided her to the bed. He laid her backward tenderly, one hand behind her head as the other slid up into her robe and came to rest in the space between her breasts.

"I love you," he said, as his mouth engulfed her own. He kissed her long and hard, languidly moving his tongue around her mouth as his hand massaged her chest.

She kissed him back, feeling her own desire for him grow. She allowed him to remove her robe, and his own, and they spent a long morning making love over every inch of the king-sized bed.

Sarah traced her finger along Alex's chest, resting and thinking about Victoria.

"Have you ever done that before?" she asked.

"Done what? Made love? Of course," he joked.

"No. I meant, with two other women."

"Once," he said. "It was a long time ago."

"Did you enjoy it then?" Sarah asked, although she figured she knew the answer.

"Actually it was the worst night of my life," Alex confessed.

"Why?"

"It was the night my mother died," he said. Sarah was quiet. The air was heavy, and she felt his body stiffen.

"Would you tell me what happened?" she finally asked.

"One night, I was out at a club and picked up a couple of women. I was eighteen, had a lot of money, we had been drinking, and I actually recall very little of what went on in the back of my car." Alex began.

"Was this in Cuba?" Sarah asked.

"Yes. I arrived home feeling like a champion. But when I walked in the kitchen, my mother was in a heap on the floor. I rushed to her side. 'Mama, what happened? What is it?' I asked. She leaned into me and sobbed. She was out of control. I just held her. I didn't know what else to do. Then I heard my father's voice.

"'It's Tomas,' he said.

"'What do you mean? Papa, what happened?' I asked him.

"Papa stood and motioned for me to follow. I stood up, but Mama grabbed my leg and dug her nails into my skin.

"She screamed at me, 'Please do not let them hurt Tomas. Please.'

"'Why would they hurt Tomas?' I asked her, but she didn't answer.

"'Alejandro! Vamos!' Papa yelled. He was so angry."

Sarah glanced at his face. She could tell that the memory of his father's anger still stung. His eyes were focused out the window, perhaps picturing the scene he carried in his head.

"I looked back at Mama, who was face down on the kitchen floor. I wanted to stay with her, but knew I had to go with my father.

"We got into the car drove into the night. Papa didn't say a word. My stomach shriveled when I recognized where we were going. There was a car waiting. It was night, but I knew the two men who were standing on the cliff. There was a third figure kneeling between them. He had a black cloth sack over his head, and as we approached I recognized the shirt the man was wearing. It was my brother Tomas."

Alex paused again and Sarah held her breath, not wanting to move for fear he would stop telling the story. Alex coughed lightly then continued.

"I looked at Papa. I am sure my eyes glowed with fear. Papa shook his finger at me, 'Not a word,' he said.

"'But, Papa,' I whispered.

"Papa turned to me and grabbed the front of my shirt. He shook me hard. 'Tomas stole one million American dollars from the cartel. They caught him trying to escape. You and I are here to witness what must take place. We cannot fight it or else all of us will be brought to the same end. Do you hear me? You, me, your sisters, your other brothers, Mama. All of us. He has shamed us all and we must comply. Not. A. Word.'

"I saw something I had never seen before in my father. Terror. I hated him in that moment. I hated what was coming. I hated the powerlessness to save my brother's life. My father worked for the cartel. There was nothing we could do. The rest was a blur to me.

"I saw the men fling Tomas from the top of the cliff.

"I saw the Cuban night pass by as I stared out the window on the drive home.

"But then, the worst of all, I saw my mother's lifeless body, hanging from the rafter in the kitchen when we got home."

Alex stopped speaking. Sarah sat up and looked at him.

"I'm sorry," she said. She knew those two words couldn't possibly be enough.

Alex pursed his lips and shook off his emotions. "I left Cuba, determined to start a new life here. One that wasn't controlled by anyone."

Sarah wiped her eyes with the edge of the sheet. She noticed Alex's eyes were dry. The clouded look passed and he reached for her again. "I never told anyone that story," he said.

"Thank you for telling me," she said softly, stroking his cheek. She didn't like the threesome and the way she felt inside as she thought about it, but she had a surge of compassion for this man she married. She sensed that he had been through much more than he told her, and she hoped it would work itself out in time.

The raw sexual pull between Sarah and Alex was unlike anything she'd ever experienced. The animalistic hunger that seeped from him made her desire and fear him at the same time. He was insatiable in bed—always wanting more. She'd never known any man who could get so hard so quickly, and every night she fell asleep spent.

Feelings of shame from the encounter with Victoria lingered. Just when she thought they were gone, she'd recall something that happened that night with a pang in her heart. And if the memories didn't come back on their own, Alex was sure to relive it for her.

"Oh, baby, remember how great it felt to have me pound your pussy while Victoria licked your hot breasts?" he would ask gruffly while they were in bed. It jarred her from any pleasure she might have been feeling and instantly draped a shroud over her heart.

The third time he brought it up, she happened to be looking at his face as he said it. His eyes were closed, and his mouth twisted into a grimace. Sarah realized he was saying that for his own benefit—to draw himself back to that moment in that room—and the thought turned her stomach. *Who was he thinking about when he came inside of me?*

She tried to be the perfect wife. She wanted him to see that she could fix the wounds his brother's betrayal had seared onto his heart. A natural first step, she thought, was to begin a family of their own. She loved children and knew that once he had his own little ones who needed him he'd feel complete.

Three months into her pregnancy with Enrico (or Eric, as they called him), her hopes for a utopian life hit a brick wall. Sarah went up to Fort Lauderdale to shop for baby clothes. She hadn't told Alex where she was going, hoping to surprise him with the cutest little football jersey ever made. Alex, however, didn't find it cute.

When she got home, she found him in the kitchen, pacing. He fumed that she had gone out for the day without telling him where she was going.

He raised his voice, yelled some things at her in Spanish, and before she could process the magnitude of his anger, she felt the crack of the back of his hand across her soft cheek. She sank down to her knees on the tile of their perfect kitchen. She raised her eyes to him, one hand holding her cheek and the other protectively on her stomach. The look on his face frightened her so much, she thought she would vomit.

Then she did vomit.

She remained on her hands and knees. He didn't move, except to inch backward from the puddle. She stared at her fingers as he spat the words for the first time: "You have nothing without me. "

She continued to stare at her hands, not wanting to give him the satisfaction of seeing her cry. "Why would you do that to me?" she wondered aloud.

"This is my house. If you don't like it, you know where the door is." He turned on his heel and left for the evening.

He didn't bring up Fort Lauderdale again, but that incident was the beginning of a new pattern. Each time Sarah caught a glimpse of the life she dreamed of, cruel words and an occasional backhand buried her dream deeper and deeper into the Miami sand.

Following one such instance, she mentioned leaving him. His laughter was laced with hatred.

"Really? And just where would you go?" He shook his head, laughed again, and went out to one of his clubs. She felt like a child who threatened to run away.

The birth of Enrico brought them together for a time. Alex took great pride in his new son, and Sarah and Enrico were inseparable. His smile filled her with such happiness that before long she was pregnant again. The rest of the kids came closely together—four pregnancies, five children. Her final pregnancy delivered twins, a boy and a girl.

Sarah's life became all about juggling children and managing Alex's moods. She came to recognize when Alex's demeanor was darkening and would be on alert against sending him over the edge. Even so, Alex's harsh words and rough nature pervaded even the parts of their relationship that were supposed to be the most gentle and intimate.

One morning, shortly after the twins turned two, Alex told her to pack a bag.

"Why?" Sarah asked.

"We've got tickets to see Holyfield fight Bates tomorrow night in Dallas. We're taking a private jet with some business associates of mine. I need you to look real nice. Go get a dress."

She grabbed her purse and car keys and headed for The Chanel Store. She made a couple of selections and took them to the fitting room.

The first dress was an exquisite one-shoulder gown that fell above her knees. The silk hugged her curves perfectly. Lead-colored sequins twinkled like stars across her body.

Any woman would have been damn proud to carry her figure, but Sarah placed a hand on her stomach and sighed. It wasn't as tight as it used to be. Head tilted, she stared at her arms, her legs. She turned to see how she looked from behind. She leaned in close and studied the face of the woman whose eyes looked back at her.

"Dammit!" she said finally to the woman in the mirror. One word came to mind. Tired. Her body, her eyes, even her hair, looked tired.

Later in life, Sarah would recall that moment with startling clarity. The moment she knew that if things were ever going to be different, something needed to change. Alex was a good provider—actually, he was a great provider—for his family. When he was calm, they had seemingly normal, fun family times. Yet the volatility of his personality and the disgust she felt each time he brought up the threesome stayed with her. Tenderness had melted away from their lovemaking and she felt dirty after each time. His crude sexual remarks weighed on her soul like sandbags and were starting to noticeably wear on her physical appearance.

"No more," Sarah said to herself. She knew then that she was not going to be one of those moms who used her kids as an excuse for why her body and life weren't how they should be. That wasn't fair to the kids or to herself. She knew what she needed to do, and she was determined that nothing would stand in her way.

That weekend, Divine Providence gave her plan an opening. One of the guys traveling with them was a fitness trainer.

"Can you train me?" she asked him outright, after they had chatted for a while.

"Excuse me?" he said with surprise. "You want to start training?"

"No, I am *going* to start training. I need a coach. Would you train me?"

"All right," he said cautiously. "When do you want to begin?"

"As soon as we get home," she said. "I'm not waiting any longer.

The decision to put less energy into trying to make Alex happy, and more toward training and to her children, ignited her spirit. She knew she would get her body in incredible shape and use her nutrition knowledge to begin her own business, one that would eventually support herself and the kids.

Her muscles remembered well the form they had before her pregnancies, and it wasn't long before she was in extraordinary condition.

She trained with the guy from the fight for a few months, then left him for someone who was a better fit with her own philosophies toward fitness. She believed strongly in getting fit using a combination of natural ingredients, clean eating habits, and hard work. With encouragement from friends at the gym, she began competing in fitness modeling competitions. Certifications in personal training and sports nutrition allowed her to formally start training clients herself, and she developed a small, but impressive private client base that included a few professional athletes.

Alex was enthusiastic about her training and showed her off to his friends and business connections. Alex saw *her* achievements as *his* success. Behind closed doors, he took every opportunity to remind her that without him she wouldn't be able to afford the trainer, the trips to competitions, or the gym that he had built at their home so that she could see clients. He also continued to take every opportunity to make her feel like nothing more than a sex object—at his beck and call whenever he got hard, which was constantly.

The more clients she gained, the more she knew she could not risk her industry reputation by having Alex throw her out. She was caged.

TWO
Miami, Current Day

The ride through Miami often made Sarah nostalgic for her carefree days when options stretched out before her, endless as the ocean. Sixteen years ago, she thought the world was at her manicured feet. Now, like a child in her room for time-out, Sarah felt she was ticking off the months of marriage, waiting for reprieve.

"One day..." she said aloud. Her stomach growled in response. She did a mental count of the weeks until she left for New York. Ten and a half.

The Natural Bodybuilding Championships Eastern Regionals were coming up fast and Sarah was entered to compete in the Fitness Model Division. She was in full clean-eating mode, which meant she had no wiggle room for anything other than chicken, egg whites, smoothies, and vegetables. Sarah's ultimate goal was to win Nationals and she knew that to do so, she needed a great placement at Easterns *and* had to be in her best shape ever. She felt cavernous inside. She only hoped she didn't gain weight over the weekend. When the scale went up after a couple of days off, she always felt like she let her trainer down.

She pulled into the parking lot at MP PowerTrain. Mark's gym was twenty quick minutes from her house. Four mornings each week, she spent an hour and a half preparing to win Easterns.

She struck a couple of poses in the locker room mirror, looking for the areas where her muscle lines needed more definition. She placed her hands on various parts of her body, feeling for tightness and definition. It seemed good, but Mark would let her know for sure.

"Well," Mark said as he checked her numbers, "looks like you behaved yourself this weekend. Good job. I was worried I'd have your ass on the stair climber all morning." It was a private joke between them. Many models think killing themselves with cardio is the way to combat calories.

"Yeah, I was worried about that, too," Sarah said. She sat at the rowing machine and began to get warmed up.

"What happened to your eye?" Makeup could not hide the bluish-black semi-circle underneath Sarah's left eye.

"Unfortunate head-butt with the dog. Don't worry, it'll heal before Easterns."

Mark stood next to her, watching her face and counting her reps. Her eyes were not focused, and her jaw was clenched. It felt like she was a million miles away. He narrowed his eyes at her. "Did he do that to you?"

"No," Sarah's lips pressed together tightly.

Mark pushed the matter. "So what did you do this weekend?"

The words were no sooner out of his mouth than her eyes brimmed with salty tears. "I can't talk about it. Can we just train?"

"You OK?"

She stopped rowing. "No, Mark. I'm not. But I will be, when I win Nationals this year. I've got to. I had a shitty weekend. I can't keep up with his bullshit anymore. He's out all night long, he hangs out at the gym or stomps around the house during the day yelling at everyone. He doesn't believe me that I want him to leave. I can't do it anymore."

"If he won't leave, why don't you?"

Sarah's maniacal laughter would have frightened Mark if he didn't know her so well. She began her rowing again, with a vengeance. "Where would I go? Pack up my five kids and move into an apartment? Pull them out of school and move to a neighborhood I can afford on my own? I can't do that. What happens to our nanny? Lila is only allowed to be in the country because we employ her. Should I throw her out on the streets or ship her back to Puerto Rico? My studio is at the house. I wouldn't be able to see my clients. He's got me trapped there."

She stopped again and lowered her eyes, "I'm hungry. I'm tired."

Mark said, "Come on, let's do punching bag."

For the next thirty minutes, she made that punching bag pay for Alex's continued crimes against her body and her spirit. As her fists connected with the vinyl, as the top of her foot completed each kick, her eyes found the clarity they lacked at the beginning of her workout.

As always, Mark knew how to redirect her energy. She had trained with Mark for three years and trusted him completely to help her prepare for competitions. What initially drew her to Mark Peña was the simple fact that his gym was not Alex's gym. But he proved to be a good coach for her.

Her shoulders were more relaxed as she began the drive back to South Beach. One quick stop at the grocery store and she would have a bit of time to get changed before her first client came at eleven a.m.

As she pulled into the parking lot at the Publix, her phone buzzed. An e-mail. It was from Marion, Alex's cousin. Marion worked at a publishing company in New York. Sarah had been meaning to contact her and let her know that she would be there in a few weeks.

Hey Sarah—Alex told me you were coming to New York next month. Can't wait to see you! I ran into a photographer who does some work for our company. He said he also does fitness magazine photography. His name is Gabe Benoit. Have you heard of him? Anyway, I told him my cousin-in-law was an awesome fitness model and that he should look you up. He wrote down your website address and said he'd check it out. Let me know if he contacts you!

Don't forget to email me the details of your visit. - M.

With a shaking hand Sarah turned off the ignition. She read the e-mail three more times. Gabe Benoit wrote down *her* website address? *The* Gabe Benoit?

Every model who ever hoped to land a magazine cover knew Gabe Benoit. His photo shoots could make or break a career. *Get a photo shoot with Gabe Benoit* was number three on her list of *Things to do before I die*, topped only by number two, *Buy a villa in Greece* and number one, *Live happily ever after*.

Her mind began to reel. Was her website up to date? Did the web guy switch out that photo she wasn't thrilled with for the new one she e-mailed him? Forgetting all about her groceries, she changed course to zoom home and check.

She dialed Alex's number on the way. He answered after only one ring. "Done training already?"

"Yes, Mark went easy on me. I just got an e-mail from Marion. She ran into Gabe Benoit—the photographer—and gave him my website address to look up. He wrote it down and everything."

"I talked to her last week and told her you were going to New York soon. When is that again?"

"June 30. Can you call the web guy and ask him to make sure he posted the new pictures I sent as well as the info on my upcoming competition? I want the site to look fresh in case Gabe checks it out."

"You sound pretty excited about this guy," Alex said.

"Alex, if I could get a photo shoot with Gabe Benoit, it would be a huge boost for my career and my business. Think of that exposure! Would you please call the web guy for me?"

"Yeah, sure. I'll do it right now."

She could picture herself on the cover of *Oxygen* or maybe even *Muscle & Fitness*. Gabe's beautiful photography on a photo spread and an article inside that would share with the world that a mom of five children can get in great shape naturally *and* run a successful business. She knew too many women who gave up on their dreams, physical appearance, and health after having children. Freedom from Alex was one thing, but equally important to her was to encourage women that they aren't alone. The spread could lead to product endorsements, commercials—the break she had been working for.

Please let this happen. The thought ran through her mind the rest of the way home. *Please.*

THREE

As days turned into weeks, Sarah's hope of hearing from Gabe melted away, along with her excess body weight. Competition prep and work consumed the majority of her waking time and, for the first summer ever, the kids were so busy with friends and activities that she hardly saw them.

When the twins weren't at surfing or tennis lessons, they could be found in the pool, with Lila's watchful eye nearby. Alexandra's tan deepened daily from long beach days with her friends, Antonio's eyes bore an unfocused glaze from too much Xbox, and Eric—who got his first girlfriend—communicated more through texts than spoken words with everyone.

Only Alex seemed to have an exceptionally high interest in Sarah's training and lurked around the house frequently, which was odd for summer—a time when his clubs did significantly more business. She felt as if he had her on a tight leash, as one would have an energetic puppy, and Sarah knew he was not about to let her run free. He alternated between pushing her away with fierce words that dripped venom and expecting her to perform sexually whenever he snapped his fingers. She could feel an undercurrent of rage building inside of him and only hoped he would be elsewhere when the lid came off and the ugliness spilled out.

On the day her competition outfit arrived, Alex was the one to greet the FedEx delivery truck.

24

Sarah was in her gym, guiding a client through his workout, when Alex walked right in with the package.

"Your outfit is here," he announced, and he began to open the box.

"Please take it to my room," Sarah requested.

He ignored her and tore the flap from the top. "No way! I paid a lot of money for this thing, I want to have a look."

Successful figure models know how to stand out from the crowd. Judges look for body symmetry, muscle tone, and stage presence as they eyeball the girls—but really it is a subjective environment; the judges are going to pick whomever they like the best. It's quite different from a race or other type of head-to-head competition, in which the fastest time or the most baskets scored clearly determine the winner.

The competitors know that how they look isn't the only criteria that will determine who comes out on top. It's about whether the judges *like* their look. Judges often determine a winner based on how marketable they feel a competitor will be for the federation. It is a tough industry, in which just a handful of really successful men and women do well because they have the potential to sell a lot of products and draw crowds for sponsors.

In Sarah's division of competition, she would be required to wear two onstage outfits: a bikini and a themed suit. She spent hours scouring past competition photos and YouTube videos, trying to locate what *wasn't* there. She wanted a theme that had never been done before. She found it.

Florida is home to Rebecca Crowling, one of the top designers for competition gear. Sarah contacted Rebecca and shared her vision for a unique themed suit. After sending her measurements and sketches to Rebecca, Sarah anticipated its arrival for days, and now she was more than a little ticked that Alex intercepted her moment. She had planned to open it privately, as one would open a secret letter from a lover.

Instead, Alex pulled her treasured suit out of the shipping box and unceremoniously ripped off the tissue paper in which it had been so carefully wrapped.

"Stop it! You'll tear the jewels off!" Sarah yelled.

"Why don't you try it on? Do a little show for us." Alex held it up and winked at Sarah's client, a baseball player for the Marlins.

"Please take it inside. I'll look at it later." Sarah's words were tightly spoken through her clenched teeth. In truth, she was dying to inspect it, but she refused to give Alex the satisfaction. She looked at her client, who shifted his gaze to his quads and continued his leg presses.

"Well, you can show me later," Alex said. "For three grand, I better be the first to see it on." He plopped the box and her suit down on a weight bench and walked out.

Sarah was mortified. Thankfully, the baseball player was just as willing as she was to play it off as no big deal.

"I'm sorry about that," she said to him. "He can be an ass."

"Hey, no worries," her client said. "Part of me was hoping you would try it on!"

"Just for that, you get to do twenty-five extra pushups," Sarah said, smiling. She was relieved that Alex hadn't ticked the guy off. He always paid on time and rarely missed training. She'd hate to lose his business.

Even though the client seemed fine, Sarah worked him through the end of his training at a faster pace than normal (including the twenty-five pushups). Her frustration hung heavy in the gym. As soon as the baseball player's Corvette was out of the driveway, she stormed toward the house, blood boiling more with every step.

As Sarah passed the pool, she gave Lila a look that clearly said "keep the kids outside."

Sarah slammed the patio door so hard, a glass that was too close to the counter edge hopped its way off the granite, smashing to the floor below. She was playing with fire, but she couldn't put down the matches.

"Where the hell are you?" she screamed.

Alex strolled down the back stairs into the kitchen, sipping an iced tea like nothing had happened. "What the fuck is your problem?"

"You, humiliating me in front of my client, that's my problem! Why would you do that? Telling him you bought my suit—and how much it cost? Wanting me to try it on? What's the matter with you?"

Alex crossed the kitchen floor, setting his glass on the table. He stood in front of her. She thought for a second he was going to smack her. His nostrils flared as his eyes narrowed.

Holding her ground, Sarah narrowed her eyes back. "You did *not* buy that suit. I did. With my money, from *my* clients. Don't ever come in my studio when I am working."

For a long moment, neither of them moved. Their bodies were mirrored. Eyes locked, fists tight, stance ready.

Alex's lips then curled into a snarl and, with a snort, he spit into her face.

His saliva splattered against her right cheek, and in the shock of the moment her right arm flew out and she slapped him on the chest.

Alex grabbed Sarah's arm and yanked it, pulling her into him. "I pay the bills around here. Without me, you have no studio. I'll enter it whenever I damn well please."

He shoved her backward, and she lost her balance. As her bottom hit the tile, Sarah's teeth clamped down on her tongue. The metallic taste of blood filled her mouth. The full-length window in the patio door rattled ferociously again as Alex left the house. Several feet behind where Alex had been standing, Sarah now saw that Antonio was there on the stairs, his cheeks wet.

A current of sadness flowed between them. Antonio went into the kitchen, tiptoed around the broken glass, reached into a drawer, and got a washcloth. He dampened it at the sink and came to where Sarah still sat on the floor. With the tenderness of a mama washing her newborn, he wiped his father's spit from his mother's cheek.

Sarah swallowed the blood in her mouth, nearly gagging. "I'm sorry you saw that," she said.

"Why does he do that?" The innocence of her ten-year-old's question drove a dagger through her heart.

"I don't know, baby."

Antonio leaned into her, and she wrapped her arms around his shoulders. As they hugged, Sarah could see the reflection of the patio doors in a large mirror that hung near the stairs. Alex stood there, watching them from outside. Sarah closed her eyes and squeezed her son.

Alex saw opposition in Sarah's eyes before she closed them tightly.

Ungrateful bitch, he thought as he watched them. *She thinks she can turn my children against me? She will never have power over me.*

FOUR

Sarah's phone rang as she put away equipment after a client workout.

"Hello?"

"Is this Sarah?" a male voice asked.

"Yes, who is this?"

"Sarah, my name is Gabe Benoit. I'm a photographer."

Sarah took a quick swig of water for her suddenly dry throat. "I'm very familiar with who you are," Sarah said. "Wow, what can I do for you?"

"I met someone who knew you, and she suggested I look you up as a potential model for a photo shoot. I checked you out. You're impressive. You've got true natural beauty." He paused, and for a moment Sarah thought they lost the connection. "Sarah," he continued, "I'm going to have to call you back. Someone just walked in here, and I need to go."

"No problem," she said. "I'll talk to you soon."

"Great. Bye." The line went silent.

Sarah sat on one of the benches and took a deep breath. *No way that just happened.* Her mind went to its happy place—where she was reading her cover story and gaining major sponsorships. She stared at her phone, willing it to ring so she could hear what Gabe would say next. She sat there for forty-five minutes, but it didn't ring back.

She went to her computer and found him on Facebook. Four thousand, five hundred and sixty friends. It looked like he was friends with anyone and everyone. She sent a friend request anyway, hoping that seeing her name come through would remind him to call her. Her request was accepted within an hour, but still no call.

That night, Alex showed up at five, just as they were all sitting down for dinner. He was in a good mood and tried to play the happy, normal family scene—as he would do every so often.

"So, what did everybody do today?" he looked around the table as he asked.

"Daddy, I got ten serves over the net," Elle said proudly.

"You did not," said Ethan. "You only got five."

"No, I got ten!" Elle shouted.

"That's enough," Sarah warned, as she piled some pasta on Ethan's plate. "Eat."

"What about you?" Alex looked at Eric, who was typing on his phone and didn't notice the question directed at him. Alex snatched it from Eric's hand and slapped it onto the table. "I'm talking to you, son. What's going on with you?"

A surprised Eric glanced at Sarah, then looked back at his dad. "Not much. Just been hanging out."

"With that girl? What's her name?" Alex smirked at him.

"Kristy. She's really cool, Dad," Eric said.

Sarah cut in. "Maybe she can come over for dinner next week."

"Sure, I'll ask her," Eric said, as if it were the last thing he wanted to do. He picked up his fork and got to work on his dinner.

"So, guys, I'm leaving next Thursday," Sarah said, aiming her words at the kids.

"You'll do great, Mom," Alexandra said. "I bet you win."

"Thanks sweetie," Sarah said. "Grandma will be here to help Lila while your Dad is at work. She's coming on Wednesday."

"Mommy, will you bring me something from New York?" Elle asked.

"Yeah, I'll bring you back some pizza. I'm starving!" Sarah laughed.

"Don't blow it now," Alex said. "You don't want your stomach to bloat."

Sarah rolled her eyes at him. "Thanks, coach. I think I can handle it."

"You sure you don't want me to come with you?" Alex offered.

Sarah nearly laughed out loud. *Was he serious?* She hadn't even spoken to him in a full sentence since the incident in the kitchen. She briefly considered jabbing her fork into his eyeball but simply said, "No, thanks. I'm good."

The kids scattered from the dinner table as soon as their plates were cleared. Without a goodbye, Alex left for the club. As Sarah was putting away the leftovers, her phone buzzed with a text message. It was from Gabe.

Gabe: Sorry about hanging up. Back 2 business. I want to talk to you more about a photo shoot. You are gorgeous.

Sarah's hand shook as she typed:

Sarah: Thx. I'm going to NY next week for Easterns. Will you be there?

Gabe: No. Will be in Philly shooting a project. If I get done early will hop plane to NY to try and meet up with you.
Sarah: Perfect! I compete Saturday. Can't wait to meet you.
Gabe: I can't wait to see if you look as good in person as you do online. So many girls don't.
Sarah: Well, I guess you'll just have to find out...LOL.

She desperately wished she could take that last line back. Was it too flirty? She hadn't meant to come off that way—but her natural inclination was to joke around. Surely he wouldn't think she was implying more?

There was no reply for a while, and Sarah was just starting to type a redaction of her comment when his next note came in.

Gabe: *We are going to have some fun together—I can tell. I'll maybe see you next week. Good night!*

Sarah breathed a sigh of relief. Knowing Gabe might be in New York was the extra motivation to stick with the last week of training and clean eating. Now she was glad she had gone all-out for her onstage wear. Things were lining up!

By the time Sarah hugged the kids goodbye and got in her truck to go to the airport to leave for New York, her feet were barely touching the ground from excitement. She had received a few other text messages from Gabe during the week. They were casual comments, dripping with overtones of something more to come.

Saturday: *Heading out to a beach shoot. We'll have to get you on the beach one day!*
Monday: *Hope you have a great week as you prep for NY!*
Wednesday: *Went on your website again today. Looked thru your photo gallery—love the boxing ring pics. Damn they're hot! But... I'll do better. LOL.*

Even Alex's bullshit throughout the week didn't bother her. He came to her on Wednesday night, wanting sex. Like everything Alex did, he never asked, he assumed. She didn't put up a fight. She wanted him to be in a good mood for the kids' sake while she was gone, and she couldn't risk a physical altercation with him; a bruise of any sort would affect her body lines and onstage appearance. Afterward, he gave her a thousand dollars in spending money for her trip, and she felt no guilt about tucking it away in her purse.

As she crossed the bridge from South Beach onto the mainland, she looked out over the ocean. Hope swelled in her chest as she thought of Gabe.

During the flight, Sarah brought Mark up to speed on her connection with Gabe, and he was almost as excited as she was. When a model got a photo shoot and article, the trainer is almost always mentioned. This could be a boost for his gym, too. They speculated on who would be at the competition and who the federation had selected for judging.

Mark asked no questions about Alex—Sarah appreciated that he avoided stressing her out—and by the time they landed at JFK, they were both focused on the task at hand.

FIVE

"Sarah Ruiz," the portly woman outside of tent number three called.

Sarah felt like a kid on Christmas Eve. The pre-show tanning and all that went with it was exciting. One more sleep, then the fun would begin. Sarah was chatting with a couple of the other contestants—well, listening mostly as they complained of hunger pains—when her name was called. She was thankful to slip away to the enclosed shelter.

Once inside, Sarah removed her baggy shorts and T-shirt and now, completely naked, faced the older woman with the spray gun. Judi (according to her name tag), had graying brown hair that stuck out in curls from around the thick strap on her plastic goggles. She wore a dark blue apron, stained brown from the overspray, and looked Sarah up and down while she pulled on a clean pair of rubber surgeon's gloves.

Sarah stood, arms spread wide, while Judi gently, swiftly, and with the precision and seriousness of a car detailer, worked her magic until Sarah's skin resembled the warm sand of the Miami beach.

"I'll be right back," Judi said when she was finished. "Don't move." Judi left to ready another contestant, leaving Sarah alone with the mirror while her tan dried.

Sarah heard her phone buzz with a text message. She hadn't heard from Gabe since arriving in New York, and she felt more than a little concerned at just how much that bothered her. She wasn't supposed to move yet, but every part of her was dying to go through her bag and see if the text was from him. Knowing how much she was paying for the tan kept her bare feet rooted.

A few minutes later, Judi returned. She walked slowly around Sarah, scrutinizing for any sign of unevenness in coloring. After a couple of touch-ups and a few more minutes' wait, Judi told Sarah she could get dressed.

"Remember," Judi warned, "only loose clothing tonight. I'll be here at six a.m. if you need anything in the morning."

"Got it. Thanks!" No chance she would smudge the tan. Sarah planned to spend a quiet evening in her hotel room, unless of course Gabe was able to jet over from Philly early. Her insides leapt at the thought—but again came the uneasiness that she was feeling something she shouldn't.

The World Bodybuilding and Fitness Eastern Championship event had taken over The Hilton in New York. As Sarah left the conference room that was the temporary headquarters for Fabu-Glam, the tanning, hair and makeup company for the show, she stopped and looked around. Competitors sat throughout the lobby, chatting in small groups. Some talked on cell phones, but most were mingling, sizing each other up for competition. A Yankees game played on a big-screen television. As she took it all in, she felt happy inside, the way you feel when you arrive at a favorite vacation spot. The intensity of competition fueled her soul. She took a deep breath, filling her head with the bitter, rancid smell of the tanning product. Although it was an assault to her nostrils, she didn't mind. She was where she wanted to be.

Sarah took her phone out of her bag and checked the message. It was, indeed, from Gabe. Her hand shook as she pressed the button to read the message.

Gabe: How's New York?
Sarah: Amazing. Just got my tan on.
Gabe: Nice. I bet you look great!
Sarah: Will you get to come & see the show?
Gabe: Not sure yet. If I can, I'll be there tomorrow afternoon. Before the nite show.
Sarah: 'K. Hope to see you!
Gabe: Knock em dead!

"Hey, nice tan." Mark walked up while she was reading Gabe's encouragement.

"Yeah. Want to get a drink?" Sarah suddenly thought she'd rather sip a glass of Cab Sauv in the bar than sit in her room alone.

"You gonna wear that?" Mark gave her baggy, bra-less T-shirt and shorts a once-over.

"I'll be right back," Sarah left him there and went up to her room. She pulled on a loose-fitting summer dress and slid on sleek, strapless sandals. While she was changing, her phone buzzed again.

Gabe: Back in my room. Just wanted to say good nite!
Sarah: You're in early. No hot date? LOL.
Gabe: It's weird. All I can think about is you. I know that's bad, because you're married. I don't know what it is, though. I can't wait to meet you.

Her heart did a flip. *He felt it too?* She wasn't sure what to say next.

Mark: Where r u? Your wine is here.

She wanted badly to tell Gabe that her marriage was at its end—but it wasn't a quick and easy conversation. She returned to Mark in the lobby, intent on responding to Gabe later.

They got comfortable in the Bridges Bar. Her phone buzzed again.

Gabe: I'm sorry. Was that wrong of me to say?

Mark saw her face when she read the text and asked, "Who is that from?"

"Gabe Benoit," Sarah said casually.

Mark's eyebrows shot up. "What does he want?"

Me, Sarah said in her head and smiled, but aloud she said, "Oh, he's going to try and make it here for tomorrow night so we can meet." She typed out a reply.

Sarah: It's ok. My marriage is complicated. I'll tell you more later. ;)

"Are you drinking wine?" Another contestant, a girl Sarah knew from prior competitions, had come over to their table. "That's so bad!"

"It isn't, really. I always drink one glass before competition," Sarah smiled.

"You're so lucky. I haven't been able to drink anything since last night," she seemed almost proud of her statement, but Sarah pitied her. Some girls just didn't get it. Why in the hell would someone not drink?

Mark and the girl-without-a-clue struck up a conversation. Mark was well-built and had a nice face—and he was single. They ignored Sarah as she went back to her text messaging with Gabe.

Sarah: Hey!
Gabe: Hey. So what's complicated mean?
Sarah: We've been living separate lives for a while.
Gabe: Same house?
Sarah: Yeah. For the kids.
Gabe: Wow. I didn't know.

Sarah took a sip of her wine and contemplated what to say next. Gabe beat her to it.

Gabe: So what happened?
Sarah: He's got a lot of problems. Violence. Anger.
Gabe: Really? Violence?
Sarah: Yeah. The first time he hit me I died a bit inside. It's been downhill from there.

The seconds seemed like hours until Gabe replied.

Tell me what happened.

The last thing Sarah wanted to do was relive everything, especially while sitting in the hotel bar. She knew, though, that she wanted to open her box of secrets for him, but once the lid came off too far, the box would be impossible to slam shut. Out would spill all of Alex's cruelty. His assaults on their marriage. Especially his unwillingness to let go of her. How she handled Gabe's simple words meant that either Gabe would become a part of her secret world, or that he would remain an outsider to her life. A need to unburden herself took over, and she began to type.

Sarah: It started a long time ago. When we got married, actually. I'm just numb to it all now. Biding my time.
Gabe: For how long?
Sarah: I don't know. I've got 5 kids. He won't let me move and he won't go either.
Gabe: Do you love him?
Sarah: He can be such an ass. I can't love him anymore.
Gabe: Can't?
Sarah: When you've taken the abuse I have you know when you've given all you've got.

She waited to see how he would react to that word, abuse. He didn't. Sarah filled the silence:

Sarah: He stays in another bedroom in the house. We're separated.

She wasn't sure why she felt the need to let Gabe know that she and Alex didn't share a bed.

Gabe: That's pretty rough. I'll try and make it there tomorrow. We'll get you a photo shoot and launch your career so high—you'll get all the things you really deserve.
Sarah: It's fate that we've connected! I can tell.
Gabe: I agree. You better get some rest.
Sarah: Yep. Good nite!

That night, while in bed, she read the messages over and over. She hadn't really confided that she and Alex were separated to anyone but her mom and one close friend. It was weird and exciting to have shared such a private matter with Gabe. It felt like he was on her side. Finally she had someone in her life to stand with her as she fought for her freedom. Within minutes she was in a deep, contented sleep.

SIX

Sarah stood firmly on her clear acrylic heels; eighth in the lineup of ten girls across the stage. It was the morning bikini judging, and before walking out, as Sarah reviewed her competitors, she felt stronger than ever. The judges had the girls do a series of quarter turns, then rearranged the girls for better comparison. Sarah wasn't at all surprised that they moved her to the prime spot—the center—of the lineup.

The girls were scheduled to appear twice onstage in the morning and twice in the evening; once in bikinis and again in a theme-wear outfit. The morning showing was where the bulk of the judging happened, and the evening show was where muscle met glamour, with more than a hint of seduction thrown in.

There were sixty-four women in Sarah's class of competition. In this kind of competition, the contestants came out in groups of ten to twelve until everyone was on stage. The judges then called forward the top ten. They lined up and were requested to go through a series of turns and poses while the judges compared and scored them. They moved the girls around so that the top three—usually—were centered in the line.

After the morning judging, Sarah felt confident that she held a top-three placement, but until the evening show was over, she couldn't know how things would turn out.

It's easy to let your attitude shine in the evening. Everything about the night event screams sexy, and the New York show did not disappoint. Even at seventy-five dollars a ticket, The Hilton was packed—the latest *American Idol* winner on the program added to the draw. Sarah thought the young black kid from Chicago had a soulful voice that made her want to scoop him up in her arms and take him home so he could sing to her every night. He revealed his new song just before her group went out in their theme wear, and the words seeped into her skin and made her want to win all the more.

> *I've got the world at my feet, it's my turn to shine.*
> *The ball is in my court, I've labeled it mine.*
> *This time I'm coming. I'm coming out on top.*
> *You do your thing—but I ain't gonna stop.*

She walked tall in the theme-wear round, forgetting how Alex had marred her excitement of the outfit she designed. Rebecca Crowling had really outdone herself in bringing Sarah's vision to life. Sarah had never seen anyone in competition do a mermaid-themed outfit. The coral-colored bandeau top was glitzed out with countless jewels that caught the light and danced it right off of her chest again. The bottom was a wrap-around mermaid tail in ocean shades that ran all the way down the back of her legs to the floor, trailing slightly behind her.

Her hips swayed perfectly to the beat with her lean, defined legs stretching forward in long, purposeful steps. Just as she reached the front of the stage, a smooth swipe of her hand pulled the tail from its spot, revealing a jeweled bikini bottom underneath. Sarah managed the motion perfectly, and she thought she actually heard a gasp from the front row. A satisfied smile radiated from her face.

Later that night, as the kid from *American Idol* hung the first-place medal around her neck, she knew the world really was at her feet.

She desperately hoped Gabe was somewhere in the audience, perhaps front row with the photographers, living the moment with her. Her eyes searched the faces, wanting to find one that matched the headshot on Gabe's website. They landed on no one who stood out.

No sooner was she offstage than she was bombarded with congratulatory hugs from the other girls. Cameras flashed as photographers milled around, snapping impromptu shots. Women crowded her in their own effort to get photographed with the Fitness Model Winner. She posed, showing her trophy and soaking in every smile that flashed her way. She tried not to let her gaze wander past the people who stopped to speak to her. She knew if Gabe were there that he would find her, yet the more people who came around who *weren't* Gabe, the more disappointed she felt.

"Mind if I take your picture?" Sarah heard a male voice ask as she gathered her things. She turned around, ready to hug Gabe, then stopped short. The man standing before her was at least four inches shorter than she was. And overweight. And, well, ugly.

Sarah reined in her emotions. "Um, do I know you?"

"Of course, Sarah, it's me," the man, who was smiling a second ago, now looked truly hurt.

"Gabe?" This man looked nothing like the picture on his website. The web pic was just a headshot, but still.

"Gabe? Who's Gabe? Sarah, it's me, John. I met you last year at the Dallas show."

"John!" Sarah exclaimed, relief oozing from her. "I'm sorry. I was waiting for someone and was lost in thought. How are you?"

"I'm great thanks. Mind if I snap a picture?" John held up his camera and took a couple of shots.

"That's perfect. You looked stunning tonight," he said, shyly. Then he added quickly, "Want to grab something to eat?" There was hope in his eyes.

"Sorry, I can't. I've got an early flight out in the morning, and I'm exhausted."

She exchanged pleasantries for a few more minutes and then politely excused herself. She had heard her phone buzz in her bag and itched to see who it was.

Gabe: How'd you do?
Sarah: You didn't get to see me win!
Gabe: Hey, that's great! Congrats. Definitely next time.
Look out Nationals!
Sarah: :)
Gabe: Going out to celebrate?
Sarah: Maybe. I need to catch up with some friends and see what's going on. I'll chat with u later.

She cut him off on purpose. She'd been in the industry long enough to know that women (and men) gushed over people they thought could boost their career. It didn't sit well in her gut that she was so frustrated and disappointed that he didn't make it to New York. Her head felt cloudy—unable to distinguish between the budding friendly banter and her desperate need for that photo shoot.

SEVEN

"Come on, Tanya. Five more!" Sarah counted out her client's remaining arm curls.

Tanya dropped the weights to the floor. "You're killing me today."

"It's been two weeks since you've trained. What do you expect?" Sarah said enthusiastically. All of Sarah's clients were in town this week, and the routine of a full schedule was calibrating to her spirit.

Sarah's chest vibrated and she pulled her phone out of her sports bra. She glanced at the screen and smiled.

"Sarah," Tanya said. "Who is he?"

Sarah looked up at Tanya and grinned. "Just a guy."

"No such thing," Tanya scolded. "Come on, don't keep him from me."

"OK, I've actually been dying to tell you, but you haven't been around," Sarah said. "I've met a guy. He's a photographer. He's charming. He's so hot. *And...* he's going to get me a magazine cover for *Oxygen*."

"No freakin' way!" Tanya gave her friend a playful shove. "Get out of here! Can he do that?"

"He's one of the top shooters in the industry. If anyone can get me a cover, it's him."

"So how'd you meet? I want details." Tanya grabbed her water bottle and sat on the mat.

"Alex's cousin told him about me, and he looked me up before Easterns," Sarah explained. "Since Easterns, we've chatted a few times and have been texting. A lot. Here, listen to this." Sarah scrolled through her phone and read aloud some of Gabe's messages.

"I'm shooting down at Malibu today. These girls have nothing on you. You're the total package."

Sarah clicked to another one. "I can't stop thinking about your gorgeous body. I can't wait to touch you. I can't wait for you to touch me."

"Sarah!" Tanya exclaimed. "So is this serious? Or what? Does Alex know?"

"I don't know if it's serious, but damn, he's sweet. We've spent hours on the phone. It's like I can talk to him about anything. Here, listen to this one. 'It makes me crazy to think you're so far away. Soon we'll meet up and you'll be my cover girl.' I swear, Tanya, the last couple of times Alex has forced himself on me, I've pretended it was Gabe to get through it."

"That's twisted, girl, but you do what you have to, right?" Tanya was married and had two kids of her own, but she also had a wild streak that only a couple of people knew about. Sarah was one of them. Of all of Sarah's friends, Tanya was the only one who really knew about Alex and Sarah's sexually dysfunctional relationship. When Sarah had told Alex she was serious about either going to counseling for his anger and volatility or else she wanted a separation, he had initially exploded and then had laughed in her face. Tanya was there to help Sarah through that rough night. When Alex began to force her to exchange sex for living expenses and told Sarah that he refused to leave the house, Tanya held Sarah's hand while she vented. A few months earlier, Tanya had helped Sarah move Alex's things to the nanny's quarters and relocated Lila to the guest room in the main part of the house.

Most helpful to Sarah was that each time Alex barraged her to participate in his warped fantasies, Tanya was Sarah's sounding board. She was the one safe place where she could unleash her frustrations. Sarah relied on Tanya to help her stay sane.

"How are things going this week with him?" Tanya nodded toward the house.

"Alex? He's been all, 'You wouldn't have won Easterns without my money getting you there. So you owe me a blow job.'" Sarah rolled her eyes. "I can't wait till I can tell him to fuck off."

Tanya laughed. "I can't wait to see the look on his face when that happens. I don't know many moms who'd put up with the shit you do for the sake of her kids."

Sarah shrugged. "After sixteen years, what's a few more months? I'm going to do this photo shoot, earn a major sponsorship, and tell Alex where he can stick his money. Who knows? Maybe I'll get a great guy out of it, too." She nodded to her phone, which buzzed again.

Gabe: *Did you get any surprises today?*

Just then, the door to her studio opened and Alex walked in carrying an enormous purple and green blown glass vase filled with white and lavender roses, calla lilies, and purple mokara orchids.

"Special delivery," Alex said unenthusiastically.

"What are these for?" Sarah asked.

"I don't know, you tell me," Alex retorted. He set them down on the ground and took the card from the center of the arrangement. "Here."

Sarah and Tanya exchanged curious looks, and Sarah opened the envelope, revealing a simple white card that read, *Congratulations on your big win. Next stop: Cover Girl. –G.*

"Who is it from?" Alex asked.

"That photographer I told you about. Congratulating me on Easterns." Sarah said cautiously.

"He must want to fuck you," Alex said.

"Can't anyone just congratulate me to make me feel good?" Sarah couldn't quite pull off the indignation. She suspected Gabe wanted more, and she did too.

"No," Alex said stoically, "not like this. Want me to leave these here?"

"Could you put them on the table by the stereo?" Sarah asked.

Alex moved the vase and left without another word. Sarah and Tanya looked at each other.

"He does want to fuck you, you know," Tanya said matter-of-factly.

Sarah smiled. "I'm sure he's around gorgeous women all day. I don't know why he'd waste his time on me, a mom of five who lives across the country."

"It's like he said. You're the total package. Three-quarters of the girls in your industry have nothing but their bodies going for them. If anyone gets a firsthand look at that, it is a photographer. He knows quality when he sees it. Have some confidence, will ya?" Tanya grabbed her things. "I've gotta go. I'll see you Thursday."

With Tanya gone, Sarah replied to Gabe's text.

Sarah: OMG. These are the most beautiful flowers I've ever seen. They're my favorite colors too. How'd you know? Thank you.
Gabe: You deserve them. And so much more.
Sarah: Why are you so interested in me?
Gabe: Sarah, I feel so close to you. It's weird, but like we are connected somehow. I meet so many women who don't get it. I want to get to know you better and see what happens.
Sarah: I'd like that.
Gabe: I can tell you deserve so much more than you're getting. I'm here for you.

Sarah pulled the card out of the envelope and read it again. "Cover Girl," she said aloud. She liked the way that sounded.

Both of Sarah's afternoon clients were traveling and had canceled their training, leaving Sarah with time to sit by the pool and plan next week's workouts so she could stay ahead of the game. Her eyes kept wandering to the flowers on the kitchen counter, which she could see through the patio doors.

Is this guy for real? Or is this bullshit? She abandoned her planning as she considered these questions to do some investigating. She looked up Gabe's website again. She had noticed before that Gabe blogged, but she hadn't had time to check it out. She opened it up on her iPad.

His posts were light on text and included lots of pictures of his projects. As she read through the most recent, she felt a bond with the words and pictures. It was like she was there, alongside him.

With a smile, she viewed the amazing pictures he shot for a fitness wear ad in Los Angeles. She looked at her phone and scrolled through to find his corresponding text message that read, *Had a shoot in LA yesterday. I kept imagining it was your body I was photographing. You are beautiful.*

She went back through the last few posts like that—matching blogs and tweets to her love notes and feeling sweet affection for this talented man. Then she got to posts that were from before she met him. These were the ones she was really interested in. What did he do before he entered her world?

It didn't look like he did anything differently—alternating posts about work, projects, and trips. Then she saw a picture of two very cute teenage boys holding gigantic vanilla ice cream cones. The caption read: *No work today. Spending time with my boys. Happy Father's Day!*

She stared at the two handsome faces. Her happiness melted, dripping away like the ice cream leaking from the cone that the younger boy, maybe thirteen years old, held. Gabe never mentioned he had kids.

Stomach knotted, she clicked over to Facebook. She hadn't really scrutinized his page—but thought perhaps she should. He didn't have any family members listed. She clicked on his friends list and scanned the names. Derek Benoit jumped out at her. The face in the thumbnail pic was the same as the older boy in the photo on his website. She clicked on the boy's name and it went right to his page. Obviously he didn't have his security set to private.

She looked at his family list.
Gabe Benoit - father
Kelly Jones - mother
She glanced again at the flowers in her house, then took out her phone.

Sarah: Why'd you send me the flowers?

A full ten minutes went by.

Gabe: I like you. A lot.
Sarah: Does your wife Kelly know you sent them?

The response came back right away.

Gabe: Wife? I don't understand.
Sarah: *Your boys are beautiful.*

This answer, too, was long in coming.

Gabe: I see you do your homework. Yes, I have two boys.
I'm divorced.
Sarah: I would have thought you'd have mentioned it.
Gabe: I don't put my kids out in the public view much.
Sarah: I've been pouring my heart out to you about my problems. I suddenly realize I don't really know you.
Gabe: Sarah, you're an amazing woman. I really like you. In time, my Princess. You'll get to know it all. I promise.

His statement seemed shallow. Sarah's mind was spinning, and she was convinced in that moment that he was toying with her—using her for something and she had no idea what.

Sarah: I bet you say that to all the models. Do you have accounts at flower shops across America?
Gabe: I have never sent flowers to a model.
Sarah: Right. Listen, you seem really sweet, but I can't be hurt. If this is just a game for you, then you can keep your photo shoot. Your messages seemed to indicate you cared about me and my life, but I don't need to be played with. I've got enough going on. Maybe we should call it quits.
Gabe: Wow.

Sarah sat back and took a sip of her tea. She inhaled deeply and let it out slowly. She closed her eyes and leaned back in her chair. *This is OK,* she thought. *I'll get a cover shot another time.*

Then her phone rang.

"Hello," she said.

"It's me," Gabe said.

"Hi," she replied sourly.

"Sarah, you've impressed the hell out of me. You are definitely the real thing. You know what you want, you have priorities, and I really do like you. Most girls would do whatever they had to for a photo shoot. I can tell you care, too. That's so refreshing. Please don't think I'm playing with you."

"Really?" she said quietly.

"Really. Trust me. We'll keep learning all about each other. I only think about you. We are closer to each other than you believe."

It was after midnight when Sarah heard her phone buzz again. Ethan had a nightmare, and she was just climbing back into bed after comforting him when she heard it.

Gabe: Don't know if you're up or not, but I wanted you to know I'm lying in bed watching porn and thinking of you.
Sarah: Should I be flattered?
Gabe: I turned on the porn because I couldn't see you. I'm sorry, but I am so hot for you.
Sarah: I'm sure you could find someone there who'd play with you.
Gabe: I can't believe you'd say that after our talk this afternoon. You don't get it. I want YOU. I am not a player.
Sarah: How can I really know you don't do this with all the pretty faces?
Gabe: That hurts. I care about you.

Sarah so wanted Gabe's affections to be for her alone. He didn't send another message. Sarah couldn't decipher if it was her mind playing tricks on her, making her doubt his sincerity or if he genuinely cared. She felt tossed back and forth like a ship on stormy waters. Guilt for doubting him swelled in her chest. Feeling bold, she removed her shirt and took a picture of herself from the waist up, staring longingly into the camera. She sent it to him.

A few minutes later her phone buzzed. It was a picture of his midsection. He had a very large and very hard dick. He also had the most gorgeous abs she'd seen in a while.

Sarah: You look like you could be a model yourself.
Gabe: I did some modeling. Before I got into photography.
I prefer working the back end of the camera. I'd love to
work your back end. ;)
Sarah: I'd like that. Shall I bring the whips? Lol.

A few minutes later her phone rang.

"Hello?" she said.

"Hi, beautiful," Gabe said.

"That's quite a picture you sent me," she said. "I don't know if I should be impressed or afraid of what you could do with that thing."

"You should be excited. The things I want to do to you will make you quiver with pleasure."

"That sounds intriguing."

"Tell me what you would like me to do to you." Gabe's voice was so low, so intense.

"How about I show you?" she suggested, her voice husky.

"Really? What do you mean?"

"Hang on," she said.

She put the call on hold, got up and locked her bedroom door. She removed her panties and tank top and snapped a sultry picture of herself, massaging her breast. She sent it to him.

"Did you get my present?" she asked.

"Oooh yes," he cooed. "You have perfect breasts. I want to massage them myself."

"Well, maybe if you play your cards right, you'll get to."

"I can't wait," he said. "What else do you have? I want another picture."

"You're awfully greedy," she said.

"I've seen a bit. I want more. Show me your pussy."

"Wow, you don't beat around the bush." She smiled to herself at the double entendre.

"Not when I know what I want," he answered.

"You owe me something first," she said.

A minute later she received a text message of his stiff cock with his hand holding the shaft.

"That's better," she whispered to him. She took her vibrator from her bedside table and placed the tip of it against her clit. She took another picture and sent it to him.

"Oh baby," he said. "I want you to use that and let me hear you make yourself cum."

She switched it on and began to massage herself, increasing the speed and intensity, and letting him hear her moan her pleasure.

"When you come, I want you to say my name," he insisted, as he sensed she neared her orgasm.

"Oh Gabe, I am coming now," she said, her voice breathy.

"Yes, babe, make that pussy come for me," he said.

"Oooh, yes," she finished, and she lay there for a moment without speaking.

"Princess, you are amazing," he said.

She sent him a final picture of her, blowing him a kiss goodnight.

EIGHT

The next morning she awoke to an e-mail from Gabe:

Sarah, Sarah, Sarah:
About that performance last night... well... I'll let you hear from the judges how you did...

From Randy: "That is a Number One smash hit. It sounded pretty exciting from here. This was your best performance yet—not too long, not too short—and you gave one hell of a finish. The question I have is, can you repeat that execution nightly?
From Ellen: I was so excited about that performance I actually forgot about Portia. What are you doing tonight? Got time for dinner?
From Kara: Truly a classy act. I am sure all the men watching were standing up and wondering if they could get "in" for tonight's show. Truly enticing for all.
Simon: Sarah, that was your best effort. I have been a fan of yours since your first audition. The pitch of your voice and your tone at the end put me over the top! I am truly your #1 fan forever. I will play this through my head multiple times, as I await tonight to CUM!

I've been walking around today with a hard-on in my pants and a smile on my face. I can tell the best is yet to CUM. This is RADICAL and off the hook!!!
                                                                     - G.

From that night on, every free moment found Sarah on the phone with Gabe—talking in hushed tones late into the night or stealing time between clients to send text messages. Her phone was her lifeline to Gabe and, as such, she had to delicately navigate her newfound attachment to it. No more leaving it on the table while she went to the bathroom. It could be found safely tucked into her bra or the waistband of her pants. Even at night, she slept with it safely cradled beneath her.

She knew Alex tried to check her phone messages when he thought she wasn't looking. It never mattered until now. She wanted to protect the passion she felt for Gabe from Alex. Gabe's compliments, every declaration of affection, the expressed concern for her feelings—all of it highlighted to her what she had been missing for years.

One morning, she received a message that threw her for a loop.

Gabe: Hey babe - want to have sex?

She stared at the phone for a minute. He usually wasn't so brash right off the bat. She typed back.

Sarah: Hey - what are you doing?
Gabe: Just feeling horny. Send me a picture.
Sarah: Excuse me?
Gabe: Come on, just one. Totally nude. Show me everything.

She felt a disconnect in his words. The tone, although inaudible, was harsh. Gabe was supposed to be traveling to a photo shoot in San Francisco.

Sarah: What's your problem today?
Gabe: No problem. Just want to see your hot body right now.
Sarah: Gabe?
Gabe: Ah - you caught me. This isn't Gabe. It's Ricky.
Sarah: Who the hell are you?
Ricky: Gabe's friend. Didn't he tell you about me? I dropped him off at the airport this morning. He forgot his phone in my car. Thought I'd try for a little fun. Guess I'll just have to scroll through the pictures on his phone.

Sarah was pissed.

Sarah: I'm sure your friend will be thrilled at you looking at his private shit.
Ricky: Oh, he won't care. He'd probably think it was hot if you and me got it on. What do you say?
Sarah: You're crazy. I don't even know you. Get off Gabe's phone.
Ricky: You didn't know Gabe either at first. Now look at you. Oh my - look at you!
Sarah: I'm signing off. I've got stuff to do.
Ricky: I'll call you from my phone. Maybe you can get me off with some of those hot words you type for Gabe.
Sarah: Good-bye.

Rage blazed from her hazel eyes. Although she felt free for Gabe to see her intimately, the thought of a stranger, to whom she had no connection, going through her secret conversations made her nauseous. She tried to remember if Gabe said where he'd be staying in San Francisco so she could call the hotel, but she couldn't come up with it.

A couple of minutes later, her phone rang. It was an unknown number.

"Hello—this is Sarah," she said hesitantly.

"Hi!" A man's voice.

"Who is this?" Sarah asked, even though she suspected she knew.

"It's Ricky, babe. What's going on?"

Sarah was furious. "Look, Ricky. I don't appreciate how you've approached me. I'm not your babe. It's pretty damn shitty of you to try and pretend to be Gabe. I'm hanging up now. Don't call back."

"Wait, wait," he begged, "I'm sorry. Honestly, I'm jealous of how happy Gabe's been lately. I wanted to meet the girl who's making him smile. I also was hoping you'd make me smile, too."

"I'm not a 1-800 number," Sarah said.

"You know, if you refuse me, I can just tell Gabe we had phone sex and he'll believe me. We go back a long way together. We were childhood friends. I stood by him at his wedding, I helped him through his divorce, and everything in between. He couldn't handle another broken heart. He really cares for you; you're all he talks about. If you give me a little pleasure, I'll never say a word." He was practically whispering.

"I'm recording this conversation, you jerk. Gabe will know how fucked up his best friend really is." Sarah looked around frantically to see if there was anything she could grab that would record. Eric's iPhone was on the counter. She quickly grabbed it and activated his voice recorder. She hit the speaker button on her own phone.

"Really? Recording me? I don't think so," Ricky was saying.

"Don't you think I'm smart enough to know how to record a call?" Sarah taunted him.

"Sarah, I know Gabe is crazy about you, but believe me, if I tell him you were talking sweet to me on the phone and getting me off, he'd believe me over you in a second. He'd kick you to the curb. He's known me for years and you for what? Weeks?"

Sarah hit the play icon and held Eric's phone up to hers.

Ricky's voice came out, picking up from "believe me, if I tell him you were talking sweet to me on the phone and getting me off, he'd believe me over you in a second."

Sarah stopped the recording. "Don't call me back," she said, and she hung up.

She didn't hear from Ricky again that day. Or the next. Gabe, either. However, knowing he didn't have his phone eased what would have been anxiety over the lack of communication. It also made her realize that she had no other way of contacting Gabe should she ever need to.

She went again to his website and looked up the phone number listed. It wasn't his cell. She dialed it.

"Hello, Gabe Benoit Studios," a perky female said.

"Hi. My name is Sarah Ruiz. I'm trying to get a hold of Gabe. I know he is in San Francisco right now, but I was wondering if you could tell me where he's staying."

"I'm sorry, I can't do that. I can leave a message if you'd like, but I can't give out his travel plans over the phone. I can't even confirm for you where he is traveling."

Little Miss Perky was trying to sound very stern. Her high-pitched, squeaky voice couldn't quite pull it off.

"I'm a good friend of his. He'd want me to know," Sarah stated.

"Listen, if you *are* a good friend then you'll understand, I get girls calling here every day looking to connect with him. I simply cannot make exceptions just because you say so. Do you want me to leave a message for him? What was your name again?"

Sarah was angry. She understood, but she was angry. "Forget it. Thanks."

She hung up.

Gabe's last blog post was from two days ago. It said nothing other than *Off to San Fran this week for a shoot. Here's a picture I took of the Golden Gate Bridge last time I was there.*

The e-mail address on his website was a generic "info@" e-mail, which she suspected Perky probably checked. She wouldn't give that chick the satisfaction of screening her message. She'd just have to wait until he contacted her, which he did, late that night.

Gabe: Hey princess! You still awake?
Sarah: I am. You're back!
Gabe: Yeah, I forgot my phone in my friend's car. I'm sorry. It was hell not contacting you.
Sarah: You could have called from the hotel.
Gabe: Sorry. I had an assistant with me the whole time.
Sarah: So, how's Ricky?
Gabe: What?

Sarah: Your friend Ricky tried to get me to send him nude pictures. He had your phone.

Gabe: LOL. He's harmless.

Sarah: He threatened me. He was going to tell you he and I had phone sex if I didn't get him off.

Gabe: He's a goofball—but he's a good guy. He's probably a little bit jealous.

Sarah: He didn't sound like a good guy.

Gabe: I've known him forever. Trust me, you'll like him when you get to know him.

Sarah: We'll see.

Gabe: He's a Calvin Klein model, you know.

Sarah: Really?

Gabe: Yup. I'll send you a picture.

Sarah: You have a picture of your friend?

Gabe: I did a photo shoot for CK's latest catalogue. I don't always just shoot women, you know. I take work wherever it comes from.

A couple of minutes later, the e-mail indicator on Sarah's phone went off.

"Damn!" Sarah said when she saw the photo. She wished her phone screen were bigger.

It was a black and white photo of a guy on an endless stretch of beach. He was on his knees in the sand with the sun low in the sky behind him. He wore white linen shorts that were a striking contrast to the brown of his stomach, which was obvious, even in black and white. He had one hand to his head, combing his fingers through thick hair. Sarah had a thing for thick-haired men. Ricky the Jerk seemed to be her type—physically, anyway.

Gabe: Did you get the pic?
Sarah: That's Ricky?
Gabe: Yeah - he's not a bad guy.
Sarah: Well...tell him not to do that to me again.
Gabe: Will do. Now... how much did you miss me...

NINE

Sarah was in her kitchen, chopping lettuce for an afternoon salad. She looked up to see her friend Tracy entering the backyard, her two kids in tow. The kids went right to the pool, where Ethan and Elle were already hard at work pounding each other with pool noodles. Tracy dropped her beach towels on a chair and entered the kitchen holding a bottle of Merlot.

"Hi!" Sarah greeted her with a big smile. They had been meaning to catch up with each other for weeks, and this was the first chance they had.

Tracy fished the corkscrew from the silverware drawer and poured them each a glass. They took their wine and salads and went outside to absorb the late-summer Miami sun.

"So what's new in your world?" Sarah asked. Tracy was a single mom who worked as a trainer at Alex's gym. Tracy had serious muscle mass—she competed in the women's bodybuilding class. More than once over the years, Sarah suspected that Alex and Tracy had something going on; but whether that was because it was true or Alex just wanted Sarah to believe it was true, she didn't know. Either way, she didn't care. Tracy had a good head on her shoulders, the kids loved to play together, and she was one of the few people who Sarah felt understood the life of a mom and fitness competitor.

Tracy furrowed her eyes and leaned toward Sarah. "Sarah," she said in a low tone, "something happened this morning."

"What happened?"

Tracy pulled out her phone and opened her text messages. She handed the phone to Sarah. "Read this."

Tracy - you don't know me - my name is Gabe Benoit. I'm a photographer. I was wondering if you and I could chat sometime about getting you into a photo shoot. Ask Sarah about me - she knows me well.

The knots that frequented Sarah's stomach made an instant appearance. She tried to play it casual. "So he wants to shoot you. He's top-notch."

"There's more. I responded to him." She read from her phone, "'That would be great. I have nationals coming up in a few weeks and maybe we could arrange a shoot following the competition.'" Tracy looked at Sarah, "We had a few back and forths like that, but *then* he said," and she looked down at her phone to read, "'You know, Sarah and I have been having a great time over the phone. Things have really heated up. Maybe you'd like to join us sometime.'"

Sarah said nothing. Her vision slowly clouded with salty tears of disappointment. When they began to spill over, she pounded her fist on the table. Wine leapt from the glass onto her salad.

"Shit!" she yelled. "SHIT!"

Tracy touched her friend's arm. "I'm sorry. Who is this guy?"

Sarah picked up a napkin and dabbed her eyes. She stared at the kids, playing in the water, carefree and oblivious to the bullshit world of adulthood.

"At what point do sweet kids become conniving adults?" she wondered aloud. She picked up her wine glass and drained it. Then she looked at Tracy. "He is a guy I thought I was dating. Apparently, he is making his way around the circuit, just looking for a good time. Do you mind if I call him?"

Tracy nodded, "Go ahead. I didn't respond to him. Sarah—I don't want any part of this. Or of him."

Sarah typed out a text message: *You need to call me. Now.*

A couple of minutes later her phone rang. She stared at it, wanting to throw it into the pool, but she knew she had to face what awaited her on the other end.

"Hello," Sarah said.

"Hey Princess, what's up?" Gabe asked casually.

"I'm sitting here with my friend Tracy, who just finished showing me a text message from you in which you invited her into our 'heated' relationship. You shithead."

"No, no, you got it wrong," he said.

"Really, how do I misinterpret 'Maybe you'd like to join us sometime?'"

"Sarah. I contacted her to do a photo shoot. That's legitimate. When I was looking through her photos, Ricky was there. He wants me to try and set her up with him. That's all—I swear," Gabe said. "Princess, I was not trying to get with her. I was trying to suggest we all get together. It came out badly."

Sarah's eyes were trying to hang onto the new tears that filled them. She blinked and they all escaped. She couldn't speak.

"Sarah, you're the kind of girl I could love one day. I'm not trying to screw that up," Gabe said, "My buddy was here prompting me, and I shouldn't have put it like that. I'm sorry. You told me she was your friend. I thought I could kill three birds with one stone: Do some work, get Ricky matched up, and find us a couple to hang out with."

Sarah wasn't having it. "Look, I gotta go. For the record, don't fuck with me. You want to play around, do so in your own backyard. Stay out of mine." She hung up.

Sarah ignored the text messages that filled her phone the rest of the afternoon. His explanation made sense, but it still hurt. And she was pissed that it hurt. Maybe she was still imagining this as more of a relationship than it was. Doubts crept in through the cracks in her heart created by his text messages.

Later that night, her fickle hopes turned on her again. She had invested so much time and energy, she was ashamed to think of it ending like this. Her pride whispered to her to continue, even though her common sense had pulled the emergency brake. She bound common sense and duct-taped it to the far corner of her mind.

Sarah: I'll give you another chance... but hear me on this: Don't fuck with me. Is that clear?
Gabe: Crystal.
Sarah: Who's Crystal? Another woman? :)
Gabe: There's no one I've got my eye on but you.

Sarah's schedule was full the following day. Workout in the morning, followed by three clients, a brief break, then two more late-day clients.

During her break, she lay on the floor of her gym and stared up at the ceiling, still considering what to do. She replayed Gabe's explanation over and over in her mind. Each time she alternated between thinking him completely believable and completely full of shit. Like a warped game of "loves me, loves me not," she plucked away at the petals in her mind.

Her studio door opened and Alex walked in.

"What are you doing?" he asked.

"Just thinking," she replied. She sat up. "What's that?" He held a FedEx envelope in his hand that he apparently tore open.

"Looks like a present from a secret admirer." Alex took a smaller envelope out of the bigger one and handed it to her. She opened it and removed a five-hundred-dollar gift certificate for The Chanel Store.

The lack of a card didn't matter. She knew who it was from.

"So who sent you that? Your photographer buddy?" Alex asked.

Sarah shrugged. "Maybe. There's no card."

Alex smiled. "Tell him to keep them coming. Saves me money." He started to leave, then turned around. "I can't imagine what you had to do for that."

Sarah sat there for a few more minutes. Her next client arrived right on time, and she had no chance over the next two hours to contact Gabe. When the second client left, she grabbed her phone and typed a message.

Sarah: Did you send me a GC?
Gabe: Depends... did you like it?

Sarah: That's my favorite store. How did you know?
Gabe: Do you forgive me?
Sarah: You can't buy me.
Gabe: I know. You're better than that.
Sarah: Damn straight.
Gabe: It is so hard not being able to touch you and hold you. Maybe you and the kids could come here for a vacation.
Sarah: School is getting ready to start. I can't. And I won't introduce my kids to any man until I know it's serious. You know I have a lot of crap to deal with here. I won't do that to them.
Gabe: Maybe you and I could meet in the middle somewhere?

Sarah thought for a moment. She was planning to go to Vegas in a couple of weeks to celebrate her childhood friend Jenny's fortieth birthday with her. Maybe Gabe could come.

Another text interrupted this thought.

Gabe: So what are you thinking?
Sarah: I'm just not sure about this. I want to believe in us, but it's hard. You're right. We need a face to face.
Gabe: Anything you want.
Sarah: I'm going to Vegas in two weeks for a long weekend. It's my friend Jenny's 40th. Meet me there.
Gabe: You got it.

TEN

The thought that she and Gabe were actually going to meet face to face both excited and terrified her. The thought of him touching her made her tingle all over, but envisioning it actually happening drove her wild. What would that be like?

She used her Chanel gift card to ensure she would be the sexiest woman in any club she entered. Nails done, hair done, and bag packed, she kissed her kids goodbye and left them in Lila's capable hands for the weekend. Alex was on a business trip to the Dominican Republic, so even he couldn't ruin her enthusiasm.

Jenny and her husband, Ty, were already in Vegas, having arrived a few days earlier. Another friend, Tina, was traveling from Dallas and would arrive around the same time as Sarah.

Sarah wisely booked her room at a different hotel from the others, so she and Gabe could have some privacy. She wasn't sure how she was going to introduce him to her friends, or even if she was going to share him at all. He wasn't arriving until Saturday afternoon, which gave her Friday night with Jenny and Tina. She figured she could always blow off Jenny and Tina for Saturday night. Sarah wasn't flying home until Monday morning.

She sent Jenny a text message to let her know she was there. Jenny responded that she and Ty were in a casino playing blackjack. Sarah put her things in her room and sent Gabe a message. He didn't respond right away, which was to be expected. He was in the studio shooting a lingerie ad that featured a large Bengal tiger. He had his hands, and studio, full!

She put on her bikini and made her way down to the pool. She ordered an iced tea and for the next hour did nothing but work on her tan. When Tina sent a text that she, too, was there, Sarah got dressed and met up with her friends.

It had been a while since she had gone out drinking and dancing. She felt so free. Ty opted to hang out with the girls, and more than once Sarah found him dancing too close for comfort. She moved away each time, but whenever she looked at him, his eyes were focused her way.

They cabbed to a few different clubs and then Sarah called it a night. The last thing she wanted was to be hung over or have bags under her eyes when she met Gabe for the first time.

"I'm going to head back to the hotel. I'm pretty tired," she said, as they came off the dance floor for a break.

"No! Come with us to just one more club, Sarah," Jenny begged.

"Oh honey, I can't. I'm really tired. We'll meet up for breakfast," Sarah promised.

"Want me to make sure you get back to the hotel?" Ty offered.

"Oh yes, good idea, Ty," Jenny said. Sarah got the feeling Jenny was sorry Ty was with them.

"I'll find my way," Sarah said, shaking her head, "I'll take a cab. I'm less drunk than you are, Ty."

Ty frowned at her. "I don't like the idea of you going alone."

Sarah closed the door firmly on the matter. "I'm fine. Stay with your wife. I'll see you guys tomorrow."

Sarah had made herself a promise not to check her phone at all while she was out with her friends. Aware of how attached she'd become to Gabe and his texts, she wanted to prove to herself she could go without checking her phone for a few hours. Once back in the cab alone, however, she gave the driver the name of her hotel, then turned her phone on. A long message from Gabe.

Gabe: I've got bad news. I can't make it tomorrow. The shoot went terrible. The tiger wouldn't cooperate and they're bringing a new one in studio tomorrow. I have to stay here and get this job done. I'm so sorry, babe. I hope you can forgive me.

Sarah leaned back in the seat. *Seriously?* she wondered. What was it going to take for the two of them to get together?

Sarah: That sicks.
Gabe: What?
Sarah: I mean, sucks. That sucks.
Gabe: I tried to reschedule, but the tiger trainer is leaving for China on Monday. We have to get it done this weekend.
Sarah: Want me to come there?

She could totally make that work. She could hop a flight to L.A. in the morning and come back to Vegas on Sunday night in time to catch her Monday flight home.

Gabe: No - you can't. I'd be so distracted. I need to get this done. You stay and have fun with your friends.
Sarah: Don't you want me?
Gabe: Are you drunk?
Sarah: Just a little buzzed. When I get back to my room, I'll give you a call...

On Saturday, she lingered in the tropical swimming pool paradise at The Mirage, where Ty, Jenny, and Tina were staying. Sarah's disappointment in Gabe threatened to ruin her weekend. To combat the brooding, she struck up casual conversations with a few different men throughout the course of the day while lounging at the poolside bar, forcing herself to be blithe. One guy, a bodybuilder, invited her to dinner, but she politely declined. She intentionally and continually had to push thoughts of Gabe from her mind and give herself the luxury of freedom.

Jenny, meanwhile, pounded back mojitos at a record pace, and got louder and louder with each passing hour. Around four p.m., Ty had to take Jenny to their room, and they all agreed to meet in the lobby of The Mirage at seven for dinner.

Tina and Sarah stayed by the pool until five-thirty. Sarah kept conversation about herself and her life on a surface level with Tina. They hadn't seen each other in a couple of years and, frankly, Sarah had no desire to talk about Alex or Gabe. Sarah was relieved that Tina did most of the talking, with plenty to say about her life, her job, and her men. Sarah felt reposed from the frustrations brought on by the men in her life.

When they met in the lobby for dinner, Jenny looked terrible. Expensive makeup couldn't hide red-rimmed eyes that glared at Ty, who couldn't take his eyes off Sarah.

Sarah's sequined halter top showed the right amount of stomach above her short black leather skirt. Her glittered Jimmy Choo sandals felt and looked fabulous on her feet. They only had a couple minutes to wait until Tina showed up.

"Damn, Sarah! You look amazing!" Tina exclaimed. "Look at those sandals!"

Sarah smiled at her. "Thanks. You only live once!"

"Got that right," Tina said. She turned to Jenny. "You feeling OK, Jen?"

Jenny forced a smile. "I'm hanging in there. Why'd you guys let me drink so much today?"

Ty muttered, "Who could stop you?" Jenny flipped him off and started to walk away.

"Ty, it's her birthday. Leave her alone!" Sarah said. She caught up with Jenny and slipped her arm through Jenny's. They headed off for dinner.

The churning of Sarah's stomach woke her, mere seconds before the vomiting began. Thank God she was already in the bathtub. She had climbed in last night and turned the shower to hot, after putting the safety lock on her hotel door.

Knees pulled to her chest, Sarah had huddled in the tub until the shower ran cold. She shut off the valve but stayed there, sobbing, until she passed out from exhaustion.

Now, she sat naked, with vomit splattered across her thighs. *Figures,* she thought.

The pain in her head was blinding. Even blinking hurt.

Her aching muscles longed to be stretched. Only her firm grip on the shower safety bar kept Sarah from collapsing as she stood and turned the water on once again.

She washed, trying to remember the sequence of events from the night before. She simply couldn't recollect anything in a logical, coherent way. Scenes strobed in her mind.

Leaving for dinner, arm-in-arm with Jenny.
Dinner at Tao with Tina, Jenny, and Ty.
Dancing with Tina—or was that Jenny? No, it was Tina.
Tina waving over her shoulder and giving a thumbs-up as she left with a large, well-dressed black man.
Sitting at a small table with Ty, asking what happened to Jenny.
Ty's eyes, staring at her cleavage. His hand rubbing her arm.

A sharp pain in her midsection snapped her from her thoughts. She flung the curtain back and gingerly stepped out of the tub, barely making it to the toilet before the second wave of nausea rolled in.

Sarah called housekeeping and told them she was ill. They came immediately to put fresh sheets on her bed, even bringing a new comforter. The kind woman at the front desk sent up an entire box of saltine crackers.

The Puerto Rican housekeeper kept her eyes on her work and did not seem fazed in the least at the pale, disheveled white woman who sat at the desk, head down on her arms. As the housekeeper had done several hundred times before, she moved quickly to make the hotel bed pure again.

With sad eyes and a weak smile, Sarah simply said, "Gracias, señora," and gave the woman twenty dollars.

She double-bolted the door again, dropped her robe, and eased her aching, naked body into the cool sheets. As she began to drift into unconsciousness, she noticed the silver-rimmed eyes on the leopard portrayed on the hideous, gold-framed picture that hung above her bed. She saw those eyes last night. The replay of what happened in her room became fresh.

She stares at the leopard print while Ty gnaws on the front of her neck, pressing her against the sharp metal frame on the picture that hung on the wall opposite the bed. His stubble shaves a thin layer of skin from the soft spot between her collarbones. In one move, he hooks his thumbs into the sides of her halter top, forcing it down to her stomach, exposing her breasts.

"Please, stop," she says through heavy breaths. "This hurts."

"I've wanted to do this for so long," he mumbles. His face presses between her mounds, and she wiggles her shoulder free from the edge of the picture. He takes her movement as in invitation to move his groping to the bed.

He spins her around swiftly, shoving her backward onto the plush California King bed, which once promised her much joy but from that moment on was going to hold only nightmares.

"*You have to stop this,*" she begs. Her eyes are blurry from tears and whatever it was that coursed through her bloodstream.

"*Shhh,*" he whispers. He opens his fly quickly—nearly bursting from it anyway—and pulls his pants down, just low enough to do the job. Her skirt is a twisted mess, so it doesn't take long for him to find what he was seeking. He doesn't bother removing the soft leather skirt, but pushes it up higher as he tugs the delicate lace of her panties, pulling them down but not completely off.

She wants to hit him, to scream, to do something, but her arms are like lead and her mind foggy. His left hand holds her wrists together, over her head, while his right hand grabs at her left breast. He assaults both of her nipples, pulling on one, while his teeth tug and bite at the other. He forces himself into her over and over. She closes her eyes and concentrates on her breathing. In and out. Slowly, so as not to panic. She holds her hips still, squeezing her vaginal muscles—as if to lock him out.

"*You're so tight, baby, oh that feels good,*" he whispers into her ear.

The shrill sound of the ringing phone slices through the air like a samurai sword. Like water on a campfire, it douses the moment in reality. Her eyes jerk open.

"*Shit!*" he snaps.

Cut by the sound, he jumps backward off of her. She takes the chance to make a wild grab for the phone. Her right hand flails toward it, and she knocks it off the hook. She rolls over, pursuing the receiver, which had fallen between the bed and nightstand. She tenses, expecting to *feel him clutch at her from behind, to stop her, but his hands never come.*

She hears the heavy bang of the hotel room door. She lets out a long exhale as she turns and stares at the empty room.

She reaches over and simply puts the receiver back onto its hook, not knowing or caring who was on the other end. Frozen in spot, she waits a full ten minutes before going into the shower.

As the images of Ty's attack became fresh in her mind, Sarah's mouth went dry and her tongue felt thick and heavy. *How did he get in my room?* she thought. That part wasn't yet released to her memory. She closed her eyes and sleep overtook the wondering.

The hotel phone woke her a couple of hours later.

"Hello," she managed.

"Where are you?" It was Tina. "We're at the pool. You won't believe what happened to me last night. That asshole I left with stole a hundred bucks from my wallet AND he took my panties! I had the cutest purple laced-back pair from Victoria's Secret and he took them! Can you believe that shit? I went into the bathroom to pee and he was gone when I came out."

Sarah rubbed her temple with her hand, "Tina, were you sick this morning?"

"Sick? No. We didn't drink that much. Why, are *you* sick?" Tina's voice was much too loud.

Swallowing down her saliva, Sarah replied, "Yeah, Tina. I'm really sick. I don't remember what happened after you left."

"Damn! What did you do, girl?" Tina asked.

There it was. The moment of decision. Not having enough time to consider how to tell Tina that their best friend's husband raped her, she said nothing. It was still lurid in her own mind. How could she expose her friend to what happened?

The sickness came again. "I gotta go. I'll catch up with you later."

For the next few hours, Sarah alternated between vomiting, sleeping, and trying to force her brain to remember something, *any*thing that would tell her how things progressed from the bar to her bed. She found her cell phone behind the dresser. Seeing that it was dead brought back the memory she sought.

She is in a bathroom stall at The Bank nightclub.
She exits the stall. Ty is standing there, with two drinks.
"What are you doing in here? This is the ladies room!" she says to him.
"I didn't think you were coming back," he replies. He extends one of the drinks to her, but she doesn't take it. His eyes wander again to her cleavage.
"Ty, you should go find Jenny," she says, and pulls her halter top up a bit. "She probably needs you."
"She went back to the room, she's fine." He steps towards her, leans in to kiss her.
"What are you doing?" She sidesteps Ty's advance and his face finds nothing but air.

"Come on, let's go finish these drinks," he says.
"I have to go to the bathroom," she says, and goes back into the stall.
"You just went. Are you avoiding me?" he asks.

In the stall, she quickly types a text message to Jenny.
> Where r u? Ur husband is looking 4 u

She hits the send key then types a second message to Gabe:
> Help. My friend's husband is all over me I cant lose him. What do I do?

Ty calls from the other side of the stall. "What's taking so long?"
"Ty—I'm going pee—wait for me at the table," she replies.

She hears him leave. Her phone vibrates. It's a return message, but not from Jenny.
> Go to a doorman. Tell him you need help. Where r u?

The low battery icon flashes and the screen goes black before she can respond.
"Shit," she says. She leaves the bathroom, intending to find a doorman and slide out before Ty sees her. No chance. Ty is waiting for her. He hands her a drink.
"Ty, I am done drinking for tonight." She sets it down on a table, but he picks it up and thrusts it back into her hand.
"Just one more," he says gently. "Have a drink with an old friend."

Sarah remembered thinking that she'd nurse the drink and slip away without him. She had never seen her friend's husband act this way toward her before. It was unsettling. However, she never had the chance to slip away. A couple of sips into that drink, her head got thick.

He follows her back to her hotel.
She pushes him off of her in the hallway.
She tells him, "No, you can't come in. Go back to Jenny."
He grabs the key from her hand and opens the door.
He shoves her roughly against the wall, jamming her shoulder into the picture frame.

Sarah got the phone charger from her suitcase and plugged it in. Six missed calls, three missed text messages.

The missed text reply from Jenny made her snort with disgust:

Jenny: Tired. Went back to my room. Just give him a blow job he'll be fine. LOL

"What the hell?" Sarah said aloud.

The other texts were within the past hour from Tina and Jenny.

Tina: We're at the pool, come join us.
Jenny: Where r u?

The phone messages were all desperate pleas from Gabe to call him. After he received her text about Ty hitting on her, he hadn't heard from her again and he was frantic. What would he say when he found out? What would Jenny say? Sarah didn't want to know. She set her head back on the pillow and cried.

By dinnertime Sunday she knew she couldn't tell anyone what happened. It would wreck Jenny's marriage, Alex would kill him, she had no idea how Gabe would react, and she didn't want to relive it—ever.

She sent Gabe a text message, saying that she was fine and that she'd call him later. She met her friends for dinner, avoiding Ty's smug gaze, and giving laser focus to Tina's adventures. She ate her pasta at lightning speed and then excused herself, blaming her abandonment of the group on an early morning flight. She couldn't wait to leave the disappointments that Las Vegas held far behind.

ELEVEN

As the plane touched down at Miami International Airport, Sarah breathed deeply. Home. It would be great to see the kids.

Maybe Alex won't be there, she hoped. It would give her time to unpack and shower. She retrieved her Suburban from the lot, paid the exorbitant fee, and let her mind wander as she traveled the short distance to South Beach.

Ethan and Elle were swimming while Lila watched from a patio chair. Salsa music tumbled from the outdoor speakers, filling the air with happiness and life. Lila waved at Sarah as she came out of the garage, and the twins scrambled out of the water when they saw her. Sarah dropped her bag and extended her arms.

"Mommy!" They bombarded her, and she enclosed them both.

"I missed you guys," Sarah said, giving them a squeeze. Their damp little bodies felt so good.

"We missed you too," Elle said. "Daddy took us bowling."

"He was home this weekend?" Sarah said with shock. Then she said, "Bowling sounds like fun."

"I got a strike, Mom! But *nobody* saw it," Ethan said. He frowned, with a disapproving look that she had seen in her own mirror more than a few times. "Everyone was goofing around, and Dad was always on the phone."

"That's OK, baby." Sarah hugged him again. "I'm sure it was great. We'll go again, and you can show me."

The twins trotted back to the pool. Elle jumped onto the raft, and Ethan grabbed his squirt gun and began to shoot at her. *Where did the past seven years go?* she wondered. Sarah picked up her bag and walked over to Lila. Sarah sat and allowed the light Miami breeze to calm her spirit.

"So how was it, Lila?"

"It was good, señora. A quiet weekend." The two women made eye contact. Lila knew what Sarah really wanted to know. They stared at one another for moment, then Lila said again, slowly, "It was a *quiet* weekend. He got home Sunday morning and took the kids bowling last night."

Sarah nodded and sighed. "Good. Anyone home?"

"Yes, Alexandra is in her room, and Antonio is out with friends. Eric is at the beach, and Señor Alex is not here."

"Great." Sarah smiled. "I'm going to go unpack." Sarah put her hand over the top of Lila's. She had grown to depend on this woman to keep the children out of the way when Hurricane Alex was on the move. "Thank you, Lila. I don't know what I'd do without you."

Thirty minutes and a shower later, Sarah still wasn't sure if keeping quiet was the right decision in regard to Ty. She played the things she could remember over and over in her mind. She listed all the things she did wrong: She didn't go to the authorities right away. If she did now, it would be his word against hers, and she had no evidence. She had left the clothes she was wearing in a trash can in her hotel room. (Except for the new shoes.) She didn't have the drink glass, so there was no way of knowing what he drugged her with. She went out to dinner with them the next night, which was a dumb thing to do when the guy you're sitting at the table with has raped you. What a mess.

A very tired woman stared back at her from the bathroom mirror. "You dumbshit," she told herself. "Why didn't you go to the cops?"

She knew that answer. Jenny. On the plane, she had deleted the texts with Jenny from her phone so Alex wouldn't see them if he were to get hold of it. She decided then to submerge this incident as deeply into her subconscious as possible.

"What's the matter with you?"

She jumped at the appearance of Alex in the bathroom doorway. "Nothing," she answered. "Nothing at all."

His body filled the door frame, and he stood staring at her for a moment. He came into the bathroom and snatched the bath towel from around her. "Come on," he said, nodding toward the bed.

"Alex, please. I can't do this anymore. Give me my towel."

"Don't give me that shit. I paid for your trip to Vegas. You've got nothing without me." He undid his pants and pulled them off. He had no underwear on, and his cock was at attention.

"You can't just fuck me whenever you want," she said. "I told you, I'm done."

She could come up with the words, but she didn't really have the energy to fight. Sensing this, he jumped on the opportunity to prey on her weakness. He grabbed her hand and pulled her to the bed. She didn't resist him. For the next several minutes her mind relived the brutal attack she had suffered at the hands of her friend, while Alex writhed on top of her.

She watched the clock and moved her hips in the way she knew drove Alex wild. She just wanted him to come and get it over with. Mercifully, it didn't take him more than five minutes.

"Oh yes," he growled as he came inside her. "You know you like that."

"Get off of me," she said.

He lingered on her for a moment, panting. He studied her face. Finally he said, "So how was Vegas?"

"Fine," she replied. "Would you please leave my room?"

He ignored her request but did roll off of her. "Did any guys hit on you?"

"Of course they did," she said. "We were in Vegas."

He stared at her for another full minute, then got out of bed and dressed. She remained where she was but grabbed a throw blanket and covered herself up. Once his pants were in place, he leaned over and put his face close to hers. "Did you fuck anyone?"

She shook her head. "I can't believe you ask me shit like that."

He straightened up and smiled. "Just wondering. You know, if you did, you could tell me." He reached into his pocket and pulled out a few hundred dollars. He tossed them on the nightstand.

She looked at it. "What is that for?"

His eyes locked onto hers. "Go get some groceries. The kitchen is empty. One way or another, I get what I want. You can't get rid of me just because you say so. I'm willing to share."

He left the room.

When Gabe called later that night, Sarah couldn't work up a passionate conversation. Gabe's disappointment that she didn't want phone sex frustrated her. All anyone wanted from her was sex. She was tired.

TWELVE

Blood pounded in her ears as she ran. The crunch of her feet on the leaves and the sound of her own breathing blended in her ears as her arms pressed forward. It felt like she was swimming—but there was no water, only thick vines and branches to push out of the way to make a path for escape.

Although she didn't look behind her, she knew the shape of her pursuer. She could feel its presence, not more than a couple of feet from her back. The gap was closing, and she had no more energy to give her flight. As she tripped and fell, she turned so as to land on her side. Its silver-rimmed eyes were inches from her face. Teeth bared. Claws out. It stretched its paw towards her shoulder. The skin begin to tear away...

Sarah sat up quickly, grabbing her arm protectively. She couldn't catch her breath, and for a moment she really thought the creature was in the bedroom with her. She looked frantically around to see who—or what—was there.

She was alone. Nothing but the haunted memory of what happened in Las Vegas. As much as Sarah tried to keep the events locked away in her mind, they often broke loose while she slept.

For two weeks after her Vegas trip, she wandered about like a child lost in a crowded mall. Alex spent long nights at his clubs, and the kids were absorbed in their various activities. Tanya and her husband were on vacation, her mom was busy with work. Gabe was distracted with back-to-back overseas photo shoots and hadn't even noticed her newly reserved demeanor. The loneliness made her feel like a prisoner in an underground dungeon, broken and forgotten.

The dream began to haunt her during the day. The bang of a door or the sudden ring of a phone would cause her to jump. The weight of the secret she carried pressed upon her, suffocating any logical thoughts. It became more and more clear that she was going to have to tell someone.

The first Friday night that Gabe was back from Paris, she worked up the courage to tell him. She began with a text:

Sarah: *Got a sec?*
Gabe: *For you, always! Hang on, I'll call you in 10 minutes.*

"Hello," Sarah answered her phone when it rang.

"Hi, what's up?"

"I need to talk to you about something," Sarah's voice cracked a little as she said it.

"What is it? Are you OK?" Gabe said with concern. *That's one difference between him and Alex,* Sarah thought. *Gabe cares how I am doing.*

"Listen. Something happened when I was in Vegas. That night I was out with my friends, my friend's husband did something to me. I don't know what it was, but he gave me a drink and I'm sure it had something in it. I tried to get away from him, I hid in the bathroom, but he came in there. That was when I had sent you that message, remember? I thought I'd slip away and see a bouncer for help, but I couldn't. My head got fuzzy and it was like I wasn't even able to control my body. He forced me back to my hotel room and..." she stopped. She couldn't say it.

"He raped you?" Gabe offered.

Sarah began to cry quietly.

"He raped you?" Gabe said again, but louder.

"I don't know," Sarah whispered.

"What do you mean you don't know?" Gabe asked gently.

"My mind was so foggy. I know he was on top of me, but I have no idea how it got to that point."

"You said he drugged you though, right?"

"I assume so. I didn't drink enough to have been that out of it. Honestly, though, I don't know what the hell happened." Sarah began to sob again. "This is my fault. I should have never stuck around after Tina left."

"Look," Gabe said sternly, "this is not your fault. Even if you were completely hammered on your own accord, he had no right to take advantage of you. And if he did slip you something so he could get with you, he should have to pay."

There was a long silence. Sarah didn't know what to say. Then Gabe said, "Why didn't you tell me?"

"I couldn't," she said. "I couldn't. I haven't told anyone, and it's haunting me. I have nightmares, I can't sleep."

"He needs to pay," Gabe said again.

"I can't do anything. Jenny is my oldest friend in the world. It would crush her."

"Sarah, this isn't about Jenny. It's about that slimeball and what he did to you," Gabe said. "You have to do something."

"I am doing something. I'm telling you. Gabe—I was so ashamed of what happened, I couldn't look Jenny in the eye the next day. It was her birthday and I couldn't even be happy for her. *He* took advantage of me, and *I'm* the one suffering. Where's the fairness in that? I feel like crap."

It was quiet for a long time.

"So what do you want me to do?" Gabe finally asked.

"Just tell me you're still there for me and this doesn't change anything," Sarah said, hopefully.

"It doesn't change anything. I have the same feelings I had for you yesterday, if not stronger, now that you've confided in me," Gabe said.

Sarah smiled. "Thanks. I feel better. I'm so tired."

Gabe said, "Maybe you should get to bed early?"

"I think I'll watch a movie. My favorite movie is on TV tonight. I wish you were here to snuggle up with me."

"Oh yeah? What's your favorite movie?" Gabe asked.

"You tell me your favorite movie first," Sarah teased.

"You'll think I'm a pussy."

"I won't. I promise."

"*Sweet Home Alabama.* It's about a woman who—"

"I know what it's about," Sarah interrupted. "It's my favorite movie, too."

"You're lying," Gabe said.

"I am not!" Sarah insisted. "It is starting here in about a half hour."

"I'm going to run to the store and get it. We can watch it together," Gabe said.

That night, from opposite sides of the country, they watched their favorite movie. Sarah snuggled down in her bed, and they stayed on the phone, laughing and chatting while they watched Reese Witherspoon come full circle. Sarah actually fell asleep toward the end of the movie, phone still on.

THIRTEEN

"You're dangerous for me," Gabe said one night, after they had exhausted themselves masturbating together on the phone. Sarah occasionally pretended with him, but on this evening she ached inside to have his physical presence accompany the emotional connection. She could imagine the movement of his mouth, the stroke of his hand, and the longing in his eyes as they spoke. He said all the right things, and her desperation to touch him was growing.

They had developed a rhythm to their relationship that ebbed and flowed between raw, passionate phone sex and sweet, gentle words of humor and affection. They flirted and laughed together and talked about everything under the sun.

"What do you mean, dangerous?"

"I could see myself really falling hard over you."

"I wish we could be together, to touch one another." Sarah responded. "I feel so alone without you here."

"Oh, Princess," Gabe said. "Why don't we get a little wild? It'll take our mind off the fact that we're so far away."

"What are you thinking?" Sarah was intrigued.

"The next time Alex comes to you for a piece, put the phone by the bed and pretend it's me," Gabe said.

"What do you mean?"

"Let me listen. Scream out when you come and I'll pretend it's my cock filling you."

"Are you serious?"

Becky Komant

"Yes, I'm serious. You've got to fuck him anyway. Might as well give me a little fun while you're at it."

Sarah was quiet. "I don't feel right about that," she finally said.

"Look, you need to keep things peaceful at home. You've said yourself you need to keep him happy for now. Why should we be miserable while you do what you're forced to do anyway?"

In a weird way, it made sense. Or maybe she was still euphoric from her orgasm.

"If he catches me, he'll be pissed," Sarah said.

"He won't. You always have your phone nearby anyway. It wouldn't be suspicious at all."

"How do you know that?"

"You respond within milliseconds of my texts. Always. I imagine you have your phone tucked in your bra everywhere you go," Gabe replied.

"Yeah, I do. You're addicting," Sarah said with a laugh.

"So let's make a game of it. Aren't you up for a game? Why should he have all the fun?"

Sarah thought about Gabe anyway when Alex pushed her into sex or a blow job. The more she thought about it, the more she thought it would be thrilling to know he was actually listening in. Besides, it would be nice to screw Alex over with him unaware. "OK, baby. Game on," she said.

"Girl, that's sick," Tanya said when Sarah told her what Gabe had suggested. They were having lunch at an outdoor café in South Beach.

"I know." Sarah needed someone to tell her if she was playing too close to the line. "But is it *too* sick?"

"Too sick?" Tanya asked. Then she laughed. "Honey, you're in such a jam, there's no such thing as too sick. Your love story is a hot mess." Tanya ticked off her points on her long, manicured fingers, "You've got five awesome kids. You're living with a maniac who's keeping you hostage because of the kids. You've got a boyfriend across the country who you've never met. So what if he wants you to let him listen in while your ex gets off on ya?"

"You make it all sound so easy," Sarah said.

"It's a no-brainer. Put in your time with jerk-off Alex and pave the way for your future. Boyfriend is still giving you a photo shoot, right?" Tanya took a sip of her vodka, leaned back in the stiff, wrought iron dining chair, and crossed her tanned legs. A couple of college guys at a table nearby fairly drooled over their pints of Stella Artois.

Sarah smiled at the conspicuous young guns. "After Nationals. Gabe is booking a local studio in San Diego, and we're going to go down to the beach and do some sunset shots. I'm so fucking excited about it. Tanya, I need this shoot."

"I know, sweetie. Screw Alex. Let your photographer listen. Take home the cash. It is that easy."

One of the studs tried to discreetly take a picture of Tanya's legs with his iPhone but did a pitiful job at hiding it. Tanya looked at Sarah, winked at her, then ever-so-slowly stood. She straightened her skirt, which fell a good inch above her knees. With a sly smile she turned to the guy—whose face suddenly got bright red. She gently took the iPhone from his hands and pushed the camera icon.

She put the camera between her legs, under her skirt, and snapped a picture. Then she looked at the screen and smiled. She raised her eyes to the speechless young man and brought the phone to her lips, leaving a perfect pink kiss on the screen.

That night, after the kids went to bed, Sarah sat in her room, anticipating Alex's knock on her door. She locked it on purpose so he couldn't barge in. At dinner he told her in no uncertain terms that he would be stopping by. He slipped up behind her and grabbed her ass while she cleared dishes at the sink.

"Don't do that," she had hissed.

"You know you want it. Just give me a piece tonight and I'll leave you alone for the rest of the weekend."

She had turned to face him. His eyes and his aura changed when he wanted to get off. She could almost hear a hungry growl brewing inside of him. It was a look that used to turn her on, but now sent shivers up her spine. He shamelessly placed a hand on her breast and pulled at her nipple.

"So I'll see you later. I've got a couple of things to do, but I'll be back."

"Don't hurry," she had said.

After she finished cleaning the kitchen she sent a text message to Gabe, letting him know that tonight might be the night. He had been asking all week when he'd get to listen in, almost to the point where it was starting to irritate her. She could sense glee as she read.

Gabe: Oh wow - this is going to be amazing!
Sarah: Are you sure about this?
Gabe: Yes - I want to hear what you sound like when you cum tonight.
Sarah: I sometimes have to fake it with him—maybe with you listening it won't be a problem.
Gabe: Just dial the phone and set it down when he comes in. He'll never know...

A half-hour later, Alex tried to enter her room. When the door didn't give, he knocked and said, "Sarah? Open the door."

Sarah dialed the phone and set it face down on her night table. She went and unlocked the door.

"What do you want?" she asked him, with more than a hint of annoyance.

"You know what I want. You haven't given me anything all week." Alex pushed his way into her room.

"I wish you wouldn't barge into my room like that. I deserve some privacy, you know," Sarah said, still standing by the door.

Alex unbuttoned his jeans and pulled them down. He was hard already. She sighed. *Maybe this wouldn't take too long.*

"Well, are we going to do this?" he asked.

"You're a pig," Sarah rolled her eyes, but she locked the door and then took a step toward him.

"See, I know you want me," Alex said.

He grabbed her around her waist and kissed her roughly. She could feel his hardness against the front of her shorts. His mouth was invasive, and his tongue pushed its way around every inch of her mouth. He pressed it against her teeth, he licked the roof of her mouth. He inhaled his breath so his tongue pulled her own into his mouth and with incredible force he sucked hard. She pulled back from it and separated her face from his.

"That hurts," she said.

"Pain is good," he replied. "It can be real good."

He pulled her shirt over her head and then pulled down her shorts. He climbed on top of her as he laid her backward on the bed.

He kissed her for a few minutes that way, pressing his cock into her thigh. Then he said, "Let me turn you around."

She turned over and clutched the pillow with her hands, resting her weight on her elbows. She was up on her knees and could feel his weight behind her as he grabbed her hips and thrust his cock into her. He continued to hold her and move in and out of her, alternating between a series of slow movements and then pounding her hard with everything he had. The pounding hurt, and yet with anyone else it might have been a turn on. He was right: Pain can be good—but with the right person.

Overcoming her disgust with Alex, she pretended it *was* the right person. She closed her eyes and placed herself in bed with Gabe. She imagined it was his hands that caressed the curve of her ass. When he reached around to stroke her clit she moaned loudly, thinking of the fingers that belonged to the man she really wanted to be with. She envisioned the picture of his long, hard dick as the cock that filled her up, stroking her. She was glad to be facing away from Alex because it made the imagining even more realistic. Even so, she kept glancing at the phone, nervous that Alex might somehow find out it was on. In her mind, she saw Gabe waiting, listening. Was he masturbating? She suspected he was. It heightened the experience for her, and when she cried out in her orgasm, it was truly for Gabe.

"Oh, Princess, thank you," Gabe said on the phone later, after Alex had left.

"Could you hear everything?" Sarah asked.

"Oh yes, I could hear you perfectly. It was like I was right there with you."

"Was is hard for you to hear me with another man?" Sarah thought that when it came down to it, maybe he'd get angry. It did feel a bit like she was cheating on Gabe, as odd as that sounded to her.

"At first," he said, "but I just closed my eyes and put myself right there with you. I liked it. What did you think?"

"Well, if I have to fuck him, it definitely was made better knowing you were there too. Is that warped?"

"No, you have to keep things peaceful there for now. We really can have fun with this."

After she and Gabe hung up, Sarah changed the sheets on her bed and stared at the ceiling for a long time. *Is this how it is supposed to be?* she wondered. It was a question that frequented her mind over the years. She knew that every time the answer was "no." She imagined having a lover like Gabe nearby to make her feel precious, instead of like a worthless sex object, the way Alex left her. She dreamt that night of making passionate love on a tropical beach. It was so intense, so real, that she woke up sweating. She was surprised to realize that it was neither Gabe nor

Becky Komant

Alex who was in her dream with her. It was someone she didn't know, and although she couldn't see his face, she knew he was beautiful.

FOURTEEN

"Sarah! Get the fuck down here!" Alex's voice boomed from the kitchen.

Sarah was just finishing her makeup and waited until she was ready before answering Alex's bellowing.

"What is it? Do you have to talk like that? The kids can hear you," she said as she entered the kitchen.

"I don't care who hears me. What is this?" He held up a FedEx box. It was Sarah's theme wear outfit for Nationals.

"Seriously? This is what you're screaming about?" Sarah reached out to take the box, but he yanked it out of her reach. "You jerk. That's my Nationals outfit."

"Whose money did you use to buy this?" Alex demanded. "You're gonna owe me big time for this. If you spent three grand for Easterns, I can't imagine what this baby cost."

"We gonna go through this again? I used my own money, you dick," Sarah said. "Now, give me my box."

"You don't have any money," Alex snorted. "You only have money because I pay for everything around here."

He threw the box on the kitchen counter and left. Sarah got a drink of water and stared at the box for a long minute before picking it up and taking it to her room. She wasn't sure why the outfit's arrival stirred such anger in him. It wasn't like they couldn't afford it. So why? Why the outburst? He should have been thrilled with her performance for him the night before. With Gabe listening, she was more into it than she'd been in a while.

Her phone rang. It was Alex.

"What now?" Sarah said.

"When is Nationals, by the way?" he asked.

"What do you care?"

"Someone's gotta take care of things around here while you go off across the country," Alex said. "I need to know."

"September thirtieth," Sarah said. "I leave the twenty-eighth. My mom and Lila will have it all under control."

Alex hung up without saying anything else.

Gabe sensed Sarah's frustration later that day as they chatted on the phone.

"What's wrong, Princess? Something bothering you?" he asked.

"You know me well," she said.

"Better than you know," Gabe said playfully. "We have a deep, deep connection. I wish it was deeper actually. So what's up?"

"Oh, Alex was such a jerk today. My competition suit arrived and he had to ruin the excitement for me by giving me crap about how much it cost. He didn't even buy it—I did. It's like he considers everything around here to belong to him. I've got nothing of my own. I'm so sick of it."

"You know, it was kind of fun listening to you have sex with him last night," Gabe put out there.

Sarah rolled her eyes. The last thing she wanted to think of was fucking Alex. She sensed Gabe was trying to change the subject, so she went along, "Yeah, you liked that?"

"Oh yes," Gabe said. "It was so hot. I don't know how you do it. It's like you wave your magic wand and you make things happen. It's one of the things I find very appealing about you."

Sarah laughed. "It was the best it's been in a while. I totally pretended it was you behind me."

Gabe gave a bit of a groan. "I can't wait to hear that again. Next time, would you say my name?"

Sarah nearly spit out the tea she was sipping as he said it. "Are you kidding me? How the hell would I pull that off?"

"I don't know. I bet he wouldn't even notice. Maybe you could ask him to do some role play or something. You're smart and sexy. I'm sure you can come up with something. You know, wave that wand and make it happen."

"I don't know. We'll see. I'm not doing that every night with him. I'd much rather be one-on-one with you," Sarah said.

"I know, Princess. In time... I promise. So what are you doing tomorrow?"

Sarah did a quick mental check of her calendar. "I train in the morning, then I've got one client afterward, my friend Tanya."

"Now remind me, who's Tanya? Did she go to Vegas with you?" Gabe asked.

"No. That was Tina and Jenny. Tanya is my wild-child friend."

"Oooh, what do you mean?" Gabe asked.

Sarah smiled thinking about her friend and was so thankful to have such a confidante who understood what she was going through. She thought about how to describe Tanya without making her sound slutty. "Well, Tanya and her husband own a hair salon here in Miami. They've got two kids, but she's always had this primitive side to her that likes to break the rules and do her own thing. She's very open with her sexuality and doesn't care who knows it."

"Are she and her husband swingers?" Gabe sounded like he liked the thought of that.

"No. Her husband is a good guy. He's pretty straightlaced. Tanya lets her inhibitions down when she's out with friends or traveling. Don't get me wrong—she isn't trampy, she's just a free spirit. You know what I mean?"

"I bet the two of you have some pretty crazy times." Gabe said.

Sarah laughed. "Oh yes. She's so good for me. She's one who I truly confide in about everything that goes on in my mixed-up world."

"Does she know about me?"

"Of course she does. She's the one who convinced me to let you listen in on Alex screwing me."

"Really? Interesting," Gabe said enticingly.

"What?" Sarah asked.

"Well, I've got an idea. Since I have really fallen for you, I've not looked at any porn or other women at all. I only have eyes for you," Gabe began.

"As it should be," she cut in.

"Yeah, but what if you send me a couple of photos of you and your friend in sexy positions. You know, something I can look at when you and I are talking. It would be less painful to see you with another woman than to see you with Alex."

"Are you serious? Take pictures of me with Tanya?"

"You don't have to do anything but pose. Unless of course you wanted to," he chuckled at his joke. "You women see each other naked all the time, don't you? It would be just for fun. A little something for me." Sarah thought she could hear him drooling over the thought.

"I'm not sure."

"Look, you enjoy my little gifts I send you, don't you? The gift cards, the flowers?"

"Yeah."

"Well, tell Tanya I'll send her something too as a thank you. You know, to make it worth her while."

Sarah playfully responded, "What? Being with me wouldn't be enough payment for her?"

Gabe laughed, "You're more than enough for anyone, but would you ask her? That would get me so hard."

Sarah did like pleasing him. Each time she knew he came on the other end of the phone, she could feel the power her body had over him, even from such a great distance. She knew Tanya would probably do it, but she thought she'd make Gabe beg for it.

"Gosh, I don't know. It could be pretty awkward," she said.

"Oh, come on, baby. Ask her. You never know. You might really get into it," Gabe said.

"I'll ask, but I'm not going to push her. She doesn't know you. So if she says no, then it's no."

"All right, we can go with that," Gabe said. He changed the conversation and they talked their way through their sexual desires into the early hours of the morning.

FIFTEEN

When Sarah arrived home from her morning training the next day, she found herself with thirty minutes before Tanya was due to arrive. She lay down on her back in her gym, stretched her arms over her head, and extended her legs as far as possible. She held the stretch for thirty seconds and then relaxed. It felt so good to lie down that she dozed off.

The dark-eyed man had an incredible smile. His teeth were stunningly white, and his lips invited her to come close and latch onto them. His arms were tight and as he wrapped his left arm around and behind her back, he let his right hand run through her hair as he kissed her. His lips were soft, but so strong, like they had a power of their own. She closed her mouth around his and tugged on his bottom lip with her teeth...

"Sarah!" Tanya called. "Sarah, wake up, honey."

Sarah opened her eyes. Tanya was staring down at her. It had been the same guy from her dream the other night. This time she saw his face... and those lips. She blinked at Tanya, not quite sure where she was for a minute.

"Tanya. Shit," Sarah said as her eyes regained focus and reality registered. "I fell asleep. Sorry."

"It's OK, girl. You gotta rest when you can get it."

Sarah sat up and ran her hand through her hair, the way her lover was doing in her dream. "Wow, I had the wildest dream."

"About your man?" Tanya asked.

"No, another guy. Someone I don't know. I've had a couple like that."

"Ooh, a mysterious third man enters into Sarah's life and sweeps her off her feet!" Tanya teased.

"Wouldn't that be something?" Sarah replied. They smiled at each other, and then Tanya got onto the stationary bike.

"How was your week?" Tanya asked. "What's new in your world?"

"Oh, man, life is crazy," Sarah said as she stood and stretched. She told Tanya about letting Gabe listen into her sex with Alex and how much Gabe loved it.

"Yeah, I can see how it could be pretty hot thinking of your lover with someone else," Tanya said.

"Really? You think so? I've never wanted to consider Gabe with another woman."

"Your situation is so different, Sarah. It's not a typical man-woman romance. You've got a love triangle that includes a psycho and a telephone in it."

They burst out laughing at that thought. "Tell me about it," Sarah said. "Speaking of not typical, I've got something to propose to you."

"What? Tell me!" Tanya said as she kept pedaling, warming her muscles for training.

"You won't believe what he's asked me to do," Sarah began.

"Who? Alex?"

Sarah laughed. "No, Gabe."

"Gabe? What does he want?"

"Well, he's got this idea that it would be really hot for him if I took some pictures of myself," Sarah began.

"Yeah?" Tanya waited for the rest of the sentence.

"With you," Sarah said. She let that register for a minute, then added. "Naked."

"Oh really?" Tanya said. "How did this come up in conversation?"

"It started with me telling him that I was training you today. Actually, I'm not sure how we ended up there—but he threw that request on the table to see if it would stick."

"He's kinky," Tanya said. "I like him!"

"Well, I told him you were probably not going to be too keen on sending that kind of image out into cyberspace, but he offered a bit of incentive."

"Like?"

"Gift certificates for both of us if we do it," Sarah said. "Is that slutty?"

"A GC? Really?" Tanya said, "He's given you some good stuff, hasn't he?"

"Yeah, actually," Sarah said. "All my favorite stores. But really, T, I don't care if we do it or not, I just told him I'd ask."

"Well, why not?" Tanya said, and she stopped pedaling. She got off the bike and took a big swig of her water. "Let's do it. Who will take the picture?"

"Hmmm. We can set up a tripod," Sarah suggested. "Let's do it on Thursday when you come in to train, and I'll think of something."

"All right."

The next night after dinner, Alex cornered Sarah in the kitchen. He pressed up against her from behind as she stood cleaning dishes. She could feel his hardness on her tailbone.

"What are you doing?" she asked.

"What? Can't I rub my cock on my wife?" Alex said. He didn't move.

Sarah slid out from in front of him and turned around. "Look, we're separated. As in, not together. You can't keep doing this to me."

"You didn't mind the other night when you were moaning in bed with me," Alex said, "and you sure don't seem to mind the stuff I buy around here for you."

"You want the truth? It's easier to let you fuck me than to fight with you," Sarah said. "But just because I let you get off on me doesn't mean I don't want out of this."

"You've got nowhere to go without me," Alex said. "Or do you? You seem to be talking on the phone quite a lot. Are you talking to your photographer boyfriend?"

"Oh please," Sarah said. "Yeah, I'm talking a lot to him, but it's about the photo shoot."

"Right," Alex said. "You don't need to talk that much about the photo shoot. I told you, I'm OK with you screwing other guys. Long as I get some fun out of it, too. What do you do, masturbate on the phone?"

"I'm not having this conversation with you," Sarah said.

"I always knew you had a dirty side. I wish you'd show it to me."

"Maybe if you treated me better than you treat your employees we'd have more of a relationship," she said.

"You're not going to leave me. I know this flirting with your photographer is just a temporary thing. You know what? I don't care. You won't leave the kids, and you can't afford to take them. Besides, once you get your precious photo shoot you won't want the negative publicity. How's this for a headline? '*Fitness Champion and Mother of 5 has Her Life Fall Apart.*'"

Alex laughed as he left the room. Sarah's chest heaved. Her lungs struggled to take in air, and she sat on the edge of her bed with her head hung forward until the feeling passed. A few minutes later she heard him leave. *Probably out to the clubs,* she thought with relief. It meant he wouldn't come looking for sex that night, leaving her free to be alone with Gabe.

SIXTEEN

A fully naked Tanya posed on Sarah's bed. She was on her back, slightly arched, with her head tossed all the way back, showing the long, sensual curve of her neck "Yeah, stay just like that," Sarah said to Tanya as Sarah looked through the camera lens and adjusted the tripod.

They had locked Sarah's bedroom door and closed the shades on all the windows. Sarah had put white sheets on her bed and removed any personal items from the background. Sarah set the timer on the camera then rushed to get into the photo with her friend. They both started laughing as the photo snapped, and Sarah had to do it again.

They wanted their faces out of the picture, so it took a few tries to hit the right pose that looked intimate and luscious.

"Let me see that one," Tanya said. They pushed the play back button and studied it.

"Ew, no," Tanya said. "My stomach looks weird in this one. Do it again."

"Oh, brother, your stomach is fine," Sarah said.

Sarah repositioned the camera and reset the timer. She got into the picture, positioning herself seductively leaning against Tanya. After a few more takes where they had wrecked the picture by laughing, they finally had a couple of pictures that looked hot.

"Done," Sarah said.

"Is he excited?" Tanya asked.

"I didn't tell him," Sarah said. "I told him I hadn't asked you yet. I thought I'd surprise him. Then if you changed your mind he wouldn't be bugging me for it."

"Ah," Tanya answered. "Well, let me know what he says."

"I will," Sarah said. "Put your clothes on. Let's go to the gym and get you training."

Sarah downloaded the pictures to her computer, e-mailed the good ones to Gabe, then deleted everything off the computer and camera. She even cleared the history and cache so Alex, who was not computer-savvy, would not be likely to find them. She reformatted the memory card in the camera to be sure they were deleted from it, too.

Within five minutes of hitting *send* on the e-mail, her phone rang.

"Hello."

"You are amazing," Gabe gushed, "truly, truly amazing." He paused. "I mean, wow. Thank you."

Sarah smiled. "So... you like?"

"Oh, I like very much," Gabe said. "And you know, I knew you were photogenic, but even from this cheap camera shot and with no airbrushing, you look beautiful. I can't wait to see you on the cover of a magazine. Shit, I can probably present you to some of the other magazines in the industry. If you think one cover will boost your career, just think what two would do."

"I like the sound of that."

"Well, then let's see what we can do. We are going to have such a great time at Nationals, you won't even believe it."

Later that night, after they talked one another through hot cyber sex, Sarah was feeling a bit frustrated. She was tired of sex without the physical connection she wanted so badly from Gabe. He sensed her mood shift.

"What's wrong, Princess?"

"I wish you were here. Or I was there. Or we both were somewhere else," she said. "Aren't you tired of this?"

"It's not forever," Gabe said. "I'm glad to get you any way I have you for now."

"I guess. I can't believe how much I miss you. I've never even been near you to know what having you there is like, yet I miss your presence. Is that fucked up?"

"No. When someone captures your heart, it's like they are right there. You make it so hard for me to concentrate on my work. Really, I think I could fall deeply in love with you. If I haven't already." He laughed hesitantly.

She wasn't ready to use the "L" word with him, so she changed the subject. "I wake up each morning and the first thing I do is look at my phone to see if you sent me a message," she confessed. "I can't wait till we can be together and see if all this is real."

"Oh, it's real, babe. Don't worry. Hey, would you ever consider moving out to Los Angeles? It would boost your career big time. In addition to the other perks I could give you every night."

"Let's see what happens after Nationals. I'm not ready to think about that. I've got to do what's best for my kids. No matter how good your perks are," she added playfully.

"Deal. By the way, you and Alex haven't had sex lately, have you?" Gabe asked.

"No. Why?"

"It's just you haven't let me listen in. I really liked that. Promise next time you'll call me so I can hear."

Her energy drained from her. Was *nothing* she did good enough for Gabe? Now *he* was pushing her to have sex with Alex, too?

"I have to be honest with you, I find it so odd that you want hear another man screw me. Especially one that you know is so awful to me. I don't get it," she said.

"Princess, it's not my fault you drive me crazy sexually. I want to hear you, imagine you, and see you as much as I can until I get to touch you myself. Talk really dirty to him next time. Pretend it's me and tell me what you want me to do to you. I want to hear it all. Please?"

She put the palm of her hand that wasn't holding the phone to her suddenly pounding head. There was a ringing in her ears; or maybe warning bells. Either way, she didn't want to talk to Gabe any more that evening.

"I'll talk to you later," she said as she hung up.

The next morning, Mark put Sarah through a tough workout. Nationals were five weeks away and it was really time to kick it into gear. As frustrated as Gabe made her the night before, she felt dauntless about Nationals.

"You look happy today," Mark said as Sarah gathered her things to head home.

"I don't know about happy," Sarah said, "but I feel ready."

"Things better at home?" Mark asked.

"Nope. Alex is the same. I'm going to get through it, though. This photo shoot with Gabe is exactly what I need. I tell you, Mark, I am going to kick butt at Nationals."

"I can tell you like this guy. Just be careful. Tread slowly. Don't give him too much information about yourself."

"Thanks for worrying about me," Sarah said. "You don't need to, though, really."

"Well, be good this weekend. We're in the home stretch. Did you get the plane tickets yet?"

Sarah shook her head. "No, I didn't. I'll get them this week. We'll leave on Thursday morning?"

"Yeah, sounds good. I got the confirmation for the hotel. We're all set," Mark said.

"Sweet," Sarah replied. "I'll see you Monday."

As Sarah began the drive home, her phone buzzed with a text message. It was from Gabe.

Gabe: OMG, OMG, OMG - I screwed up.
Sarah: What happened? Are your kids ok?
Gabe: They're fine. I accidentally hit reply to the email of the pictures you sent me.
Sarah: What?
Gabe: I replied to the email—so my message went to your home computer.
Sarah: SHIT!

Sarah punched the accelerator and started talking out loud to herself. She knew there was no chance of the kids seeing Gabe's message—they never went into her e-mail—but she knew Alex checked it all the time and he was home.

"Maybe he'll be out," Sarah kept praying over and over.

She came to a screeching halt in her driveway. She ran through the door, into the kitchen, and flew up the back stairs to the office. Her blood froze in her veins when she saw Alex at the computer. His back was to her. She could see that e-mail was open and he was reading a message.

She walked up behind him and said quietly, "You have no right to read my personal e-mails."

Alex spun the desk chair around slowly to face Sarah. His arms rested on the arms of the chair, and his fingers were intertwined. He leaned back in the chair, looked up at the ceiling, and took a deep breath before meeting her angry gaze.

"So it *is* more than just a photo shoot for you," he said. The tone of his voice gave her a shiver as she racked her brain to think of what to say. If he thought she cared for Gabe, he would find a way to wreck it. Maybe she could pull it off that she was using Gabe for what he could do for her. There was a slim chance that Alex could understand, and even appreciate, that.

"Look," Sarah began, "I told you from the start that I really wanted this photo shoot. You know a magazine cover would be a shot of adrenaline for my career. Yeah, Gabe and I have been goofing around on the phone, but it isn't like I'm going to run off with him. I need this cover."

"I guess that explains the reasons for all the gifts," Alex said. "Flowers, gift cards. You've got him whipped."

Sarah remained still and quiet. The last thing she wanted to do was fuel the fire she could smell burning inside of her ex-husband.

Alex stood and said, "Here, sit down. Read your e-mail from your lover."

Sarah sat. It said:

Hey Princess! Thank you again for the amazing photos. You are truly one in a million. I am so hard from just looking at them. I can't wait to make sweet love with you tonight. I'll call you at 10.

- *G.*

Sarah sighed.

"So what were the photos?" Alex wanted to know. "Let me see them."

"Sorry, I deleted them all after I sent them."

Alex laughed. "Well, at least I get the real thing. So what's this guy into?"

"I don't want to talk about that with you!" Sarah said.

"Well, if he needs more photos taken, you know I'd be into it," Alex said. "Besides, he's saving me money by buying you things."

Alex left the room. Sarah heard the door slam. It was only after she heard his car leave the driveway that she realized she'd been holding her breath. She exhaled.

"Shit," she whispered.

She sent Gabe a text message.

Sarah: He saw it.
Gabe: I'm so sorry. I forgot I wasn't supposed to reply to u. Only phone.
Sarah: It's ok. He had to know I'd find someone else eventually anyway. He needed reminding that he and I are done.
Gabe: Forgive me?

Sarah: Of course. Hey - I have a client coming soon - I'll talk to you later.

That afternoon, as Sarah finished up with her last client, Alex came into the gym. He slapped a manila envelope onto her stereo case and walked out.

Her client, the Florida Marlins baseball player, raised his eyebrows. "He isn't as talkative today, I guess."

"Nope. I like it better that way," she said, laughing.

"Things going rough?" he asked.

"Oh, we're separated and it gets a bit intense sometimes."

"That's too bad." Her client looked truly saddened for her.

"Trust me, it's for the best," Sarah assured him.

When she was alone, she looked inside the envelope. Two gift cards from The Chanel Store with a value of seven hundred and fifty dollars each. No note, no card.

She took the envelope and went into the house where Alex was fixing himself a drink.

"Where'd this come from?" Sarah asked.

"I assume your boyfriend," Alex replied without looking at her.

"No, I mean how did it get here? This isn't a mail envelope," Sarah held it up—her name and address were scrawled on the outside of the envelope, but there was no postage and no return address.

"A guy rang the doorbell and asked if you lived here. I said yeah, and he gave me this envelope. What was inside?"

"Gift cards from The Chanel store," Sarah answered. She immediately wished she hadn't said *cards*.

"How many cards?" Alex asked.

"Two," she answered.

"Why two? Were you extra good? Or is there someone else involved, too?" Alex stared at her. She knew she didn't want Tanya brought into this with Alex.

"Both for me," she lied. "At least he appreciates me."

She went to her room and locked the door. She was angry for telling Alex anything. The envelope wasn't sealed well, so he had probably looked inside anyway. She texted to Gabe.

Sarah: Hey. I got your GCs. Thank you! Wow.
Gabe: You girls deserve them.
Sarah: How'd you get them here so fast?
Gabe: I called the store to order them and paid to have them personally delivered so you'd have them today.
Sarah: You didn't have to do that.
Gabe: I feel bad about sending my message to your email.
Sarah: It's fine. Really.

That night, Alex came into her room after the kids went to bed. He shut the door behind him and stood over her while she lay in bed, reading.

"You need to tell me what's going on with this guy," he said.

"What are you talking about?" Sarah asked.

"Don't play dumb with me. Your photographer. What are you doing with him?"

Fear gripped Sarah's chest. She smelled booze on Alex's breath and could practically see the venom dripping from his words as they hung in the air.

"What do you want me to say?"

"You're not as smart as you think you are. I've had your phone tapped for weeks. I already know about your conversations, the phone sex, the promises to be together one day. I want to hear it from you to me now."

Sarah's face turned white. She slid out the other side of the bed and headed for the door. He quickly stepped in her path, blocking her exit. He put his hands on her shoulders to stop her from moving.

"Let go of me or I will scream," she said. "You want the kids to see this?"

"Go ahead." Alex laughed at her. Spit flew from his mouth, landing on her cheek.

"You're disgusting," Sarah said as she wiped her face with the back of her hand, "and you smell like a toilet. I thought you didn't care what I did."

"You'll do anything to get that cover shoot, won't you?"

"I told you—I'm trying to keep this guy happy until after Nationals." Sarah tried to say it calmly. She didn't want him to think she had any feelings for Gabe. She forced her breathing to stay level.

"I don't care. Now that I know for sure you're dicking around, though, I've got news for you," Alex said. "Unless you let me in on what you're doing, you won't get anywhere near Nationals."

She was near full-on panic, yet her body ached to keep it together. She dug her fingernails into her palms to keep from crying, but she knew this would only work for a couple of minutes. "What do you mean?" she asked.

Alex took his hands off of her shoulders and sat on the edge of her bed. The path to the door was free, but Sarah didn't move. She turned to face him.

"What do you mean?" she said slowly.

"You want something. I want something," he said. "Come on, I want to hear from you what he wants you to do with him. Tell me what he told you."

It took every ounce of Sarah's willpower to keep her hands from reaching out and grabbing his throat. She knew he'd overpower her. She was thankful that a sudden surge of rage overpowered her desire to cry. Her eyes went cold.

"You bastard," she said. "I hate you. No way. If you have me tapped then you already know."

"Oh, you'll tell me," Alex said, "and here's why: I will call your little boyfriend and tell him you are just using him for his damn photo shoot. I'll tell him that you have been playing him all along. I'll tell him that you and I have been laughing behind his back at what an idiot he is. And I'll tell him that I'm going to blow the whistle to the magazines he works for on what he's been doing—trading sex for promises of a cover shoot. How do you think that will make him look?"

Sarah leaned her head back and closed her wet eyes. He had her trapped.

"So," he began again, "tell me what he wants you to do. I want it from your mouth."

She kept her eyes closed as she spoke, "He wants to listen in while you fuck me. He wants me to call out his name."

Alex grinned. "You know what? That doesn't bother me. I don't care what name you say or who is listening. I'd let ten guys fuck you while I watch. I can't help it you turn me on so much. So you're going to give him what he wants, and you and I are going to have a great time doing it."

"I can't believe you'd blackmail the mother of your children like this. You're sick," Sarah said. She felt defective. No matter what she tried in order to slip through Alex's grasp, he had a new scheme, a new rope ready to pull her back. Her attempts to get away were futile.

"I can't believe you'd think I wouldn't. This is my house. You want to play around in here, you play by my rules. You don't like it, you know where the door is."

"Look," Sarah said, "if you screw Gabe's career, you screw mine too. Then *you'll* look bad. It will come out in public that your wife was cheating on you. Remember, your friends don't know we're separated. You're keeping up the image. Is that what you want?" She thought that if she had a card to play, this was it.

Alex laughed. "It wouldn't get that far. I'd threaten Gabe, he'd pay off in return, and it would all be over. Nothing would ever get public. Remember, I'm one step ahead of you, Sarah. I always am."

"You're sick," she said.

He rose from the bed and straightened his shorts. For a horrifying moment she thought he was going to remove them. He smirked, knowing what she was thinking, and walked slowly out of the room, leaving her standing there in her humiliation. She fell face first onto the bed and cried herself to sleep.

SEVENTEEN

For the next week, Sarah existed in a state of heightened alertness that damn near killed her. The awareness of Alex's presence blocked out all other thoughts. Each time she saw him, she expected him to cash in on his scheme to exchange her body for his silence to Gabe.

Yet he never advanced. She didn't know if he was allowing the tension to build to screw with her mind or if he was letting the sexual energy grow in his own loins for his pleasure. Either way, she was ready to snap.

Sarah couldn't help but be reserved in her words to Gabe during their conversations. Knowing Alex had a bug on her phone changed everything. She chose her phrasing carefully, so as to give Gabe a bit of sexual passion, but not too much, so Alex could read between the lines and think she wasn't emotionally attached.

She couldn't properly get into their phone sex and ended up mentally exhausted and very frustrated. Even when she knew Gabe was coming on the other end of the phone, she couldn't bring herself to orgasm.

Sarah toyed with the idea of telling Gabe about Alex. Should she give him the heads-up that Alex was threatening to bring him to ruin? Or should she play along and pray it all worked out?

She caught a break and gained a couple of days to ruminate on the next steps. Gabe had a big photo shoot scheduled and would be traveling with limited phone access. When Alex informed her that he was going to Vegas to watch a pro fight, she gave thanks out loud to

God. The potential for three full days of peace lifted the weights from her shoulders. She also took the opportunity to get a new phone.

"So why do you want a new phone?" the store employee asked. He was a kid, maybe eighteen years old. "This one looks brand new."

"My idiot husband bugged it," she said.

"Are you freaking serious?" The kid laughed as he said it. "That's so cool."

Sarah raised an eyebrow at him. "Cool?" But then she laughed too. "Yeah, he's a bit crazy. This is why I need a new phone. Do you know anything about bugs?"

"No way, ma'am." He took the back off the phone and removed the SIM card. "I don't see anything back here that looks out of the ordinary."

"Hmm. I need to find someone who can check it out for me. Do you know anyone?"

"Sorry, I have no idea," the kid said.

An idea came to her. "Wait a minute. Actually, put that SIM card back in the old phone."

"You don't want a new phone?" he asked.

"I do want a new one, and I am going to keep this one," she said. "If he thinks I removed the bug, he'll just do the same thing to my new phone. If I get a second phone, with a new number, and start using that, he can continue to listen all he wants to these calls."

The kid shrugged. "Hey, whatever you want. This is awesome. I feel like we're all James Bond and shit." He put the old phone back together and got Sarah a new phone account set up. Forty minutes later, she walked out.

The new phone looked exactly like her old one. She even bought two new matching covers so there would be virtually no difference. She gave each a different password to get in—using Alex's and Gabe's birthdays—to help her remember which was which. A satisfied smile crossed her face as she exited the store and made the left turn to head toward Chanel, where she met Tanya. They spent their entire gift cards on hot new clothes that Sarah had every intention of letting Gabe see her in (and hopefully out of) when they met at Nationals.

While she and Tanya shopped, Sarah brought her up to speed on the events of the last two weeks, including Alex's phone bug and his threats against Gabe.

"Sarah, he is whacked enough to call Gabe's work. You know that, right?" Tanya said as they paid for their clothes.

"I know. Makes my stomach hurt to think about it. It wouldn't just fuck up Gabe's career, my name would be splashed all over it too," Sarah said.

"Girl, you better keep Alex happy. Does he know it was me in the pictures?"

Sarah quickly answered, "No, I told him it was only me." As she said it, a realization came to her. "Oh shit," she said, "I talked about you with Gabe on the phone. Alex would have heard everything."

Sarah never had seen Tanya look frightened. Until now. "Sarah, if Josh ever found out, he would leave me."

Sarah took a deep breath. "Let's think about this. Alex didn't bring you up at all, and I'm sure he would have if he'd really known. The kid at the phone store didn't find anything in my phone. Alex didn't actually tell me anything—he made me tell him. So is it possible he was lying about the bug?"

Tanya shook her head. "I have no clue, but we better find someone who does."

Next door to Chanel was a Starbucks. They sat at a table, pulled out Sarah's iPad, and Googled local businesses with "phone bugging" in the name. A shop called Spy Supply was not too far away.

The outside of the shop had no signage to give a hint as to what business took place inside. A small banner with the shop's logo hung above a nondescript door. If they hadn't seen the logo on the internet, they wouldn't have even realized what it was. The logo was a pair of black sunglasses with an S in each lens—for Spy Supply.

Inside the shop, a short, narrow hallway opened into a thirty-by-thirty-foot space. Industrial warehouse shelving lined the walls and clustered in the center of the room. At a quick glance they could see night vision goggles, surveillance equipment, pen recorders, locksmith supplies, GPS trackers, even something called "wireless Nanny."

"Damn," Tanya said. "I need me one of these Nanny Cameras. I think Evelyn has been napping during the day instead of watching the kids."

"First, let's figure out my phone," Sarah said. "Then we can bust your nanny."

"Helloo?" Tanya called out.

"How can I help you fine ladies?" a male voice said from behind them.

They both jumped and turned around to find a skinny black man standing there. He held an armload of boxes that indicated there were voice-activated phone recorders inside. He set them down on a shelf and smiled at Sarah and Tanya.

"Well," Sarah began, "here's the thing..." She explained that Alex told her he was bugging her phone, but she had no way to know if it was true. She asked the guy if he would be able to tell.

"That's an easy one," he said. "There are a couple of ways he might have done it. He could have installed a listening device on the phone—possibly attached to the battery to draw from its power. It would be voice activated, so when you began to speak into the phone, it would begin to record. The recording would transmit to a device that he held in his possession."

"What's the other way?" Tanya asked.

"If it is a smartphone, there are applications that he could have installed onto the phone to do the same thing—transmit voice or text messages."

Sarah pulled the phone from her purse and offered it to the guy. "Can you tell if he's done either of those things?"

"Absolutely," the guy said. "Follow me. My name is Ben, by the way."

"I'm Sarah, and this is Tanya," Sarah said. "Thanks for helping us."

He led them through a narrow door in the back corner of the store into another room that held a workbench with a laptop on it and some tools.

Ben opened the back of Sarah's phone and removed the SIM card and battery. "Your phone is pretty slim," he said. "Not a lot of room to hide anything back here. If he had put a bug into the phone, we would see it here—or here." With the tip of a screwdriver he indicated where the bug would be. "But I don't see anything."

Sarah sighed relief. "That's good, right?"

Ben shrugged. "Let's check the phone's software."

He plugged her phone into the laptop, "I'm going to need to run a diagnostic program on your phone. It won't show me your private messages and stuff and it will not download anything onto my laptop. It will check for very specific types of programs. Do I have your permission to do that?"

"Please. I need to know if he can hear what I'm saying on that phone," Sarah answered.

Ben punched some stuff into the laptop and then sat back and waited. It took only a couple of minutes.

"Nope," he said. "You're clean."

Sarah and Tanya looked at one another and smiled.

"You're sure?" They said simultaneously.

Ben laughed. "I'm sure. There is no recording device or listening software on this phone."

After they left the store, more relieved and with one new Nanny Camera in tow, Sarah let out a long breath.

"That fucker lied to me to get me to tell him what Gabe was saying to me," Sarah said. "I'm gonna kill him!"

"Now just wait," Tanya said. "If you call his bluff now, you have no leverage later should you need it. Go along with him. Sarah. You still need him. You have to be able to walk away cleanly with no need of his finances for you and the kids. You aren't there yet. You have to fuck him a bit longer. Both men get what they want."

"But what about me?" Sarah said sadly. "Doesn't what I want count for anything?"

"Oh, sweetie," Tanya said, and they stopped walking. Tanya hugged Sarah and let her sob for a minute.

Then Sarah pulled back and looked at her friend, "I can do this. I've got under four weeks till Nationals. I'll make it."

"Thatta girl," Tanya said. "Come on, let's go set up my Nanny Cam. I can't wait to see what that bitch does when I'm not home."

Even though Sarah didn't need the new phone, she kept it anyway. It felt masterful to be one up on Alex as she planned to switch her connections over to the new number. She knew she'd have to tell Gabe some reason for the number switch. She gave him a partial lie about Alex, based on what he had told her about the bug. She hoped this would give Gabe the heads up that Alex was a crazy SOB. She sent him a text message from the new phone.

Gabe: Hey, Princess. Why the new number?
Sarah: I found out Alex was bugging my old phone.
Gabe: Seriously?
Sarah: My old one is under Alex's account anyway—I needed to get a new one set up. I got the billing to go to my mom's house.
Gabe: Oh. Smart thinking.
Sarah: We'll have to still use the old number from time to time so he doesn't get suspicious, ok?
Gabe: Did he tell you he bugged the phone?

Sarah thought about that—she didn't want to concern Gabe that Alex would do something crazy, like call his work, but at the same time she wanted him to understand that Alex *was* crazy enough to call his work. And she really didn't want to scare him off.

Sarah: I think after he got the email the other day he planted it to see what I was really up to.
Gabe: Oh really?
Sarah: I tried to blow it off like there's nothing big between us. If he thinks I care for you he'll be a pain in the ass.
Gabe: Oh, ok. Is he ok with you and I talking so much?
Sarah: He knows I'm moving on with my life. Yeah, we fight about it. He thinks I want him, but there's no going back.
Gabe: I'm sorry to hear it.
Sarah: How's the trip going?
Gabe: Not bad - sorry I can't chat at night - I'm sharing a room with one of the lighting guys for this project.
Sarah: It's ok. Do you miss me?
Gabe: Like crazy. I'll call when I get back.
Sarah: Talk to you soon. xox

Sarah was proud of herself for determining that Alex didn't have her phone bugged. It was a heady feeling to have some power. If he wanted to pretend he could hear her conversations, she'd play along. For now.

EIGHTEEN

Come lie next to me. Let me wander my hands over the soft, sensual curves of your body. Let me kiss your shoulder as I reach down, between your legs and slowly start to rub your inner thigh. Let me gaze into your eyes and kiss you deeply, so I take your breath away. I want to hear that you want me. Then I will fill you up, pushing my throbbing cock deep inside your wet pussy. Let me hear you moan with every stroke. I want to watch your face light up with pleasure as I bring you to climax and then look at you and say, "Good morning, Beautiful."

Gabe's text message brought a longing to her chest. Why oh why was he so far away? Endless texts and phone calls that promised loving tenderness yet seemed to always end up in nothing but sex left her empty and unsure what this relationship was all about. No matter how many times he typed the words, they couldn't replace the feeling of having a body there, hot skin on skin, sweat dripping all over each other. She was especially tired that although he said he wanted to bring her to pleasure, again and again, she was the one fulfilling the act.

"Shit." She sighed and put her phone down on the nightstand. Three more weeks until Nationals. The end was in sight. She would finally meet up with him. She would finally know the warmth of his hand on her back and the feel of his lips on her neck. Then she'd know for sure if this long-distance thing was worth it. She stood from her bed, stretched, and went to shower.

When she returned she saw she had missed a message from him.

Gabe: Good morning, Beautiful. Whatcha doin?
Sarah: Hi. Just had a shower.
Gabe: Did you like my other message?
Sarah: Sure did. Made me miss you.
Gabe: Soon, Princess.
Sarah: What are you up to today?
Gabe: Aside from missing you, going to do a family shoot down by the beach.
Sarah: I wish I was at the beach.
Gabe: I'll get you on the beach one day soon.
Sarah: Lol. Can't wait.
Gabe: Hey - I had an idea. The other night, when you screamed out my name, it got me so hard. I came within seconds of that.
Sarah: I couldn't believe I actually did that.
Gabe: You never stop amazing me. Maybe, just maybe, you can do something else for me?

The hair on her arms stood up as she read his words. *Something else?* What now? She already did everything he wanted and then some. Alex had come looking to get laid the day before, and he had the nerve to spank her ass when she called out Gabe's name, even though he told her ahead of time she'd better do it. It wasn't a pleasurable spank for Sarah—it really hurt. She punched the keypad angrily.

Sarah: What?
Gabe: Maybe you could somehow sneak your phone to snap a picture of his cock entering into your wet, soft pussy.

Sarah read the words three times, incredulous. Furious sparks leapt from her fingertips:

Sarah: Are you kidding me?
Gabe: I'd love to see what you look like at the moment you are being penetrated.
Sarah: That makes no sense whatsoever.
Gabe: I'm sure Alex wouldn't mind getting a little kinky with the camera.
Sarah: Alex would have a dozen guys lined up with cameras. That's not the point. I don't want to capture that memory. I don't want to keep having sex with him, let alone take a picture of it.

The voice in her head was screaming at the screen. How could he be so inconsiderate?

Gabe: Oh but Princess, the picture would be of you and your hot pussy. I want to see it and think about my cock filling you up.
Sarah: I can't do that Gabe. Sorry. That's not going to happen.
Gabe: Aw. Can't you wave your magic wand for me?
Sarah: If I could wave my wand, I'd make you not be an asshole right now.

It was degrading for her to keep having sex with Alex. Could Gabe not see that? Or maybe she was wrong and he had no concern for her feelings. All he thought about was his pleasure and getting off. If that was the case, he was no different than Alex.

She was more than a little disgusted with the whole thing. His lack of response infuriated her.

Sarah: Don't you care how I feel about it?
Gabe: Of course I do. Your pleasure is always first in my mind. I wish I could be with you so badly, I want to see what it's like to go inside of you. It's cause I want you so much.
Sarah: This is such a wild relationship we have.
Gabe: I've never been so hot for anyone. Ever. I can't get enough of you.
Sarah: I know what you mean. I want you continually throughout the day.
Gabe: I just wanted to see your sweet body. I guess it was too much. I'm sorry for asking you to do that. I'm an idiot.

His apology struck a chord. She could understand him wanting to see her. She was dying to know what he would feel like in her arms. She never wanted to see him fuck another woman—but, in a strange way, she felt like she could understand what he was saying. The confusion made it tough for her sort through what was really going on. Was she acting out of desperation? The unknown distance between them was filled with so many emotions. She didn't want to overreact or underreact, but she wasn't sure which way to tip the scale.

Sarah: No need to apologize. Tell you what, I'll try.
Gabe: No, I was wrong. Just forget it.

Sarah: I understand. Believe me, I do.
Gabe: Really? Oh sweetheart.
Sarah: I'll try, ok?
Gabe: You and that magic wand of yours will come through, I know it.

She rolled her eyes to herself. This was tiresome. Three more weeks.

Sarah threw all of her frustration once again into her morning workout.

"Easy there, killer," Mark said. "You're lifting the weights a little too fast. I want these to be slow reps."

Sarah slowed her movements.

"That's better," Mark observed. "You're gonna rock it at Nationals."

Sarah finished her set and gently set the weights down. "Damn straight," she said, "This is a turning point for me, Mark. You have no idea."

"Is Gabe still going to shoot you after?"

"Yep, he is." Sarah smiled. "He booked a small, private gym to do the shoot on Sunday morning. Then we might go down to the beach for some surf and sand pictures."

"Are you pacing yourself with him?" Mark asked.

"Mark, come on, I know what I'm doing," Sarah said. His question annoyed her, though, because she knew she had not paced herself.

"You have so much going on in your life, Sarah. This guy could be another complication for you. I just say it because I care."

Sarah raised an eyebrow at him. "I appreciate that. You are a great trainer and a great friend." She picked up the weights and began her next set.

"How's Alex been lately?" Mark asked. "I saw him the other night, you know."

"Really? Where?" Sarah asked.

"It was weird. You know that restaurant down by the Miami port, Docks?" Mark said.

"No, never been there."

"They have awesome clams, you should try them. After Nationals. Anyway, I was sitting at a booth having dinner and Alex walked by with these two guys. He didn't notice me—but they sat at the booth behind mine so his back was to mine." Mark said.

"He goes out a lot. Why do you think it was weird?" Sarah wondered.

"Well, they were talking about a shipment that would be coming into port next month, and Alex was quite aggravated at the men about whatever was coming in. He must have told them a half a dozen times that if they didn't take care of the security problems he'd make sure this was their last assignment. It reeked of illegal importing."

"What the hell would he be importing?"

Mark shrugged. "You're his wife. What kinds of things does he do in his businesses?"

"Oh, shit. I stay out of it. He's got the three nightclubs and a couple of apartment buildings that he owns. Then of course there's the gym. I know he and a partner bought a little Cuban restaurant on Calle Ocho a couple of months ago. Maybe the shipment was for the restaurant?"

"I don't know, but it was a very odd conversation," Mark said. "Anyway, let's get back to it. We've got legs next."

Even though Sarah didn't really care what Alex did with his businesses, something about the conversation with Mark stayed with her, even after her workout was over. *Was he involved in something illegal?*

She recalled the sad tale of his mother's death and the flippant comment about his father's cartel involvement. It had never come up again, but were there still ties? If not, the only thing she could think it could relate to was Club Fuego. Club Fuego was high-end, very upscale, and offered guests the pleasure of watching fully nude women dance in pairs and alone on any of several staged areas. Gentlemen paid high premiums to get in. Alex often boasted that his was the only liquor-licensed strip club in Miami to offer enclosed private rooms. Sarah never really asked, but it was known that the clientele also paid premiums for what happened behind the closed doors.

Other than the prostitution, she couldn't imagine Alex being involved in contraband activity, like dealing illegal substances. He was outspoken against drugs, and if he caught any of his employees so much as smoking pot while on the job, they were canned immediately.

She put those thoughts aside, but felt that she should pay more attention to what went on at the house. If he was into something bad, she sure as hell didn't want it around the kids.

That night, Gabe was extra attentive, perhaps feeling badly about upsetting her earlier in the day.

Gabe: Hi my Cover Girl! How are you tonight?
Sarah: Hey. I'm doing ok. 21 more sleeps until we meet.
Gabe: I know. I'm counting too.
Sarah: I hope you like me when we finally meet. Actually, I hope you more than like me. Lol.
Gabe: Too late—I'm in love already.

Sarah froze up for a minute. The "L" word again. Shoot. She wasn't ready to go there.

Sarah: That's a sweet thing to say.
Gabe: You're my sweet girl.

She wasn't sure how to answer. So she waited.

Gabe: Are you really committed to me? No bull shit?
Sarah: You have all of me. No bull shit.
Gabe: Maybe after Nationals I can come to Miami and meet your kids.
Sarah: We'll have to figure it all out. I really have to get everything dealt with here. And I won't introduce my kids to any guy unless I know 100% that it is serious.
Gabe: I'm pretty serious. How about you?
Sarah: Oh my Gabe. We haven't even met yet. I care so much for you, but I want to feel you and touch you. I want to wake up next to you and see your face in the morning smiling back at me. Can I ask you... what about me makes you so serious about us?
Gabe: It's you. All of you. You are funny and passionate. I enjoy talking to you. Throughout my day, when something happens I can't wait to share it with you. You are gorgeous

and that makes me want to fuck you hard (LOL) but you are the total package.

Sarah: So you're pretty hooked.

Gabe: You have no idea. Aren't you?

Sarah: I do want to be with you so badly. I want to stroke your face and kiss your lips.

Gabe: I want you to stroke something else.

Sarah: Really? What's that?

Gabe: You know exactly what it is. I want to feel you stroke my cock with your lips. Sucking and tasting every part of me until I cum fiercely into your mouth. Then I want to lie you back on the bed, with your sweet head resting on the softest pillow. I just really want to be on top of you, kissing all over your neck. I would move my way down, kissing around your breasts, then your stomach and then to your waist, spreading your legs apart and gently taking my tongue and putting it against your slit. I would gradually move all around it and then kiss your clit. I would slowly begin sucking on it and run my tongue up inside you, sliding it in and out, kissing and kissing you...

Sarah: Mmmm. Please come do that to me right now.

Gabe: In time, Princess.

Sarah: My body just got instantly hot.

Gabe: Good. I want you to want me... and only me. After I suck on you, starting at your pussy, I would move my way back up, kissing on your body right back up to your neck, and then your lips, sucking on your tongue. While kissing on your tongue, you would feel my rock hard cock moving against you, with your legs spreading further apart so I can slowly enter you, with the head of my cock moving into your pussy, my cock would spread your pussy apart, pressing in, sliding in, going in and out. With each stroke, going deeper and deeper, then you grab my butt and pull me deeper into you with each stroke I make, you moan with pleasure as I continue to kiss your neck and ears...

Sarah: I need to get a drink of water. To cool off.

Gabe: I would love to take an ice cube to you. First, I would blindfold you and tie your hands together above your head.

Sarah: I like where this is going...

Gabe: Beginning at your lips, I would trace the ice cube down your neck and let it drip in the soft spot at the front of your neck. Then I would run it around each of your breasts, pulling your nipples between my fingers. Then I would glide the ice down to your stomach and let it rest a minute on your belly to form a little pool in your belly button, which I would lick up with my tongue.

Sarah: That would drive me wild.

Gabe: Good. Cause then I would place it in my mouth and suck on your pussy, letting the cool water escape while my hot breath devoured your amazing wetness until you came for me.

Sarah: I bet you have the most incredible mouth.

Gabe: I guess you'll find out, won't you Princess?

NINETEEN

Alex went away on business again for a couple of days, allowing Sarah the freedom to engage in her own sexual fantasies with Gabe without interruption. She was leaner and more fit than she'd ever been before, and feeling good physically heightened her feelings of arousal.

Gabe asked her to send a headshot of her beautiful face, smiling at him through the camera. It warmed her to receive such a basic request from him. A simple photo of just her with no other women and no dicks pounding her, brought her emotions back to the place where she first felt affection for him.

She got a little playful and took several of herself naked, with her hands touching herself across her breasts and between her legs. Gabe responded with several photos of himself from the waist down—damn, he had a long, hard cock.

She was glad to have something to look at during their sex. She sometimes wondered why Gabe never wanted to use the video chat on the computer, but he insisted that he would prefer to meet her in person before they saw each other over video.

Darkness surrounded Alex when he arrived home from his trip. When his car pulled up, Sarah was sitting on the back deck, while Ethan and Elle frolicked in the pool. She had been daydreaming of an idyllic family life, one where she was valued. He slammed his car door so hard that it scared the twins and snapped her thoughts back to reality.

The twins looked to Sarah for reaction. She shook her head subtly, and they went back to playing, but kept an eye on their dad, who headed toward the house in strides that screamed, "Stay the fuck out of my way."

Sarah didn't follow him, sensing that they'd all better steer clear. She told the twins to get dressed because she was taking them out to dinner and a movie. She instructed them to find Antonio and tell him to get ready, too, then she sent a text message to her oldest children that read:

Dad's home. He's in a bad mood. Anyone who wants to go out to dinner and a movie with me, meet me by the garage in 15 minutes.

All five children showed up, ready to go. They managed to avoid Alex that evening—he was out when they returned home—but Sarah's years of living with his personality swings told her from the second she looked at him walking from the car to the house that he was due to erupt.

He left her alone for two days before even speaking to her. Sarah finished up with her last client of the day and was spending a few minutes cleaning the mats in the gym when Alex opened the door. He stood there, saying nothing, watching.

"What is it?" she asked, trying to sound casual.

"When do you leave for Los Angeles?"

"Not next Wednesday but the Wednesday after. Why?"

"Whose money are you using to go?"

"My ticket is bought already, and I just have to pay my entrance fees and hotel and stuff."

"I hope you don't plan on me giving you anything."

Sarah threw down her towel and walked to Alex. She poked at the air in front of him, bottle of cleaner still in hand.

"What's your problem?" Sarah asked. She was ready for this battle.

"You think you can come and go as you please, taking my money but not giving me what a wife should give her husband."

"Alex, I've told you, I can't take your mood swings anymore. I want you to move out."

The laugh that churned her stomach slipped from his angry lips. "That's funny. You know where the door is. You've known for years. Yet here you are."

Sarah shook her head at him. "You know I can't afford to raise five kids. And I won't leave them here."

"Well, then, I guess we're stuck together."

Sarah stood tall. "You know you have a legal obligation to provide for me and your children."

Laughter burst from him. "Ha. I have things set up that you would get nothing. Do you hear me? Nothing."

Sarah shook her head.

"So I guess we are stuck together." He seemed to purr it.

Sarah's anger was unmistakable. "We might live in the same house, but we are *not* stuck together."

"We are if you expect me to keep supporting your expensive tastes." He locked the door and pulled his shorts down low enough to free his hard cock. He began to rub himself, stroking up and down.

"What are you doing?"

"Come on, baby. Talk me through this," he said. "Better yet. Why don't you come over here and use those luscious lips on me."

"I'm not going to talk you through anything." She turned and walked back to the mat she had been cleaning. She picked up the towel and moved to another mat, further from him.

"You better take care of me another way, then."

"I've got a client coming soon," she lied.

"No you don't. I know your schedule," He walked around the gym and closed the shutters. He removed his shorts completely. Sarah put down the cleaning supplies and headed for the door, but he grabbed her arm and spun her around.

"No, Alex."

"It turns me on when you struggle against me."

She stopped struggling. "You make me sick."

He pulled her shorts down and turned her toward a weight bench. She bit her lower lip to keep from saying anything that would piss him off. He roughly grabbed the sides of her ass and slammed his hardness into her. It hurt like hell, but she grabbed the side of the weight bench and hung on.

"Damn, you are so tight right now. I love when you are ready for a show. Every inch of you is tight," he said.

It took him only three minutes till he came to orgasm. He slapped her on the ass and said, "Thanks, babe."

He put on his shorts and left. She sat on the floor in the center of her gym and looked around, tears strangulating her. This was *her* gym. The gym she loved. The gym she enjoyed watching her clients get fit in. The gym she worked so hard to set up just perfectly. For three years, every birthday, Christmas, and every Mother's Day that had come around, she requested nothing but equipment for her gym. She had saved her money to buy the mats and weights. His discount of her hard work would not break her.

A fire burned in her belly for success. Success to buy him out and kick him to the curb in the way he kicked her spirit time and again.

When she returned to her room to have a shower, there was five thousand dollars on her dresser. *Bastard*, she thought.

TWENTY

Sarah's insides were in a frenzy. It had been two full days since her last message from Gabe. She sent a couple of texts and left three voice messages, but nothing. His blog didn't indicate a photo shoot or trip, and neither did his Facebook status. In the few months they had known one another, it wasn't like him to fall off the grid—and especially to not respond to a message from her.

Near desperation, she sent Gabe a Facebook inbox message. She typed: *Hi my Gabe - What's up? I miss you. Where'd you go? - your Princess.*

There was no contact until the following morning. She received a Facebook reply:

Ummm - I think you've got the wrong Gabe. Not sure who this is?

Sarah stared at the computer. She picked up her phone. Her fingers shook so much, she could barely type.

Sarah: If that's your idea of a joke, I'm not laughing. What kind of crap are you pulling on me?

Another excruciating hour went by until she finally saw Gabe's name appear on the phone screen:

Gabe: What are you talking about?
Sarah: I sent a message on Facebook.

Gabe: Why would you do that? My assistant checks the Facebook account. I get so many inbox messages, I've told her no one I'm really in touch with will ever use f/b to reach me.

Sarah: Well you've been out of touch for 3 days, what the hell?

Gabe: I was in bed with the flu. It was bad.

Sarah: You could have told me.

Gabe: My mom came to stay with me cause it was my turn to have the boys. She took my phone away so I couldn't work.

Sarah: I was worried.

Gabe: About me?

Sarah: It's getting close to Nationals. 9 more sleeps. I'm worried something will keep us from meeting again. It always seems to.

Gabe: Oh Princess. Nationals will be a trip to remember for a loooong time. Hey, can I call you?

Sarah: Sure.

A couple of minutes later her phone rang.

"Hi, babe."

"So are you feeling better now after being sick?" Sarah asked.

"Much better. In fact, I feel so good, I could wrap my arms around you and give you the most extreme pleasure you've known. For at least two or three hours anyway." he said, laughing.

"That's it?" Sarah laughed too.

Gabe whined a little for effect. "Prin-ceeess, I've been sick. I need to build my strength back up."

Sarah smiled. "Hmmm. I guess I could do the majority of the work then."

"What would you do to me, my Cover Girl? Tell me..."

Sarah lay down on her bed before answering. "For starters, I'd remove all your clothes and make sure you were nice and comfortable, laying in our bed. I would glide my hand along your hips, massaging your thighs for a few minutes to get the blood flowing. Then I'd move my hand to your balls and rub them softly until you couldn't stand it. I'd slide my hand up to your hard cock."

"I would really like that," Gabe said quietly.

She continued, speaking more slowly, drawing out each word with perfect seduction. "I would go down on you and lick every inch of your thighs, your balls and your cock before taking you completely in my mouth. I'd straddle your leg and let my one hand massage your balls while the other strokes you with my mouth."

Gabe groaned. "Yes, baby. What else?"

"I would keep taking you in and out and licking the head of your cock," she crooned. "Over and over. Stroking, sucking, and licking you..."

"Mmmm. Can't wait for you to suck me good."

Sarah kept on. "I'd go as deep as possible."

"Yes," Gabe whispered. "I'd love that."

"You could press that cock deep, deep down my throat. My lips would massage you everywhere, and we would go hard until you were about to explode." Her voice got more forceful, like he was pounding into her mouth and about to come.

"Oh babe, I want you to do that."

"Then I'd let you come over and over into my mouth and I'd take it all in and suck you a little bit more gently while rubbing your balls—until you got it all out," she said sweetly.

Gabe's breath came hot into the phone. "My cock is so freaking hard. I need to totally just fuck you right now."

Sarah smiled. "Mmm. I want to feel that cock slide between my legs."

"Are you playing with that pussy right now?"

"Maybe."

"Send me a picture."

Sarah took her other phone and put it between her legs, where her hand was holding her vibrator. She snapped a shot and e-mailed it off to him.

"You are so freaking hot. I can't believe you're all mine," he said.

"Can't wait to see you," she said. "Barely over a week to go."

"Yes. It is," Gabe replied.

Mark scheduled Sarah for a six a.m. workout Monday. As she drove across the causeway, the sun was just beginning to peek over the horizon, blasting a span of yellow and orange into the deep violet sky. Her breath was momentarily halted at the sight, and the intensity of her reaction to seeing the morning blossom surprised her. So much so that she knew she had to pull over and take it in. She left the road on the other side of the bridge, parked on the shoulder, and got out.

She snapped a picture with her phone. It didn't do the canvas before her justice, but was good enough. Then, standing with the driver's door open, she stood on the side step of her Suburban and rested her elbows on the door frame, placing her chin on her arms. She watched the sky transform. Night and its darkness had no choice if it wanted to stay or go. The sun was coming no matter what.

She envied the sun's power over night. Alex was her darkness. Although she knew she didn't yet have the strength of the sun to cast out his shadows, she knew as sure as she stood there that it would happen. She prayed again that Nationals would be her turning point. There were so many unknowns about Gabe. She tossed between wanting to believe he was her knight in shining armor and the caution that he would disappoint her.

His insatiable sexual appetite reminded her of Alex, but Gabe mixed in the right amount of sweetness to keep her coming back for more. His words had filled her bucket time and again over these past few months, and she knew part of her attachment was to the kindness and care he displayed for her. Whereas Alex sucked her dry with degrading ugliness, Gabe's value of her as a person enriched her spirit. She was confident that when she met him, touched him, hugged him, she would be able to judge his sincerity.

She sighed deeply, then got back in her truck and continued on to Mark's. The workout was light; she was ready for Nationals and just needed to have a good clean week. She and Mark both felt she was in the best shape ever.

On the way home, her phone buzzed with an e-mail. She glanced down and saw it was from Gabe. It was rare for him to send e-mail, so she pulled into a strip mall parking lot to read it. Five minutes later, her head was on the steering wheel and she was sobbing uncontrollably.

Sarah -

My Princess. You are such an amazing person and this has been an incredible adventure for me. I wanted to tell you that first, because what I am going to reveal may make you doubt my sincere belief that you are truly one of a kind.

For the last few months, all of our interactions have been monitored. My name isn't Gabe Benoit. I work for a unique kind of company. Our staff members begin relationships with women and then post our live conversations and texts through our website. Our subscribers pay to watch, read, and listen in to what our staff is doing.

Sarah - all of our conversations and texts were viewed by thousands of subscribers. But it's over now. I have to end it because this week you have Nationals, and obviously the real Gabe Benoit is not going to have you scheduled for a photo shoot. Please don't let this squash your ambition. The humor and passion you've shown is unique. No other girls have ever had the following you've had. We posted this morning that Sarah's story is over as of today and we're getting hundreds of angry emails from subscribers who want to know what's going to happen next in your life. Will you stay with Alex? Will you leave him?

Everyone wants to know.

You don't have to worry about anyone coming after you. We have the live posting on a brief delay and we remove any mention of city or state location. We also never let your last name go out.

Sarah, I am sure you are disappointed about the cover shoot, but hear me on this—with everything you've accomplished, your fabulous children, your career, your business—you are on your way to great things. You don't

151

need a cover for that. I say that because I do care what happens to you. The team is really going to miss you around the office.

You won't be able to find us. We are a discreet company with private clientele. And anyway, you were a consenting adult who was sending information willingly. In doing so, you know there is always the risk that someone is listening. The way technology is today, I do hope you will be more careful in the future with whom you engage digitally.

This account will no longer be active once I see that you've read this email. I really will miss our daily interactions. They've become my favorite part of the day.

Good-bye from the Team.

The wail that escaped from her lips was a sound she'd never made before. Her cries echoed off the windows of her truck. A man walking by tapped on her window and asked if she needed help. She shook her head no, and tried to catch her breath.

She stared at the dashboard and for the first time ever had no idea what to do next. She looked over at her phone. The betrayal that phone delivered stung her chest. She spoke words of hope into it, and it twisted her hope and left wreckage behind.

An urge to be at home suddenly overpowered her paralysis. She threw the truck into drive and pulled forward so fast she nearly hit an elderly woman walking to her car. She stomped the brake in time, and the lady shot her the bird.

She drove home on autopilot, not really seeing the road or other cars. Sarah's breathing escalated as she pulled up into her driveway. She took her phone and ran to the house. *Thank God the kids left for school already.*

"Alex," she screamed as she entered the house. "Alex, are you here?"

She ran to Alex's bedroom and burst through the door. He was coming out of the bathroom and was clearly shocked to see her standing there.

"Alex, oh God, Alex," she moaned, and fell into a heap on the floor.

"Sarah, what happened?" He squatted down next to her and placed a hand on her back. She didn't pull away. Her shoulders heaved with her cries.

"Is it the kids?" he asked.

She shook her head. "I-I-can't- b-believe—" She took a breath. She stopped trying to talk. Instead, she handed Alex her phone, with the e-mail on the screen.

After reading the message, Alex said, "Who the hell is this guy?"

Sarah sat up. "I don't know. What the fuck am I going to do?"

Alex sat next to her on the floor. "Look at me," he said. "It'll be OK. I'll find him."

Sarah snorted, "People paid to listen to me get off with this guy. You too, for that matter. That's humiliating."

"How much did you tell this guy about our lives?" Alex asked.

"Enough to keep a relationship going. I wanted him to like me. I wanted him to help my career. You tell me all the time I don't have enough money to live on my own. I wanted to be on my way to my own freedom. You don't understand how fucking hard this all is! You are impossible to live with." Her voice escalated as she spoke, and she screamed the last words at him. Expelling them from her head made her burst into tears again. She put her head down on her arms and wept.

Alex took a deep breath. "Sarah."

Sarah lifted her head.

Alex shook his head. "I will find this guy. Leave it to me."

Sarah said, "How are you going to find him? He said the company is private."

"I have connections you know nothing about." He stood up. "I want you to write down the phone number you used to call him and his e-mail address. Write down everything he said about himself."

"It was all lies. It won't be true," she said.

"Doesn't matter," Alex said. "It's possible he slipped up in his info and gave you some bit of truth. No one will beat me at this game. I play better than anyone, and I'm smarter than anyone. I'll figure it out."

"You'll help me?" Sarah said. "I really want to find out who this is."

She gave him what she could then went to her room and lay down on her bed. Her phone rang. It was an unknown number. She let it go to voicemail and then listened.

"Sarah, it's me. Look, I'm calling from my personal cell, not the company cell I had been calling you on. Listen, I had to send the e-mail earlier, my boss made me. He stood there while I typed it. Please talk to me. I want to explain. Please answer your phone."

Sarah listened to the message three times. *Is he fucking kidding?* He didn't leave a number. *I guess I can't track him then,* she figured. A few minutes later it rang again. Then again. Then again. She finally shut it off. She told Lila she was going to bed for the rest of the day and asked if she'd please take care of the kids until tomorrow.

A light tap on her door woke her. It was dark outside, and she was still in her clothes, face down on her bed.

"Come in." she called.

Alex opened the door.

"Since when do you knock?" she said.

"How are you doing?"

"What time is it?" she couldn't see the clock through her cloudy eyes.

"Nine o'clock. You've been asleep all day. Kids are in bed. I won't go out tonight."

"Thanks. Really. That's decent of you."

"Any other messages?" he asked.

"I shut the phone off. He called a few times in a row and I didn't want to hear it anymore."

"No, Sarah, you've got to talk to him," Alex insisted. "We need to get more information. Get as much as possible. You must do your part so I can do mine. You know you need me on this one, right?"

"Alex, I'm humiliated. Thousands of people listened to me on the phone. He posted pictures of me. Shit, they listened to you having sex, too—doesn't that bother you?" Her eyes bore straight into his. "Probably not. I'm so embarrassed."

"I'll get this guy. But I need you to talk to him. See if you can get him to slip up and pass on anything that will help me find him. You know I can find him."

"Not tonight. I'm exhausted. I'm going to have a hot shower and then climb right back into bed."

She did just that.

TWENTY-ONE

Mark received a text message from Sarah the next morning.

Sarah: I won't be able to meet with you today. Sorry. I'll see u tomorrow.
Mark: What's going on? We leave in two days.
Sarah: I can't make it. Too much going on around here.
Mark: Everything ok?
Sarah: Please don't ask. Had the worst day ever yesterday. Just need to rest. I'll practice my posing in the gym here.
Mark: Sarah... you know I'm here for you.
Sarah: Thanks. You're terrific. See u tomorrow.

Once the kids were safely off to school, Sarah took a cup of tea and sat on the back deck. She went back through her phone, reading and re-reading the expressions of affection and the warm sexual encounters from the stranger called "Gabe." Knowing what she now knew, she could trace from the beginning how he started small and then escalated things to build her confidence. She did whatever he wanted. Even when she hesitated, he persuaded her to step out of her comfort zone and into his twisted sexual ploy.

How could I have been so stupid? she thought.

Alex came outside with his coffee. "So how ya doin'?"

"I can't believe this is happening," she said. "I also can't believe I leave the day after tomorrow."

"You think this guy will show up there?"

157

"I have no idea who the hell it even is. He could be anywhere."

"Has he called today?"

Sarah shook her head. "No. Nothing. I want to get this fucker."

Alex stood up. "Don't worry, I will. I gotta go. I've got to make the rounds and see how everything went at the clubs last night."

"See you later," Sarah said. She watched him cross the deck and enter the garage. *Why is he being so nice?* she wondered. She couldn't let her guard down too much with him. During his next mood swing he would likely throw this right back in her face as one more screwup in her life.

The phone's ring pierced the air and made her jump. She swallowed the lump in her throat and looked at the display. The unknown number.

"You can do this," she said out loud. She answered the phone with as flat of a tone as she could manage. "Hello." She wanted to remain stripped of emotions but knew it would be hard.

"Oh Sarah, you answered," so-called Gabe said.

"Who the hell is this?" she growled. *So much for keeping emotions out of it.*

"Sarah, listen, I am so sorry about all of this."

"WHO ARE YOU?" she wanted to reach through the phone and rip his tongue out.

"My name is Ricky. Ricky Jameson."

"Bullshit. You said that was the name of your friend. The Calvin Klein model, remember?"

"No, that's really my name. Another guy in the office pretended to be Ricky for that episode," he said. "Sarah, I'm so sorry."

"How could you do something so slimy to me? This can't be legal. I'm going to find out who you are and I'm going to string you up by your balls. And I'm going to video it and put THAT on the Internet, you motherfucker."

"Look, I know this won't help, but I'm calling you now because I really do care for you. I'd only done this with two other girls and they were both so stupid it was easy to play the game. You're different, though. You've got substance to you that most girls don't even understand. When I told you I was falling in love with you, it wasn't an act." He was talking quickly, as if trying to squeeze all the words in before she hung up on him.

Mascara streaked her face. She had really grown to care for the voice on the other end of the phone. The promises made. The daydreams of having someone like him in her life.

"I'm sorry, I don't believe you," she said through clenched teeth.

"How can I convince you?" he asked.

"I don't see how you can."

"There must be something I can say so you'll believe how much I do care for you. I'm taking a big risk even calling you. Once a play is up we aren't supposed to have any further contact. I'm taking a huge risk here."

"What? A risk of being fired from your shitty job where you deceive innocent women with your lies? Yeah, that's a great career path. You want me to believe you? Then tell me the name of the company you work for. Where you're located. Everything. I want to know how to get these bastards."

"I can't. You don't know who these guys are. They don't play by the rules in any walk of life. It's the kind of organization you can't go after," he said.

"What, like Mafia?" she snorted. "Yeah, right."

"Sarah, how else do you think they'd get away with this kind of thing? The private connections. The exclusive, expensive subscriptions. They make serious coin from people who want to listen in on live sex by unsuspecting victims. It is bewitching to follow the drama of real people who have no clue their every encounter is being played out for the pleasure of others. And the biggest bucks are from *men*. Reality television and the Big Brother shit—that's all for chicks. Men want sex. Men want porn. And this puts the two together in a reality venue that can't be matched. You'll never get to these guys."

"How did you get involved?" she asked. "And why?"

"Same reason everyone does everything they do, Sarah. Money. It's the reason you were drawn to Gabe. It's the reason you continued on, even when your own common sense had you doing things you didn't think you'd ever do."

"Fuck," she said. He was right. She became addicted to the sex, but if she was honest with herself, it was the possibility of getting out, free from Alex's financial clutches that hooked her hard. "So, now what?" she wondered aloud.

"Sarah, I am sorry. I started this because it was my job, but my feelings for you are so real. After I sent that e-mail yesterday morning, I went into the bathroom. I was so nauseous I couldn't eat all day. It killed me to imagine your beautiful face reading it."

"What do they do when the story is over?" she choked out.

"Everyone who subscribes knows it's a game. They know each story has an expiration date to it and at some point the woman will be told she was played. The reaction is part of the game. Subscribers can bet on how a scene will end. Will the woman call the guy screaming? Will she send a text? What will she say? People will bet on anything."

"What is being said about me?" She wanted to know, and yet she didn't. This was surreal.

"The gallery is pissed that we pulled the plug on your story. The discussion board is getting hate mail by the dozens of guys who wanted it to continue with you."

"What's the gallery?"

"It's our term for the subscribers who are locked in to a particular story," he said.

"What a sick fucking world."

"Yeah. It is. You were my last one. I see now that I can't do this anymore."

"Will they let you stop?"

"Oh yeah. It really is a job for me. I have to be careful not to get caught talking to you. It's a big no-no."

"How did you know all that stuff about Gabe? And whose body was in the pictures you sent?" she asked.

"The pictures are all stock porn photos. We never use any face shots. Gabe is easy to pretend to be. A lot of the guys actually use his character because he posts all of his schedules and things online before he does them. And, fitness and bodybuilding models all know his name instantly."

"So I'm not the only one?"

"No. You aren't. The team knows the girls will never tell because they are so humiliated and don't want others to find out they were duped." His matter-of-fact tone made her once again want to reach through the phone for his tongue.

"Fuck you," she said.

"Sorry, I didn't mean that to sound harsh. I'm just trying to explain. Thought you'd feel better if you knew you weren't the only one who'd been sucked into the game."

"I want to hate you. Part of me does hate you, you know."

"I will do everything I can to earn your forgiveness, but I can't tell you where they are located right now. Do you understand why? They'd kill me."

"I don't know what to think," she said. "Give me your telephone number. This one."

"Can't. I know you'd trace it, and I can't risk it. But it doesn't change how I feel. I'll call you later, I'll call on a number you can have."

She hung up.

She felt a little better after talking to him, which surprised her greatly. Knowing there were others *did* take away some of the sting. Somehow, some way, she would get to the bottom of this and bring those assholes down. Right now, she felt she could focus on Nationals and perhaps it would all be OK.

Alex beat the kids to the dinner table, and she took the few minutes to bring him up to speed on her conversation with Ricky.

"Ricky Jameson, huh?" he said. "That's his name?"

"I guess," Sarah said. "How could we really know?

"I'll look into it," he said. The life and laughter of five kids came barreling into the dining room, ending the conversation.

Ricky sent a text message from a new number with a San Francisco area code.

Ricky: Hi - you can contact me on this number.
Sarah: Sure. So... you live in San Fran?
Ricky: I have a handful of phones from different places. I'll tell you where I live, though.
Sarah: Where?
Ricky: Seattle.
Sarah: Is that where you work?
Ricky: No. It's all done through technology.
Sarah: You said your boss was standing with you to send the email.
Ricky: I flew in to do the breakup. We always do.
Sarah: I don't know what to say. I'm so angry.
Ricky: Would it help if I said I'm sorry again?
Sarah: You may have to say it a bunch.
Ricky: Oh Princess.
Sarah: Don't call me that right now. I leave tomorrow.
Ricky: I know. I've had the date marked on my calendar.
Sarah: I thought I was going to get to meet you.
Ricky: Maybe I'll come anyway.
Sarah: What?
Ricky: Honestly, I thought about it.

Sarah began to type that she didn't think it would be a good idea. Then she stopped. If he showed up, she could see what he looks like. She could probably access his wallet, something to tell her where he lives. This could be promising.

Sarah: I'm not sure if this is crazy or not, but if you come, I'd want to meet you.
Ricky: Really?
Sarah: I think so. I need to sort out my feelings. If I can see you, I think I'll know.
Ricky: Let me try, ok?

She started to ask if he had the boys this weekend, then stopped. *Right. Gabe Benoit has two boys, not Ricky Jameson.* That thought annoyed her anew. She suddenly didn't want to talk to this virtual stranger anymore.

Sarah: I've got to go finish packing.

TWENTY-TWO

Sarah shifted uncomfortably in her seat. The room was stifling, the air weighing down on her chest like a wool blanket. She fanned herself with the envelope that contained her contestant's package, but it was like blowing hot air on a campfire.

Every chair in the conference room was filled, and people lined the aisles and stood along the back wall. Those who had already been to their first spray-tanning session were trying not to lean or rub against anyone, and the scent from the spray added to the heat of the room, giving Sarah a dull headache that threatened to worsen if the meeting lasted much longer.

Mercifully, the competition director wrapped it up. "Thank you, ladies and gentlemen, that's it for now. You guys look great, and we are so excited that this year's Nationals is our biggest competition yet! We'll see you tomorrow morning."

Like kids released for recess, a mass exodus of some of the fittest men and women from across the country swarmed to the doors. As Sarah made her way out, she bumped into a guy who was going in.

"You don't want to go in there," she said. "I don't think the air conditioning works, and it is stinking hot."

The man laughed. He had perfect teeth. "I'm looking for my friend." He didn't push past her, though.

Sarah smiled. "What class are you competing in?"

He laughed again. Damn, he was cute. "I'm not competing. I'm here to watch. My buddy's girlfriend is competing."

His features were exquisite. A woman came up and grabbed his arm. "Joseph, here you are."

"Oh, hey, Steph. I was just looking for you. This is—" He fumbled as he realized he didn't know Sarah's name.

"Sarah." She extended a hand. "Nice to meet you."

"Hi, I'm Steph," the woman said.

Sarah smiled at them both. "Well, I am going to the bar for a glass of wine. My tanning appointment is at midnight, so I need to amuse myself until then."

"You know what, I'll join you," Joseph said.

They began walking the long hallway back to the hotel lobby. Steph tagged along, too.

"Do you really have a glass of wine before competition?" she asked Sarah.

"I do. Always."

"I can't imagine," Steph said. "I'm afraid to drink anything the night before."

Sarah just smiled at her and kept walking.

"I think it's great you are so confident," Joseph said.

"It's not so much confidence as knowing proper training principles," Sarah said, "but thanks."

The lobby was filled with cozy tables of chatting competitors. Steph guided them to a table and planted her lips firmly on the guy seated there.

"Sarah, this is my fiance, Mike," she said.

"Hi, Mike," Sarah said, and they all sat.

The banter of these strangers was a balm to her wounded sense of trust. This circle of friends were all so comfortable together that she nearly forgot that mere days ago she believed she would be meeting Gabe tonight for the first time. She learned that Joseph was a doctor at the

Children's Hospital of Los Angeles, and Steph and Mike lived in Chicago.

Although she enjoyed listening to their anecdotes, Sarah couldn't help but look around the room every so often, searching the faces for someone who might appear to be more focused on her than the others. *Would Ricky show up?* At this point, she had no idea what Ricky might do.

She suddenly realized Joseph had said something to her. "Oh, I'm sorry, what?" she said.

Joseph laughed. "Boy, you were lost in thought there for a minute. I asked if you are married."

Sarah grinned, "I'm sorry. No, I'm not married. I've got a lot going on. I guess my mind was elsewhere."

"I'm sorry to hear that," Joseph said, frowning. "Why don't you hang out with us this weekend? Tomorrow night a bunch of us are going out to celebrate my birthday after the show. Would you like to join us?"

Sarah shook her head. "I'm sorry, I can't. You have no idea what a week I've had."

Steph took her hand. "Oh come on, Sarah, it'll be fun. We won't get too crazy—we are just going to have a good time!"

Joseph agreed. "Join us. The more the merrier. Let's turn that bad week around."

Sarah felt at ease with them already. It did seem like it would be a delightfully fun time. "You know what? I'll come. Thanks!"

She scribbled her cell number on a napkin and gave it to Joseph. She and Steph were competing in different classes, so Sarah didn't know if she'd get to see Steph in the morning, but she hugged her goodnight. Steph seemed to be a genuinely kind person, with brains too, and spending time with nice people had great appeal.

A giant yawn cast from her lungs as she delicately climbed into bed that night after her midnight tan. As weary as she felt physically, her brain resisted being shut down. Each time she told it to shut up and go to bed, it came back at her with more accusations and things to consider about the guileful drama Ricky led her through. Her emotions raged as she lay in bed. She watched the shadows on the wall and despised the ones cast on her spirit by men she most wanted to trust. First Alex, years ago with his disappointments. Now Ricky. She could feel her bones vibrating.

At two a.m. her phone buzzed.

Ricky: Are you asleep?
Sarah: It's 2 am - why are you messaging me?
Ricky: I was just thinking about you.
Sarah: WTF - I compete in the morning. Are you here in town?
Ricky: No I couldn't make it. Sorry.
Sarah: I'll talk to you tomorrow.
Ricky: Did you hook up with anyone tonight?
Sarah: Go fuck yourself.

That encounter ensured that sleep would elude her completely. *What an asshole!* She could almost hear his mocking tone, prompting her to angry, fighting words. She might not be able to sleep, but she sure as hell wasn't going to play his game tonight.

"Fuck you, Ricky/Gabe!" she said to the shadows. The shadows remained silent. As she stared into them, she could almost envision Ricky, stalking her from the audience tomorrow. *Did he send the text only to make her think he wasn't there?* It was possible. For that matter, Ricky could have been making up the whole online monitoring thing and simply be a crazed lunatic, worming his way into her life only to ambush her.

This thought was suddenly more terrifying than that of thousands of people listening to her have sex. She got up and checked to make sure her hotel room door was double bolted. She called down to the front desk.

"Hello?" the night operator said.

"Hi. This is Sarah Ruiz in room eight-one-four. I need you to do me a favor," Sarah said.

"Yes, ma'am, what is it?"

"Could you put a note on my account that if anyone asks what room I'm in, no information would be given?" Sarah asked.

"Ma'am, we never give out our guests' room numbers. That's against our policy."

"Would you make a note anyway? I've had some trouble with a stalker and I want to make sure he can't find my room if he tries. Actually, can you make it so no calls come through on the phone for me, too?"

"Yes ma'am. We'll take messages for you if anyone tries to call."

"Thank you," Sarah hung up and looked at the clock. *3:16 am.* She was wide awake. *This is not good,* she thought.

Months later, as Sarah tried to recall the events of the competition day, she found that she remembered very little. The mind games haunted her all night. At five o'clock she couldn't lie there anymore. She was ridiculously early for her six-thirty chair time for hair and makeup. The stylists made her look gorgeous, tired eyes and all, and afterward, she went back to the tanning booth for some touch ups.

She ate a small bowl of oatmeal while envying Mark's bacon, eggs, and hash browns. *One more day,* she thought.

Mark asked, "So, have you run into Gabe yet? What time is your shoot tomorrow?"

The realization that Mark didn't know what happened hit her in the gut.

She widened her eyes to make room for the tears to dissipate. "Mark, I can't say anything or else I'll cry and wreck this five-hundred-dollar beauty job I have. All I can say is no, Gabe's shoot isn't going to happen."

Mark's eyes reflected the kindness she longed for from a friend. "I'm sorry. I won't ask anything else. Don't you dare cry. Here, look at this." He took his coffee stir stick and put it in his nostril. He made a goofy face and crossed his eyes. "There, does that make you laugh?"

"You dork." Sarah laughed. The tears stayed at bay.

She flowed through the morning on autopilot. Her countenance was clouded, her eyes were heavy, and although she felt in better shape than she had ever before, she knew something was lopsided in her spirit. She was surprised that she was called out for the top ten in her class during the morning judging. She knew she was off, and Mark could tell, too.

"Sarah, what's going on? You seemed lost up there. Your eyes are not focused," he said after the morning competition ended.

"I know—I'm trying. I didn't sleep last night and everything is whirling around me like I'm in a tornado. I've got to get it together."

"You will. You're in top ten so far. That's amazing." Mark was always so encouraging. He knew what to say, when to say it. Like a good coach should.

"Thanks. I'll bring it hard tonight," Sarah promised. "I'm going to go back to my room and rest for a bit."

She had just dozed off when Ricky cut into her moment of peace.

Ricky: So how'd it go?

Fuck! He seemed to know just when she didn't need to hear from him. She shut her phone off for the next hour and a half, while she rested her body as best she could without messing up her hair and face. It felt good to be still.

She had two new texts when she turned it back on.

Ricky: WTF - don't you answer me anymore?

Unknown number with an L.A. area code: Hey - you looked incredible on stage! Good luck. See you later—we should have more than one thing to celebrate tonight.

Sarah did a double take. *Who would she see later? Was Ricky there?* Her breath caught and the hair on her neck stood up as she considered his presence in the same room, watching her. She simply didn't know what to make of him. Which story was real? That he cared? That he used her? Or something else? After the torment the shadows put her through the previous night, she didn't know how she should feel.

Then it dawned on her. She had given her number to Joseph. Perhaps the message was from him.

She sent a quick reply:

Sarah: Joseph? Is this your number?
Joseph: Yes, sorry, I should have said who I was. Lol.
Sarah: No problem. I'm looking forward to hanging with you guys tonight.

Sarah held nothing back for the evening show. ESPN was there to televise it and the energy backstage was electric. Sarah's theme wear outfit was, in her opinion, even better than the Mermaid costume. It was a translucent jumpsuit with circular cutouts across the left side of her torso and her right thigh. A silver, sparkled spider web pattern accentuated her muscles and worked its way up her arms, across her breasts, around her right side, and covered her lower back—making her a sexy Spider-Woman that would capture anyone's attention. The web thickened in just the right spots, but left enough to the imagination that one wanted to keep staring.

Her shoes were silver, strapless, and six inches high, which towered her a good inch above the women on either side of her in the lineup. She clearly dominated the stage in this round of competition and the cameras spent a lot of time pointed in her direction.

However, even with the incredible showing her perfect outfit projected, her demeanor was still not as confident as she felt at Easterns. The judges felt it too, and Sarah came in fifth place. It was an impressive finish, especially considering the level of competition gathered in L.A., but Sarah still felt disappointed. This was supposed to be *her* year, and *her* show to rule. Ricky had sucked the energy from her, and as she left the stage, she resented him more than ever.

Mark found her and hugged her tightly. "I'm so proud of you."

Her eyes were moist, but damned if she was going to cry backstage. "Thanks. You have no idea what I've been through."

He took her hand. "You can tell me when you're ready. Or never. I'm still thrilled for you. You looked great up there."

"Oh dear God, Mark, look," Sarah said. "There's Gabe Benoit."

They turned and saw Gabe in friendly conversation with a group of contestants.

"That jerk," Mark said. "I want to give him a piece of my mind."

"No, Mark, it wasn't him," Sarah said.

"Come again?" Mark narrowed his eyes.

"It was someone pretending to be him," she said.

"Holy shit. You're kidding."

Sarah looked at the man she thought she had developed a passionate relationship with. He had no idea that someone was impersonating him, leading women on with unfulfilled promises and lies. Her throat was tight, and she felt a pain in her heart.

"Are you OK?" Mark asked.

"I think I need to go talk to him," Sarah said.

"Bad idea," Mark said. "Don't even think about it."

"Not to tell him anything that happened, but for my own sanity's sake. I had built up the moment when I first saw him live in person for so long, I can't just walk away."

She didn't wait to hear what Mark said next. If she didn't act right away, the courage would evaporate. She walked purposefully to where he stood. He glanced at her and smiled when she reached him.

"Congratulations," he said.

"Thanks. I wanted to introduce myself to you. I'm Sarah Ruiz. I am the crazy girl who sent you the message on Facebook a couple of weeks ago."

"Oh right, Sarah!" Gabe said with a laugh. "My goodness, that was funny. My wife and I were lying in bed together when that came in. I was wondering if I had done something I couldn't remember. I had been in Vegas the weekend before."

Sarah laughed. "I'm sorry. I meant to send that to someone else in my friends list, I actually have two friends named Gabe on Facebook, but my fast fingers picked the wrong one. So I want to apologize." She babbled nervously, trying to squash the discomfort of the situation.

"No worries," Gabe assured her, "it's totally fine."

Sarah walked back to Mark and breathed a sigh of relief. Facing the real Gabe took every ounce of strength she had at that moment. Although Gabe would never know the humiliation, the disappointment, and the hurt she endured in the days leading up to their meeting, she was thankful for his graciousness and relaxed attitude. Perhaps she could move forward.

While these thoughts played in her mind, Steph approached and hugged Sarah tightly, "Oh wow! Congratulations!" she exclaimed. "You looked beautiful."

Sarah hugged back. "You look amazing, too. How'd you do?"

Steph shrugged. "I came in eighth. I'm thrilled to make top ten my first time out."

"Awesome," Sarah said.

"You still going to come out with us tonight?" Steph asked.

"Definitely," Sarah assured her. "Mark, you want to come?"

"Why not?" Mark said. "When are you leaving?"

"Meet us in thirty minutes in the lobby," Steph said.

In her room, Sarah stood in front of her mirror. She sought her eyes for the hope she felt just a few days ago. Faintly, it was still there. Cloaked with disappointment and confusion, her dream was dimmed but not extinguished.

She changed and met up with her new friends. It was subtle, but she noticed that Joseph's eyes traverse her figure while she chatted with Steph. Gabe Benoit walked by with a beautiful woman tucked under his arm. She sidestepped behind Mark, hoping Gabe wouldn't see her. However, Gabe did see her and steered the blonde over to where Sarah stood with her throat tight.

"Sarah! I want you to meet my wife, Kelly," he said.

"Kelly, this is the girl who sent the Facebook message to me a few days ago. Remember? When we were in bed?" he laughed, and Kelly joined in.

"Yes, of course, oh my gosh, that was funny," she said.

"I'm so sorry," Sarah said, "I want you to know that was completely sent to the wrong person."

"No problem. We had a good chuckle," Kelly said.

As she watched them leave the hotel, Sarah was once again thankful for their kindness and simultaneously furious at Ricky for placing her in the position to have to apologize for something he caused.

The limo arrived, and they all piled in, off to experience nightlife Los Angeles style.

The limo was loud with music and laughter and if her phone didn't vibrate, she wouldn't have noticed the text from Ricky. She felt the anger bubble up again.

Ricky: Why aren't you answering me? I need to talk to you. I'm not happy at all that you haven't responded.
Sarah: I've been a little busy.
Ricky: You could have sent a note.
Sarah: So what's up?
Ricky: What do you mean what's up? What are you doing? How'd you do?
Sarah: I placed top 5.
Ricky: That's great. I bet you were awesome.
Sarah: It was good. Look I can't chat, I'm heading out.
Ricky: What do you mean? Where are you going?
Sarah: I met some friends. We're going to celebrate someone's birthday.
Ricky: A guy?

Sarah: Yeah - I met a hot doctor and he's really nice. It's his birthday.
Ricky: Is that really responsible of you? Going out with someone you just met?
Sarah: Srsly? You're lecturing me?
Ricky: You have 5 kids. You shouldn't be out tramping around.
Sarah: Fuck you.

She shut her phone off and laughed to herself. *Let him think about that one.*

She looked up. Joseph was checking a message on his phone, but he looked up and met her eye. He smiled at her, and she couldn't help it. She gave him her sweetest smile back.

"So are you excited at how it went tonight?" he asked.

"I am. Top five is really great. I hoped to win. Maybe next time," she said.

"I loved your Spider-Woman outfit. That was so cool," he said.

"Thanks. I wanted something I had never seen before onstage," she said.

"Well, nothing else up there compared. I was surprised you didn't win. Those judges must have been blind."

Sarah smiled again. "Now you're just being nice."

"No, I'm serious. You've got great stage presence," he said.

She didn't feel like he was flirting. He truly seemed to mean what he said. It warmed her heart and helped push the anxiety to the back burner for a while.

After three bars, a whole lot of dancing, several drinks, and many laughs, they found themselves back in the limo on the return trip to the hotel. Steph, Sarah, and another girl who was out with them all had photo shoots in the morning. Sarah had gone to one of the vendor tables and signed up for a shoot with a local photographer the day before. She didn't want to waste the great shape she was in by not capturing her figure on film.

The group scattered once they returned to the lobby. Steph and Mike went to the hotel bar. Mark had hooked up with a girl and immediately disappeared. And the others went their separate ways. Sarah and Joseph found themselves alone, in the elevator.

Sarah pushed the button for the eighth floor and Joseph the eleventh.

Sarah turned to him. "Thanks so much. I needed this night out more than you know."

"Well, I'm glad you had fun. Thanks for sharing my birthday with me."

He stepped partly out of the elevator behind her at the eighth floor and held the door open with his arm. "Can I ask you something?"

"Sure," she replied.

"Would you have dinner with me tomorrow night? I mean, if you're still around. I really enjoyed your company. I'd like to take you to dinner."

She cocked her head to the side. "Yes. I'd love to. I go home on Monday."

"Great. I'll meet you in the lobby at five," he said. Then he smiled, stepped back into the elevator and the doors closed.

She turned on her phone. Three text messages.

Ricky (11:45 pm): That wasn't cool at all.
Ricky (12:45 am): I guess you're still out. Can't believe you.
Ricky (1:30 am): I'll be up waiting, text me when your doctor leaves.

She shook her head in disbelief. *He has some freaking nerve.* As she thought about it, she realized he really was sounding more like a jealous boyfriend than a guy who pranked her for the hell of it. Maybe he did care. She had invested so much of her emotional health in that relationship, if she were honest with herself a teeny small part of her wanted it to be real. She wanted to be able to rely on her judgment. She didn't know which feeling to trust.

It didn't take her long to fall asleep from the sheer exhaustion of her life.

TWENTY-THREE

It was 3:45 p.m. Sarah's day had been nearly perfect. The photo shoot with Darren Ashe went so well—his camera skills were far beyond what she'd hoped. She didn't know it beforehand, but he had rented Gabe Benoit's studio for her shoot. Once again, Sarah ran into Gabe and faced yet another reminder of her annihilated dreams for the weekend.

Gabe brought a few people over to her as she was looking at the unedited proofs with Darren.

"Sarah, I want to introduce you to Madeline Bruno. She is one of the editors at *Oxygen* magazine."

Sarah shook Madeline's hand. "So nice to meet you."

"You, too," Madeline said. "Congratulations on a terrific performance yesterday."

"Thank you so much."

Madeline looked at the pics. The angles and positioning of Sarah's body in the frames were so striking. She looked every bit as sultry as she felt. Darren had done fabulous work.

"Those are exquisite!" Madeline said. "Nice job."

Sarah was on cloud nine. Back in her room, she sipped a glass of wine, watching the minutes tick by toward her dinner with Joseph. She knew she didn't want to take things beyond the friendly rapport they had established, but it was comforting to have met some friends this trip.

Her phone rang. Her breath halted when she saw the number. It was the number Ricky used when he was Gabe.

"Hello?" she answered tentatively.

"Sarah, it's me," Ricky said.

"Why are you on this phone?" she asked cautiously.

"We have a problem," he said.

"Yeah, you're the fucking problem."

"No. Sarah, the team wants more," he said. "They want more, and they're willing to fuck you over to get it."

"Fuck the team. Oh, but you'd probably enjoy that if I fucked the team, wouldn't you?"

Ricky's voice was low and the tone sent a wave of fear through her as he spoke. "There is a problem and you need to listen very closely to what I'm saying. Some of the elite members threatened to drop their subscriptions if we didn't find a way to get you back online. They're furious, and I got a call earlier today that I am to get you back in the game or else they'll go to Tanya's husband and to Jenny with information about what happened."

"What the fuck do you mean?" Sarah, panicked, shouted into the phone. "They can't do that!"

She was suddenly in a vortex, while scenes from her life spun around her as she felt again the weight of the emotions that accompanied them. The spit on her face from Alex's spewed hate. The weight of Ty's body smashed on her as he raped her in Las Vegas. The ring of her own cry in her ears after she had read Ricky's confession e-mail. It all flooded her brain, and there was no room for even one more bit of new information. Like a punch to the gut, she knew in that moment she had absolutely no control over any part of her life.

Ricky kept talking. "Listen, they can. They will. Sarah, I am supposed to put you on live in about thirty minutes to tell you what you need to do. Please understand, I'm doing this to protect you. If you don't go along with it, they'll tell everyone you know. They'll fuck your life up."

"I can't let Tanya's life be ruined." She pushed the words through dry lips. "What do I do?"

"When I call you, play along," Ricky said. "It'll be OK. I promise. Please trust me."

"Trust you? Trust *you*?" She downed her wine.

"I gotta go. I'll call you in a while. Look, you really have no choice but to trust me. I'm your friend in this—and the only one who can save you from the humiliation. Whatever you do, when I call back, don't act like you've talked to me since I broke up with you. Remember, the team is listening." He hung up.

With hands wrapped around the toilet, doubled over, she began to cry. "Not again!" she said to the porcelain in between heaves. "Please not again."

Twenty-five minutes later her phone rang. She was waiting, perched on the end of the bed with a glass of water.

"Hello?" she answered.

"Hi, Sarah, this is Ricky," he said.

"I can't believe you're calling me," she said.

"Yes, I am surprised myself," he answered. His voice was so cold. So emotionless. "So how was Nationals?"

"I did all right." She didn't want to say her place, now that she knew others were listening; she was cautious about giving too much information. "Didn't do as well as I wanted. I was a bit distracted from the news you gave me last week. I am so hurt by all of this."

"Well, you were quite the superstar around the Internet," Ricky said calmly. "We did hate to end it."

"Look, you asshole, what do you want?" she demanded.

"A trade. You give us some live sexual action tonight and we won't e-mail the nude pictures of you and your friend to her husband. From what I understand, he wouldn't believe that his wife could engage in such behavior."

"Our faces aren't visible in those pictures. Send all you want," Sarah said.

"Oh, but the sweet tattoo on your friend's hip shows up quite nicely," Ricky said.

"Shit," Sarah said. He was right. Tanya's butterfly was uniquely hers and very clear in the photo. "Look, I've got dinner plans with some friends soon. I can't go out and fuck someone just because you want me to."

"Oh, I'm sure you'll wave that magic wand of yours and a hot guy will appear," Ricky said seductively. "You can do it, baby. We're rooting for you."

"I'm hanging up now," Sarah said. "Don't call back."

"Sarah, you have until midnight to give us what we're waiting for. Or else the e-mail goes out to... Joshua is his name? And don't forget about Jenny."

Sarah stared at the phone in her hands. It was pure evil. It brought her nothing but grief.

"Fuck you!" she said to it, and threw it across the room. She looked at the clock. 4:45 p.m. She went into the bathroom and cleaned up her face. She retrieved her phone from the carpet and tucked it in her purse. *What the hell is this night going to hold?* she wondered.

Joseph took her to a quaint seafood place in Marina Del Ray. He had hired the limo again, and on the way to the restaurant he kept a respectable distance as they chatted like old buddies. She told him about her kids and her work, and he shared tales about his patients at the Children's Hospital.

Over dinner they sipped wine and ate oysters. Her body was relaxing, and she would have been content to talk the night away with no expectations or demands. At one point during dinner, Joseph left to use the washroom and almost immediately her phone rang.

"Hello?" she answered.

"What are you doing?" Ricky asked.

"Having dinner with a hot doctor. Leave me alone!" she hissed.

"Oh, the doctor?" Ricky crooned. "Perfect. You are going to fuck him tonight, and you are going to leave your phone on so we can hear."

"You're sick," she said.

"You know what'll happen if you don't. I'll be waiting for your call."

She hung up and put the phone in her purse. Joseph returned to the table and looked concerned.

"Are you OK?" he asked.

"I'm fine," she said, forcing a smile. "Just got a call from home. My ex was giving me shit about something."

"I'm so sorry," Joseph said. He reached across the table and held her hand. "You seem much too lovable for any man to give you shit."

"You have perfect bedside manners, Doc."

"I try."

After dinner they walked along the beach. He carried the sweet stories of the kids he treated in his heart, and he shared quite a few of them with her. She found herself admiring the strength of these children she would never meet, and she longed for the same fortitude in her own life. Joseph's casualness felt dreamy and genuine, but inside Sarah was fidgety and restless each time she thought about Tanya. Her heart was heavy as she considered how to delicately transition their friendship to what Ricky was waiting for.

When they returned to the limo, Joseph said, "Thank you for having dinner with me."

"No, thank you, Doc. I loved hearing the stories of your work. This was one of the nicest dinners I've had in a while."

They sat a little closer in the limo. Part way back he leaned in softly and kissed her, which was a relief for Sarah.

"Is that OK?" he asked. "I don't want to do anything inappropriate."

She wasn't ready—and yet, the thought of Tanya's marriage wrecked over her stupidity pained her chest. She knew she needed to go through with this.

"It's fine," she said, smiling. "You're a great guy, and I'm having a wonderful night."

They continued to kiss in the back of limo, controlling the urge to do more by keeping their hands in respectable places.

Once in Sarah's room, however, all bets were off. Joseph went to use the bathroom and Sarah dialed the phone to Ricky's number. She set it facedown on the nightstand.

She went to her mini-bar and opened a bottle of Jack. She caught her reflection in the hotel window and for a brief moment was transported to eighteen years earlier and a room at the James Hotel. She sighed to herself. *At least it's not sex with another woman.*

She looked over at her cell phone and momentarily considered hanging it up, but then Joseph came out of the bathroom naked, and seeing his Adonis form made her forget all about Ricky, Gabe, and the thousands of faceless assholes who were going to listen to her have her way with this gorgeous man before her.

They didn't make love. They *fucked.* He drove his tongue deep into her mouth and pressed his body against hers, while his hands roamed along her neck, down her back, and grabbed her tight ass, pulling her even closer to him.

She could feel the hardness of his cock against her. He wanted her, and her body reciprocated. As steam built between them, she worked out the tension brought on by Ricky, Gabe, and Alex. They fell onto the bed, sucking on each other's lips and necks, with their hands at a frenetic pace to touch every inch of one another.

Her body shivered at the touch of his cock against her clit. She was ready to explode from wanting to feel him inside of her. He didn't disappoint as he gently spread her legs apart with his hands and then not so gently thrust himself into her. Their hips made a fabulous slapping sound as they came together, and it was as if neither of them had ever had sex before. They were primal, animalistic in their moans, and when they finally came it was at the same time, leaving them exhausted and full of pleasure.

They lay side by side on the bed, panting. After several minutes he reached over and stroked her face.

"You're beautiful," he said.

"So are you," she replied. They looked at one another for what seemed like eternity. Then Sarah could feel her body begin to ache for him again. He felt it too, because he was suddenly once again kissing her neck, her breasts, and her stomach while she ran her fingers through his thick, dark hair.

"I want you again," he growled. He turned her over and placed his hands on her hips. He slid himself gently into her from behind and she moaned with the incredible feeling of his hardness once again inside her.

After two more orgasms, they finally lay spent.

"That was amazing," he said, for the fifth time.

She laughed. "Happy birthday to you."

"Yes, happy birthday to me!" Joseph agreed. "Would you be offended if I went back to my own room? I've got to check out early and drive the hour and a half back home. I'm on call."

"Not at all," Sarah said, relieved.

They showered together and then said goodbye with a long kiss that, for a minute, seemed like it was going to lead to yet more sex, but they pulled away from each other in time and Sarah closed the door behind him. She was surprised to see that it was only midnight.

She had turned the phone off when they went to shower. She turned it back on to see if there was any news from Ricky.

Ricky: Guess your magic wand still works. Call me on my private line when your medical exam is over.

She considered ignoring the text but feared that pissing him off would inspire him to do something rash. She dialed his number.

"So, it sounded like you had a wild time," Ricky said.

"Was everybody there happy?" Sarah asked.

"Oh your performance was divine," Ricky said. "The numbers were through the roof tonight."

"So they aren't going to contact Josh?" Sarah asked, "That is all I care about."

"You know, I don't believe you. I think you also care about hurting me. I can't believe you degraded yourself the way you have." His voice was icy again, and it made her shiver.

"What do you mean? You threatened me."

"I think you liked being with that doctor. It sounded like he got you off." Ricky's voice was loaded with anger.

"Oh he got me off good, you jerk," she said. "You blackmailed me."

She swallowed the saliva in her mouth. The room was beginning to suffocate her. "What the hell do you want from me?"

"I was just thinking back to all the things you did in order to get that magazine cover. You really were desperate to win my love, weren't you?"

Sarah's head felt like it was going to explode. What the hell was he doing to her? "Are you shitting me? Yeah, I was stupid. We've all been stupid at one time or another in our lives."

"You seem to have taken the prize for stupid these days," Ricky said with a laugh so evil that she knew she was listening to the devil himself.

"I'll admit I was stupid. And, yes, desperate for a better life, one free from assholes," she said calmly.

"Great. Well, you have a good sleep and think about the assholes you want to be free from. And by the way, tomorrow, Jenny and Tanya are going to need new men in their lives. It's all gonna come down on you, baby. I'll make sure and copy Alex when I send out the other e-mails and the link to you having sex with your doctor tonight. Hope the moaning doesn't upset him the way it bothered me."

"Ricky, please don't send those messages. Please," she whimpered. "Why are you doing this to me? Why?" She repeated her plea over and over, until the words were barely intelligible.

The sound of an e-mail whooshing off into cyberspace filled her ears. It was the most horrible sound she had ever heard.

"Too late," Ricky said. "Prepare yourself. Oh and by the way, I hope Alex has a fabulous fiftieth birthday." The line went dead.

Sarah trembled. She put a hand to her throat, which was closing at an alarming rate, as if a clamp were being tightened around it. Breath had vacated her lungs. Icy shivers ran up her legs and through her midsection and pierced her heart. Her eyes saw nothing but gray. For a moment, she thought she had died.

She looked at the vibrating phone in her hand. *Why was it vibrating but not ringing?* she wondered. It took a minute to realize *it* wasn't vibrating, *she* was. Her hand shook out of control.

She pressed the speed dial for Alex's number and held the phone to her face.

"Hello?" he answered. "Sarah, it's almost four a.m. here. What the hell?"

She didn't say anything. She sat with the phone to her face.

"I can hear you breathing," Alex said. "Why are you panting?"

"I-I-I'm going t-to d-d-die," she stuttered. The faces of her children flashed before her eyes. Ethan and Elle jumping into the pool. Alexandra waving goodbye as she went to the beach. Eric and Antonio as little boys, learning to play baseball. "Tell the kids I love them."

"Sarah!" Alex yelled into the phone. "What happened? What's going on?"

"Ricky," she said. Her voice was low, monotone and had the creepy calmness of a serial killer about to strike. "He's ruined everything. I fucked the Doc. You'll know all about it as soon as you check your e-mail. Tanya's husband will know, too. I ruined their lives. Me. My bad decisions. He blackmailed me. He called my bluff. I can't take it. I'm through with it. I can't face myself or anyone else anymore."

"Sarah, please stop saying that," Alex begged. "Whatever happened, I will fix it. Don't talk that way."

"No, Alex, I *am* talking this way. My life hasn't been my own for a while now. And I want to kill myself. I want to take control of what happens to me. I'm done." Her voice got stronger as she began to form the plan. She had a bottle of muscle relaxers in her bag. Mixed with tequila and whatever else she could find in the minibar, this could really all be over very soon.

"The kids need you," Alex said. Actually, he whined it at her. "Please don't do anything to hurt yourself."

The kids need you. Those words gave her a moment of clarity. *The kids need you.*

She raised her arm back and projected her phone with alarming force toward the wall. Pieces flew in every direction following the impact. One actually came directly back at her and landed in her lap. She looked at it. The phone. It betrayed her for the last time. Now, it was dead. And although she wished she were dead too, she knew those four words spoken by the man who caused her much pain would be the words that kept her from harming herself. *The kids need you.*

She lay back on her bed. She stared at the ceiling for what seemed to be ages. Then her head began to pound. She realized the pounding noise was a knock on the door. She went to answer it and then realized she was still naked. She pulled on a T-shirt and shorts and went to the door.

"Who is it?" she asked.

"Mrs. Ruiz, it's the hotel manager."

"How do I know this?" she asked.

"Ma'am, your phone is off the hook and we got a frantic call at the front desk from someone claiming to be your husband. He insisted that you are in danger and we should check on you immediately. Is everything OK?"

She opened the door. It was the night manager. "Yes," she assured him. "I'm sorry my husband bothered you. I'll put the phone back on its hook, but please don't put any calls through. I'm going to go to bed now."

"Will do, ma'am. Sorry to have disturbed you." The man bowed slightly and walked off.

Sarah re-bolted the door. She went to the bed and fell asleep before her body even came to a full rest on the mattress.

TWENTY-FOUR

With each mile the airplane soared, the knot in Sarah's stomach got bigger and tighter. What awaited her in Miami? Tanya? Jenny? Alex? She went to the tiny airplane bathroom and vomited for the fourth time. The paper towel was rough on her dry lips, but the cool of the bathroom mirror on her forehead eased her headache a bit. She leaned that way for several minutes.

What am I going to say to Tanya? she wondered. She was concerned about Jenny too, but less so, as Jenny's husband deserved whatever pain was coming to him. Alex already knew some of Ricky's bullshit, but now he would know she had sex with Joseph. The thought of Alex listening to her enjoying an orgasm made her shut her eyes tight and want to die all over again. *And how did Ricky know Alex's fiftieth birthday was today? Was he who he said he was?* She shivered.

Alex's dark eyes were the first thing she noticed as she came out of baggage claim. He stood, arms akimbo and legs planted apart. She'd seen him stand like before last summer, in their kitchen, waiting for Eric one night as he blew way past curfew. He had been furious then. She took a deep breath and approached him.

"What are you doing here?" she asked.

He took her bag from her and set it down. He clasped both her shoulders and stared her in the face. "Don't you ever hang up on me like that again," he said. "I was sick wondering what happened to you. Why haven't you answered your phone today?"

193

"My phone is in a dozen pieces in a Los Angeles garbage can," she said. "That fucking phone has caused me enough pain."

"I thought," he stopped. His voice cracked as he said it. *Cracked?* She'd not seen him choked up in... years? Ever?

He cleared his throat. "I haven't heard a word from Tanya," he said. "Are you sure he called Josh?"

"He e-mailed them," Sarah said, frowning. "I can't believe she hasn't called." When Tanya couldn't get Sarah on her own phone, surely she would have called the house. Or Alex. *Wouldn't she?*

"Come on." Alex picked up her bag and headed to the door without waiting for her. She followed.

On the ride home, she dialed her voice mail from his phone. Ten messages. All from Alex. She shut it off.

"Look," she said to Alex, "you have no idea how hard this past week has been. I'm walking a thin line, and at times I'm not even sure which side is sanity and which is the edge."

Alex kept his eyes straight ahead. They rode the rest of the way in silence.

Once home, she retrieved her other phone from its hiding spot in her closet. She was desperate to hear Tanya's voice.

"Hi babe!" Tanya said. "You're home. How was Nationals?"

"Tanya, did you check your e-mail today? Did Josh?" Sarah asked.

"Yeah, why? What's wrong? You don't sound good," Tanya said.

"I need to see you. Now," Sarah said.

"Sure, sweetie. I'll be there in forty-five minutes."

Sarah collapsed in Tanya's arms as she told her everything. She started by showing her Ricky's e-mail and talked for twenty minutes straight—right through to the swoosh of the e-mail sailing off into the night.

"Holy shit." Tanya stroked her friend's back as Sarah sobbed hysterically against her chest.

"I'm so sorry," Sarah said, weeping. "Tanya, I never meant for it to get this crazy."

"I know, darlin'," Tanya said. "I want to kill that guy for making you cry."

"Tanya, what are we going to do?"

"I don't know. Look, he hasn't sent anything to Josh. What e-mail address do you have in your phone for him—home or work?"

"I'm sure it is his Gmail account," Sarah said.

"OK, he doesn't know a lot about computers. I'll tell him he was hacked and has to change his home account. He doesn't use that e-mail much, he won't care."

"What if he gets it before you do all that?" Sarah said. "You should go switch it now!"

"Sarah, I'll fix it," Tanya assured. "This isn't your fault. I'm a big girl. I was there, too. Don't tell anyone that I'm switching e-mail. I won't delete the account, I'll just change the password and I'll keep checking it."

"What if he calls him? What if he texts the picture?"

"One thing at a time," Tanya said. "How are you holding up?"

Sarah sat up and wiped her eyes. "I'm hanging by a thread." She looked at her friend. "Tanya, I really liked Gabe. I wanted that to be real so badly."

"I know, sweetie. I know."

"I can't even trust my own judgment. What the hell was I thinking?"

"Sarah, go easy on yourself. Alex has beat you down so much, of course you wanted something real."

"He isn't real, and that's the point. I fell for a fake. And not only that, thousands of voyeurs have followed my life. They listened to my private conversations. They heard me have sex, Tanya! I'm humiliated." Sarah and Tanya were sitting at the patio table on the deck. Sarah folded her arms on the table and put her head down. Her eyes were finally dry. She closed them, willing the Miami heat to burn her up into a pile of ash. Tanya rubbed Sarah's back and stared at the still water of the swimming pool. Alex watched them from the kitchen.

He wandered outside and sat down. "How's it going?"

Head still on her arms, Sarah replied, "They didn't get an e-mail."

Alex said, "Well, that's good. I wasn't so lucky."

"Look, I said I was sorry," Sarah said.

"She feels bad enough, Alex," Tanya warned. "Leave her be."

"I'm just saying, he sent me everything. All the pictures, all the texts, links to the recordings. It'll take months to go through it all." Alex spoke casually, as if he were talking about something to do with the nightclub and not the most intimate parts of Sarah's life.

Sarah looked up at him. "I wish you wouldn't. I mean, I'm sorry you had to get all that crap in that way, but I wish you'd delete it all without reading or listening to a single bit."

"Look," Alex said, "you need my help to catch this guy. I'm going to go through and see if there is anything there that will give away who he really is or the name of the company he works for. You make sure you keep talking to him on the phone."

Sarah plunked her head back onto her arms and sighed. Tanya watched Alex cross the yard and go into the garage. "Why is he trying to be so helpful?" she asked Sarah, as Alex's Porsche backed out of the garage and sped off down the road.

"Damn if I know," Sarah said. "Probably to show me that I need him."

"Do you?"

"I just don't know. Alex knows people. If anyone can locate Ricky and the sickos, it's him."

"Look at me," Tanya said. Sarah looked up. "You are a smart woman. You've been manipulated, yes, but you are intelligent and have a lot going for you on your own, without Alex. You don't need him to do your investigation. I know you, Sarah. You need to step up and take control of your life."

Sarah saw the love in her friend's eyes and felt stronger as she looked at her. She thought back to what Mark had said to her about Alex and his odd meeting at The Docks. *What was he up to anyway?*

"I seem to have all these men with secrets in my life," Sarah said. "You're right, T. I don't need him, do I? I don't even know half the shit he is up to."

"So figure it out. I'll help however I can," Tanya said.

Long after Tanya left, Sarah was busy making a plan. She made a list of everything she knew about Ricky based on what he'd told her.

Lives in Seattle—maybe.
Company he works for is in another city—maybe.
Has a San Francisco telephone number.
Has played the game on two other women—maybe.

Then she stopped. She realized everything else she knew about him was really info about Gabe. She didn't even know what he looked like. She knew well what Gabe looked like. She knew Gabe's home life situation. She didn't even know if Ricky was married.

"I am not going to be discouraged," she said aloud. She was tempted to call the San Francisco number and drill him for more answers, but she resisted. He hadn't called her or texted all day. Even though her other phone was trashed, Ricky had her second number. He had to know she'd be furious. Or was he giving her time to deal with Alex's anger? For all Ricky knew, Alex could be flipping out on her right now. He did indicate his intent to ruin her life.

She set aside the brief list of things she knew about Ricky and turned her focus to Alex. Sleuthing into his ventures would be a bit more complex. *Was Alex into anything illegal?* She started with a list of his businesses:

Miami Muscle Gym.
Las Palmas Apartments.
Las Faldas Night Club.
Club Fuego.
Jugar Night Club.
Calle Ocho Restaurant.

She stared at the list, considering just how much she didn't know about what went on behind the scenes at the establishments that provided for her children's well-being. She knew Alex kept a main office at Jugar, the hottest dance spot of all his clubs. If he had anything to hide, he would keep it there. Last year, he gave her specific instructions to purchase a grade VI safe for the office. He said he didn't have time to shop around and gave her cash for the purchase. She had arranged the installation at Jugar, and had been there with Alex when the safe went in. When it came time to receive the combination, however, Alex had taken the slip of paper from the installer. She pictured herself sneaking in and going through his desk, his files, even the safe—if she could figure out how to pull it off.

The next morning she got a text message from Ricky as she drove into downtown to pay a call on Miami Safe and Vault. She pulled over to read it.

Ricky: So how are things at home?
Sarah: How do you think they are?
Ricky: You had to know he'd find out eventually anyway. I saved him and you the trouble of waiting.
*Sarah: He's not mad at **me**. He's mad at **you**.*

Ricky: Really? Well, good thing he can't find me.
Sarah: You just wait. You'll get yours. Now fuck off.

She had nothing left to give him but hate. Alex wanted her to play him up, to sweet talk Ricky for more info, but she didn't have it in her. With the swoosh of the e-mail he sent, a vacuum sucked all her tenderness for him. In the hole left behind was bitterness and rage.

She heard another text message come in, but she pulled back onto the road and didn't look at it until she arrived at the safe company.

Ricky: Come on, Princess. Don't be mad.

She walked into Miami Safe and Vault with an air of confidence. Cool, calm, in control. She needed to be believable.

"Can I help you?" asked the clerk, Craig.

"My name is Sarah Ruiz. I bought a safe last year and had it installed in my business. I've not used it in a couple of months and I can't seem to remember my combination."

"Well, ma'am, we do have copies of our client combinations. However, only the original purchaser can receive this; so your name has to match our records. I'll need two forms of photo ID from you as well as your original receipt for the safe."

"I've got those things." Sarah retrieved the receipt, her passport and her driver's license from her bag. Her hand shook slightly as she handed them over.

"Ok, thanks. I'll be right back," Craig took her ID and disappeared into the back of the store, leaving Sarah to wait. She strolled nonchalantly, looking at the different safes, trying to hide her nervousness.

After several minutes, Craig returned. "Mrs. Ruiz? I did match your name and driver's license number to the original purchase. So it will be no problem for us to give you the safe's combination, as long as you sign this form stating you have not sold the unit to another party."

Sarah exchanged her signature for her ID and a printout of the combination for Alex's safe. She nearly squealed with glee as she tucked it all back into her bag and left the store.

Her next challenge would be to get Alex's keys so she could make a copy of his master. She stopped by the Spy Supply to see if Ben was working.

"Hey, nice to see you again," Ben said as she entered the store.

"Hi. I've got another problem I need some help with."

"Another bug?" Ben asked.

"Not this time," Sarah said, laughing. "I've got a question: Is it possible to make an impression of a key and then get a key made from that impression? I've seen it done in movies and was wondering if something like that can really happen."

Ben smiled. "Absolutely." He took a small tin from a nearby shelf. "This is what you'll need. It's a special clay. Don't open the tin until you are ready to make the impression. The key should be free from a key ring to get it flat as possible—but there is a cut-out in the edge of the tin right here in case removing the key from its ring is not possible. Press the key flat and so the key is level with the clay. Don't push down too hard."

"How long does it have to stay there?" Sarah asked.

"Just for a moment. Then lift it back up as straight as possible. Put the cover back on and bring it here to me."

"That sounds easy enough," Sarah said.

"Now by law, I am required to tell you that it is illegal to make an impression of a key that does not belong to you."

"Got it," Sarah said. She paid Ben. "I'll see you in a few days."

She left the store feeling braver and more like her old self than she'd felt in a while. She treated herself to her favorite sushi for lunch.

The next couple of days were quiet. No texts from Ricky. Alex left her alone. She could tell he was preoccupied with something. One night at dinner she tried to get some information from him as to why he was so frustrated, but he just got up and left the table. He tossed his plate into the sink so hard it broke. His feet were heavy on the stairs, and there was no denying the slam of his bedroom door. Sarah noticed he'd left his keys on the table.

"Kids, I need you guys to go to your rooms right now," she said urgently. "Quickly and quietly."

"But Mommy, I'm still eating," Ethan whined.

Sarah looked at Alexandra and said in a low voice, "Take the twins and go. Right now."

The older kids, fearful that her tone meant that their Dad was going to blow up, ushered the twins away from the table and up to their bedrooms. Sarah didn't want them to see what she was about to do, so that Alex couldn't question them later.

She had been keeping her purse close to her, with the key tin inside, in case she got her chance. She swiftly retrieved it and opened the top.

Alex's key ring only had six keys on it. She hadn't considered that she wouldn't know which one was his master office key. Two different car keys and the house key were easy to eliminate. The other three posed a problem. *Which was it?*

Her breath was rapid as she tried to figure out which was which. She fumbled and dropped the keys. The clank as they hit the tile made her jump. She picked them up quickly, paused and listened, but heard nothing coming from Alex's part of the house.

"Get it together, Sarah. Breathe," she told herself. She looked at the three keys again. *What could they be?* Then it dawned on her—one of them had to be her gym key. She went back to her purse and got her own keys. She held her gym door key up to Alex's keys. One was a match.

"Two to go," she said. She looked at the keys. One seemed to have fewer bumps and ridges than the other. *Would that make it a master?* she wondered. She heard a noise from upstairs and knew she didn't have time to think about it anymore. She was about to press the less bumpy key into the clay when she realized if she turned it at an angle, she could possibly get both impressions done.

The first one was easy enough to do, fitting the second was tricky, but she managed to angle it with no room to spare. She heard Alex's heavy footsteps in the hall above and knew he was heading toward the stairs.

She had scarcely placed the tin back into her purse when he appeared in the dining room doorway.

"Where'd the kids go?" he asked.

"I sent them upstairs. They were done," she said.

"They didn't even finish eating. KIDS!" he bellowed. "GET DOWN HERE!"

"I'll go get them," Sarah said. She took her purse with her and went up to the kids' wing upstairs. They were all in Alexandra's room.

"Hey guys, Dad wants you to come down and finish eating. I'm sorry—don't say anything, just do what he says, no complaining, got it?"

"Sure, Mom," Antonio said. "What's going on?"

"Dad's just in one of his moods, right, Mom?" Alexandra said.

"Yes, but be polite, don't tick him off," Sarah said.

Elle began to cry. Sarah scooped her up and hugged her. "It's OK, baby. We'll go out for ice cream after he leaves for work. Please don't cry."

Elle buried her head into Sarah's shoulder and they all trooped back downstairs to the dining room. Alex was standing at the table, holding his keys and Sarah's keys. She put Elle down and didn't look at him.

"How'd your keys get here?" he asked.

"How should I know?" Sarah responded coolly. "Did you pick them up before instead of your own?"

"Hmm. Must have. You kids need to finish your supper. I pay good money for the food around here, and it shouldn't go to waste. Do you understand me?"

A small chorus of "yes sirs" satisfied Alex, and he put down Sarah's keys and left.

TWENTY-FIVE

In the week leading up to Sarah's birthday, the text messages from Ricky started again.

Monday: *How are things going?*
Tuesday: *Guess you aren't answering me anymore?*
Later Tuesday: *WTF? You know the team wants more action, right?*
Wednesday: *This isn't funny. Answer me please.*

She also had a handful of phone calls from Ricky's San Francisco number. She ignored them all. Let him stew. There wasn't anything he could do to hurt her any more than he had already. Tanya had not only changed Josh's e-mail, but she also changed his cell phone number. She told him his number got used in a long distance phone scam and they had to switch it. Josh, being the easygoing guy that he was, switched everything with no questions asked. Knowing Tanya had things under control gave Sarah great peace.

On Thursday morning, Sarah's thirty-ninth birthday, Alex brought a bouquet of roses into the gym where Sarah was prepping the equipment for her morning client.

"What's that?" she asked.

"Just arrived," he said.

"From Ricky?" she asked.

"I don't know. Open the card."

Sarah read, *Happy birthday. You deserve these.*

"Wow, you must have him reeled back in," Alex said.

"I haven't heard from him in a couple of weeks."

"Really? He stopped calling you?" Alex was surprised. "I told you you need to keep talking to him."

"I'm not going to pursue him. I can't take it, Alex. He makes me sick. I can't believe you want me to keep talking to that animal. He has hurt me so much. You know, I don't think I want your help any more on this. Leave it be. I want it to go away."

"That's not going to happen," Alex said. He left the gym. A few minutes later, her phone rang. It was The Chanel Store.

"Is Sarah Ruiz there?" a voice asked.

"This is she," Sarah answered.

"Hi, Ms. Ruiz, this is Lacey from The Chanel Store. I wanted to let you know that we have a gift card here for you in the amount of five hundred dollars."

"Really? From who?" Sarah asked.

"From a Ricky Jameson. You can come pick it up anytime."

"Ok, thanks," Sarah said. She wanted to vomit. *What was he doing now?*

The kids took Sarah out to dinner for her birthday and had precious gifts that they made or bought with their allowance. She felt truly blessed as she tucked them in that night. She took a gloriously long bubble bath, sipped a glass of wine, and gave thanks for her kids.

She exited her bathroom, naked, and let out a scream. Alex was lying in her bed. Also naked.

"What are you doing in here? How'd you get in? My door was locked," she said. She went back into the bathroom and grabbed a towel. Wrapping it around her, she went to the door and opened it.

"Get out," she said.

He didn't move, except to pick up a glass of wine from her bedside table and extend it to her.

"Come on, have a glass of wine with me. It's your birthday," he said.

"I know it's my birthday. Which is exactly why I want to be alone. Please leave."

He set the wine down, got out of the bed, and walked over to where she stood holding the door open. He closed and locked it. They stood facing one another again, Sarah poised for battle. Alex had that hungry look in his eyes that scared her so. He took her hand and walked her over to the bed. He pulled her down next to him.

"I know you want me," he said.

She was not in the mood for this. It was her birthday. She knew if she started the fight, she had to see it through to calling the cops. The kids were so happily sleeping and she'd had such a lovely evening. She couldn't imagine the scene that would play out if she dug in her heels and forced him off.

She allowed him to climb on top of her. He held her hands up by her ears, pressing down on her wrists with his palms. He kissed her neck and her chest as he pumped himself in and out until he came. He didn't even have the decency to carefully pull out of her, dripping his come all over her bed.

She lay there for a long time after he left, crying. *This is exactly why I wanted out.* She heard her phone buzz with a text message.

Tanya: Happy birthday, beautiful friend! I am so proud of you!

Sarah smiled, and the feeling of thanks she had earlier in the evening returned in a small dose. She changed her bedsheets, took another bath, and when she fell asleep, she did so thinking of how she was going to execute her plan to break into Alex's office.

The next morning she drove to The Chanel Store. She was glad to see that Lacey was working. Lacey helped her often when she shopped.

"Hi, Mrs. Ruiz!" Lacey said.

"Hi, how are you today?" Sarah asked.

"Great. Here for your gift card?"

"Yes, I suppose. And actually, I need your help. I need to know the address of the guy that bought this card."

"Hmm. Let me see if I can tell," Lacey said. She typed some information into the computer. "There was a five-hundred-dollar gift card purchased on Wednesday. That was two days ago. It was bought by a Mr. Ricky Jameson."

"Yes?" Sarah asked.

"Yes, here, look." Lacey turned the monitor so Sarah could see the screen. "It shows that the card was bought either online or over the telephone for you to pick up here. All I can see are the last four digits of his credit card, though. And there is no address information on file."

"You don't know if it was online or over the phone?" Sarah said.

"Looks like the information was typed into the computer after the sale—so I think it might have been over the phone. That's also why they didn't put an address in. They would have processed the purchase differently," Lacey said.

"This guy has been harassing me for a few months. I desperately need to find out his address. Is there anything you can do to help me?"

"I can make a phone call to the head office and see if they'll tell me," Lacey offered.

"Do it. Please."

Lacey dialed the main number for Chanel and explained the situation.

"Yes, the customer is here now," she said. She handed the phone to Sarah.

"Hello," Sarah said.

"Hi, there. Ma'am, I'm sorry but I am not able to give you the billing information for the credit card that bought your gift certificate," the voice on the phone said.

"Please? I really need to find out where he lives," Sarah begged. "I won't tell anyone where I got the information."

"I really am not allowed to divulge anything about it. I'm sure that's frustrating, but we are bound by laws regarding billing privacy. The only way information can be released is with a police warrant. Is there anything else I can help you with?"

"No, not if you can't tell me the address. Thanks anyway." Sarah was disappointed. This was as close as she'd been to someone who knew Ricky's address. She took the gift card from Lacey, tucked it in her purse and left.

She sent Ricky a text.

Sarah: Why the gifts?
Ricky: For your birthday.
Sarah: I don't want your gifts.
Ricky: You never minded them before.
Sarah: That's before I knew you were screwing with my head.
Ricky: You know I care for you.
Sarah: Well, I no longer care for you. Don't contact me anymore. Ever.

On a whim, she called the phone company and asked if they could trace the two telephone numbers she had for Ricky. Both numbers came back as pay-as-you-go numbers with no identifying records attached. One of the numbers he had given her to use had a 415 area code; which was Northern California. The other was 206—Washington state. She wasn't sure he'd be stupid enough to use phone numbers from his home city to call her, but just in case, she checked the directory assistance for both those areas. No Ricky Jameson in either place.

Facebook held some Ricky Jamesons, but none had a profile picture that was visible to the public. MySpace and Twitter both turned up fruitless searches. There were a few there, but it was impossible to tell if any were her Ricky Jameson.

She got a text message from Ricky.

Ricky: OMG! What did you do?
Sarah: What?
Ricky: I got a call from the police today.
Sarah: Really?

Her phone rang. An unknown number. Curious, she answered it.

"Hello?"

"What the heck?" Ricky said. "I've got the cops calling me."

"What did they say?" Sarah asked.

"They wanted to verify if I was Ricky Jameson and were asking questions about my employer and shit." He sounded panicked.

"What did you tell them?"

"I said Ricky wasn't here right now and I hung up. I'm going to have to dump this number. Sarah, they knew my address. They asked to verify it. My real address. Did you do this?"

"I told you, my ex was pissed. Maybe he found you after all."

"Well, I guess this is goodbye then, Sarah. I can't take this risk. I can't believe you." Ricky was angry.

"*You* can't believe *me*? That's really rich," Sarah said. "One of these days you're going to mess with the wrong person. Maybe you already have."

"Don't worry, you can tell your ex that I won't be calling you again," Ricky said. The line went dead.

Sarah shut off her phone. *Did Alex really find him?* She would be impressed if he had. The thought of it all being over with Ricky opened the floodgate that had held myriad emotions at bay. She wept—not sure if it was relief, anger, a sense of love lost, or something unidentified that brought the tears to the surface.

When Alex came home late that night he found a note Sarah had left on the door to his room. It simply said, *It's over with Ricky. Don't know if you had anything to do with it or not, but thanks.* Alex smiled to himself and tucked the note into his dresser.

"So was it you?" Sarah asked him at breakfast.

"I've made some calls, had some people looking. One of them must have struck gold. I'll find out today who," Alex said.

"I think we can back off. I don't think he'll be bothering me again. You spooked him."

"Good. He better watch his step."

"Well, thank you. I appreciate it."

"No problem. I guess you do need me."

Sarah rolled her eyes, but Alex was studying his iPad, not looking at her.

"I'm going out of town tomorrow," Alex said. "I'll be gone two days."

"Oh, where are you going?"

"I've got to go to New York for a meeting."

"What kind of meeting is it?"

Alex looked at her. "Since when do you care about my business meetings? I'm looking to expand the gym and may have found a potential partner."

"Make the gym bigger?" Sarah asked.

"I'm going to open a second one north of the city," Alex said. "There's a good market there, and the other gym in that area sucks."

"Wow. Well, good luck with that," Sarah said. Inside, she was bursting with excitement. This would be her opportunity to have a peek inside Jugar. She'd been anxiously waiting for him to go out of town again.

She knew as she approached Jugar that she'd need to maintain the same assertion of authority she carried when she went to get the safe combination. Sarah felt confident she could handle the local club manager, Javier, if he came around, and she brought Tanya to help calm her nerves even more.

They arrived at the club at noon. Sarah guessed Javier wouldn't arrive until around three, so they had a good window in which to explore. The first of the duplicate keys Sarah tried opened the door easily. They were immediately met by the high-pitched tone of a security alarm. Sarah hadn't even considered the security system. The keypad was right next to the door.

Without hesitation, Sarah punched in the four digits of Alex's bank card PIN: 0811. It was the month and day of his deceased brother's birthday. The tone didn't cease.

"Crap, Tanya! It didn't work," Sarah said. "He uses that code for everything."

"Reverse the numbers," Tanya said. "That's what I do sometimes."

Sarah punched in 1180. The noise stopped immediately. They looked at each other.

"Wow. I nearly peed my pants," Tanya said.

Sarah shook her head. "Wait here. I'll go down to his office. If anyone pulls up, call me immediately."

The club was to the right of the entry doors. To the left was a hallway that led to Alex's office, Javier's office, a small staff room and a storage area. The same key opened

Alex's office. She paused and waited to see if she had another alarm to deal with. No sound. She exhaled and went inside.

She began with the safe. The office had walnut wainscoting, and the safe was concealed behind one of the panels. She was glad she had been there for the installation so she knew exactly how it worked. She pushed on the side of the panel to release the spring-loaded door. It opened easily.

She pulled the combination and a pair of rubber gloves from her purse. The safe door also opened with no hesitation. She stared at the contents inside for a good thirty seconds. She could see a gun, cash, and a whole bunch of papers. Using her phone, she took a picture of how the inside looked so she could put things back exactly.

She carefully removed the gun, which was on top, and set it gently on the floor pointed away from her. The cash was in bundles, and she let out a low whistle after counting it out. Twenty-five thousand dollars. The papers were randomly and messily stacked on top of each other.

She took them out as one big stack. She looked at each page and turned it upside-down to keep them in order. The first few were club bills—electricity bills, liquor bills and such. *Why keep these in the safe?*

The next few bills were cell phone bills. She turned them into the pile also, not really caring about their content, but then something caught her eye. September 30. The day of Nationals.

She took the phone bill and stared at it. Something was off, but she couldn't clearly see what.

She took snapshots of the phone bills with her camera. She'd have to study them later to see what was bothering her about them. She continued through the pile. A spreadsheet caught her eye. It wasn't labeled as to what it was, but across the top were the months of the year—twelve columns dating June 2011 through May 2012. Along the left of the page were some letters and numbers that meant nothing to Sarah. SW-54, SW-87, N-27, and others. She counted twenty-five of them. Written in the cells of the columns were names and more numbers. She took a picture of that too.

She put the papers back in the safe, placed the money and gun on top, making sure to match them to the picture she took and she closed the safe door. She opened his filing cabinet. Employee files and files that contained more bills for the businesses. She wondered again about the phone bills and couldn't wait to get home and have a closer look.

She opened his desk drawer and quickly saw that it was nearly empty. Nothing but pens, scissors, a jackknife, a few AA batteries, and gum.

"Sarah!" Tanya called down the hall. "Someone is here!"

"OK," Sarah called back. She closed the desk drawer.

She looked around. Everything looked put together. She pulled off her gloves and stuffed them into her purse, made sure she had her keys and phone, and locked the door behind her. She had just reached Tanya when Javier opened the club door and came in.

"Oh! Sarah, hi," he said.

"Hey there, Javier," Sarah said. "This is my friend Tanya."

"Hola," Javier said.

"We were just leaving," Sarah said.

"Anything wrong?" he asked.

"No, I was looking for the kids' passports. I couldn't find them at home and thought maybe Alex had them in his desk."

"Did you find them?" Javier asked.

"No, I didn't," she said, "but I'm sure they'll turn up somewhere."

"Want me to call Alex and see if he knows?"

"No, no, it's OK. I'll talk to him later. Don't worry about it at all. I am thinking about surprising him by scheduling a trip for all of us to Jamaica for Christmas." She even feigned excitement in her voice.

"Oh, I get it," Javier said. "No problem. I won't say a word."

"Thanks, Javier. We'll see you later."

When they got in the car, Tanya burst out laughing.

"Wow! You are go-*ood*!" she said. "You make quite the actress. I totally believed you!"

Sarah held out her hand. It was shaking. "Look at this."

"Did you find anything?" Tanya asked.

"I found a bunch of weird cell phone bills. And a couple of other things. I took pictures with my camera. I need to study them."

TWENTY-SIX

Tanya and Sarah downloaded the pictures of the phone bills to Sarah's computer and printed them. There were fifteen pages, covering August 18 to September 30.

"Sarah, look how late at night these calls were made," Tanya pointed to a line. "This one began at one a.m. and lasted just over two hours."

Sarah looked at Tanya. "What date was that? What day of the week?"

"August twenty-seventh. Saturday," Tanya said. "Why?"

"Holy shit! I know what they are!" Sarah said.

She got up and ran to her bedroom. In her closet she had a locked file box in which she kept all of her bills. She opened it and located her cell phone bills for the past few months. She brought them back to the dining table and spread them out.

"Ok, let me find August... here. August twenty-seven. Look at this. Incoming call, unknown number, at one o'clock a.m. Duration one hundred and twenty-four minutes." Sarah said. "Find another one."

Tanya looked at the page and said, "August twenty-eighth, outgoing call made to your number at ten thirty-five p.m. Lasted forty-seven minutes."

Sarah looked at her phone bill. "Incoming from unknown number at ten thirty-five p.m, forty-seven minutes. Do another."

"September fourteenth, twelve-fourteen a.m., fifty-six minutes," Tanya read.

Sarah scanned her bill. "Same."

"Oh wow," Tanya said. "He got a hold of Ricky's phone bills. How did he do that?"

Sarah furrowed her brow and thought about that. *How would he get Ricky's phone bills? Unless...* Sarah shook her head. "No Tanya, he didn't get Ricky's phone bills. It's more fucked up than that. What if he *is* Ricky?"

Tanya's eyes got round. They both felt a shiver run along their spines.

"Could he... how would he...?" Tanya couldn't finish a sentence. The two of them stared at one another, wheels turning in their minds.

The only thing more horrifying to Sarah to say the words out loud was the knowledge that they were probably true. "Alex is Ricky."

They continued to look at one another, eyes studying each other's faces, thinking through the implications of it.

"Sarah," Tanya finally said, "do you really think it's him?"

Sarah shrugged. "What other explanation is there for these phone bills?"

"Talk it through," Tanya said. "Was Alex ever there when a call from Gabe or Ricky came in?"

Sarah thought for a bit. "I don't think so, but I can't say for sure."

"Didn't you say Ricky had you online with him while Alex was screwing you?"

"Yes, but I never talked to him during the sex. I dialed the phone and set it down."

"OK," Tanya said, "didn't you say Alex was worried about you after Ricky sent him the e-mail? Did you see the e-mail?"

"I never saw it," Sarah said. "Yes, he panicked when I almost killed myself in Los Angeles."

"So if he was really scared that Ricky pushed you over the edge, then he couldn't be Ricky," Tanya said.

"Unless his real fear was that *he* pushed me over the edge."

The words hung heavy in the air. Sarah mulled them over.

"Why would he do that to you?" Tanya asked. That was a million-dollar question for which Sarah had no answer.

"I don't know."

"What are you going to do? Are you going to tell him that you know?"

"How can I? I can't tell him I broke into his office and opened his safe. You're going to have to take these phone bills with you," Sarah said.

"Sarah, I think you should talk to a someone about this. Sweetie, you need professional advice about how to proceed with this. And you need to be careful. If he is crazy enough to screw with your brain like that, who knows what he'd do. And you have five kids upstairs to worry about."

Sarah nodded. "I know. I do have a good counselor that I saw a couple of years ago when I first needed to talk to someone about Alex. I'll make an appointment this week."

Tanya hugged her friend with all her might. "Be careful."

The next day, Sarah went back to Miami Safe and Vault and purchased a small safe for herself. She had it delivered and installed in her bedroom closet. It wasn't completely hidden, but a casual observer wouldn't notice it. She needed something that Alex couldn't get at. She felt so vulnerable.

She telephoned the therapist and was thrilled to learn she could get in immediately. Sarah saw Dianne two years earlier when she first had realized that she needed an "out" plan from Alex. Although Dianne didn't understand how Sarah could stay under the same roof with Alex after the distorted sexual relationship he had created between them, she supported Sarah in her decision to stick things out a while longer for the children. She had helped Sarah keep clarity between her feelings of worthlessness as a used-up sex object for Alex's pleasure and the truth—the strong qualities Sarah carried that made her who she is.

Sarah began her story with the first contact from Gabe and talked for an hour straight, pausing only for sips of water, and ending with the information she and Tanya discovered in Alex's office. Dianne began taking notes, but at some point the pencil remained frozen midair and Dianne's mouth dropped open, where it remained for the rest of the story.

"So here I am," Sarah said, wiping her eyes with a tissue.

Dianne put her notepad down and went to where Sarah sat on the couch. She sat next to Sarah and hugged her tightly. Sarah leaned into Dianne and sobbed.

"How is it you are still functional after all you've been through?" Dianne asked.

Sarah smiled weakly. "I don't know. Strong will?"

"The strongest I've seen in a while. Sarah, I don't give out diagnoses without having spent a lot of time with someone, but if what you are telling me is true, you are dealing with a very disturbed individual. What you've described indicates elements of narcissism, sexual dysfunction, psychopathy. And probably other things, too. These are dangerous, serious conditions. When found all together in the same person—it's a ticking bomb with no way to be defused."

"I'm not in a position to leave," Sarah said. "Not yet. I can't take the kids and run. We have nowhere to go."

"How long has this been going on? When did Gabe first connect with you?"

"This summer. End of July."

"So for four months, he has been pretending to be this other man?"

"I think so. I mean, I've got some evidence, but I can't say with one hundred percent certainty."

"He is holding your psychological state in a delicate balance. He is tormenting you as one person so you'll run to him as your husband to rescue you from your tormentor. He pushes, you go to him. He backs off, you back off. This angers him, so he unleashes on you sexually, then starts the cycle again. Sarah, you can't go on like this. Something is going to give. Gabe made sure to be the complete opposite of what turned you off about Alex.

"You told Gabe your preferences and hates and he used those to suck you in emotionally. He was the complete opposite of Alex in word and emotions, but he couldn't hide the sexual dysfunction. That isn't as easy to turn off. So Gabe brought Alex back into it, so he could be sexually satisfied."

"When you say it like that is sounds even more disturbing," Sarah said. "Could it really have been Alex all along?"

"Why are you not convinced that it is?"

"For one thing, I am not sure that I never got any messages or contact from Gabe when Alex was in the room. I just don't remember. We texted and talked so much back and forth that I would find it hard to believe he was never around for that. Second, wouldn't I have known Alex's voice? His way of speaking or something would have given him away, wouldn't it?"

"Not necessarily. If he is psychopathic, I guarantee you he can chameleon his emotional state to suit his purposes. Psychopaths are parasitic. In your case, he feeds off your dependence on him. He'll create whatever situation he has to so that you will need him. And voice-altering devices are easy to acquire. He likely used one when he called you."

"What do I do?" Sarah asked.

"Unless you are ready to go to a women's shelter, you need a plan to get away from him. I would ask if you feel you are in imminent danger, but I think you would tell me 'no' even though I suspect the answer is 'yes.'"

"Honestly, I don't think he'd hurt me physically. Other than the sex, which hurts, but isn't life-threatening."

"Would you come back and see me later this week?" Dianne asked. "I think you and I should be in constant communication for the time being."

"Am I a horrible mother?" Sarah asked. Her eyes pleaded with Dianne's for affirmation.

"Oh, Sarah, you are a terrific mother," Dianne said. "Those kids need you whole and healed from all of this. They know they can count on you."

Alex was back from his trip when she returned home. He was in the kitchen, making a sandwich.

"Hey, where've you been?" he asked.

She willed her voice to have a casual tone, "I went back and saw Dianne, the therapist. I thought, now that this whole Ricky thing is over, maybe she can help me feel good about myself again."

"I was thinking about something," Alex said, "I have been going through the e-mails that Ricky sent to me. I spent last night listening to you screw your hot doctor in L.A."

"Look, I don't need your judgment," Sarah began.

"No, what I was wondering is, what if *he* was Ricky? What if he played you so you would have sex with him?" Alex sat back in his chair with a satisfied smile.

"No way, I met him with Stephanie and her boyfriend," Sarah said.

"How did you meet him?" Alex asked.

"I bumped into him after the registration meeting," Sarah said.

"You bumped into him—or he bumped into you?"

Sarah thought about that for a minute. She wasn't sure how it went.

"Did he continue to have contact? Or did you pursue it?" Alex asked.

"He invited me out for his birthday," Sarah said.

"Was he there when Ricky called?"

Sarah replayed the evening. Ricky called just before she went out. Then he rang again while Joseph was in the bathroom. *Could it have been?*

"No, he wasn't there when Ricky called," Sarah admitted.

"I'm only suggesting, maybe you fucked Ricky and you don't even know it. Wouldn't that be something?"

"I need to go get some air," Sarah said. She went for a walk to the beach. If it was true, Ricky was more disturbed than she even considered, and it would also mean Alex wasn't Ricky.

Thinking about it made her head ache, but whether Alex was Ricky or Ricky was Doc, her course of action was set. She was filled with gratitude that Dianne was going to help see her through this and felt more determined than ever to bring her emotions back to a healthy place. For her future. For her kids.

TWENTY-SEVEN

The next eight weeks were peaceful for Sarah. Her wounds began to heal, with the help of biweekly appointments with Dianne and Tanya, who checked in with her every day. There was no further contact from Ricky, and even Alex left her alone for the most part.

Her safe began to accumulate cash. An extra bit here and there from the bank account when she bought groceries or paid for other household expenses wasn't missed. One January day she got a text message from Jenny, asking if she would go with her to Las Vegas the first weekend in February. Sarah's friendship with Jenny had faded in the months following the last Vegas trip. Sarah didn't go out of her way to call. Jenny, always a bit self-absorbed anyway, either didn't notice or was too busy with her own life to think twice about Sarah. Sarah talked it over with Dianne.

"Does Jenny know what Ty did to you?" Dianne asked.

"I never told her, and obviously Ricky never e-mailed her," Sarah said. "I've thought about how to tell her so many times, but with everything else going on, it just never happened. I probably should have told her straight away, but I didn't. Do you think I should go?"

"Why do you think she wants you to go with her?" Dianne asked.

"I'm sure she is thinking 'Girls Weekend Away.' Possibly none of her other friends could go, so she figured I'm a good fallback friend. I don't know."

"Do you want to go?" Dianne asked.

"No. Not really. Perhaps this would be a chance to mend some of the damage that's been done to our friendship. Damage Jenny isn't even aware of."

"You haven't been away from home in a while, have you?"

Sarah shook her head. "Not since Nationals last year. That was September."

"Why don't you sleep on it, then let her know," Dianne suggested. "Go with your gut feeling."

Sarah's gut told her that Jenny would hate her forever if she found out what happened with Ty. It would be delicate navigation to explain it all, and she couldn't imagine any presentation of the events that ended well, but if she never saw Jenny, she'd certainly never have the chance to bandage the wounds. She decided to go.

They arrived in Vegas on a Saturday afternoon. The Vegas strip is always rocking with activity, and the weekend promised big fun. There was a UFC fight that day at the MGM *and* it was Super Bowl weekend. The crowds were aroused even more than normal. Sarah exited the cab in front of their hotel and, as soon as her foot hit the pavement, she felt the electricity of Las Vegas course up her leg and into her chest. She suddenly realized part of her hesitation about this trip was that she felt betrayed by a city she loved. She and Vegas had a long history together— good times, many laughs, relaxing poolside drinks and warm conversations. Yet last year, she left Vegas with nothing but anger and shame. She determined right then that the weekend would be a catharsis for her, a chance to reconcile with Las Vegas so they could be friends again.

She and Jenny put their things in their shared room, freshened up, then went to the House of Blues, one of Sarah's favorite spots. Blues music was balm to Sarah's soul. Many people misunderstand the blues, thinking it to be all about loss. Your husband cheats on you? You sing the blues. Your best friend betrays you? You sing the blues. Down on your luck? You sing the blues. But Sarah didn't hear the loss in blues music. She heard hope and felt the overcoming spirit that rose to the surface and poured from the guitars, saxophones, and pianos. Blues music always left her confident that success lay around the next bend.

After the first band left the stage, Jenny was itching to go dancing. While pausing at the bar for a drink, Sarah heard a voice behind her. "Can I buy your drink?"

She turned and saw a handsome black man who had to be all of twenty-five years old. He was with three other guys.

"No, thanks, I got this one," she said.

"No really, allow me." He indicated to the bartender to put the drinks on his bill.

"Thanks," Sarah said.

"I'm Derek," he said. "This is Jack, Brandon, and Steve."

"Sarah. This is Jenny," Sarah said, motioning to her friend.

"Nice to meet you ladies. So what brings you to Vegas?" Derek asked.

"We're just here for a couple days of R&R," Jenny said.

"We were just heading to an after-party for the UFC fighters," Jack said. "Maybe you ladies would like to join us?"

"Sure!" Jenny said before Sarah could even respond.

"We don't want to intrude," Sarah said. Jenny smacked Sarah playfully on the arm.

"Of course we do!" Jenny said, giving an eye roll.

"You aren't intruding. We can bring eight people," Derek said. "We'd be honored to bring such beautiful ladies with us."

"Where is this party?" Sarah asked hesitantly.

"The Palms," Jack answered. "We're going to take a cab over. Join us. It'll be fun."

Jenny looked at Sarah and shrugged. "Why not?"

Derek made sure he was squished up against Sarah on the cab ride to The Palms. He placed his arm behind her on the seat back and allowed it to touch her a bit more firmly with each bump of the cab. Sarah almost laughed out loud at his audaciousness.

Derek's VIP passes bought them an elevator ride to a party at the top of the hotel, where Sarah saw many people she'd seen only in the headlines. She spotted Forrest Griffin right away and then did a double take to the guy to whom he was speaking. He had a shaved head, deep chocolate eyes, and dimples that she had an impulse to touch. Their eyes met briefly, and he shot her a smile that made her blush.

As she made her way around the party, more than once she realized that the guy with the dimples was watching her. Derek made it a point to never be more than a step or two away from her, and he touched her shoulder or back frequently enough that anyone who didn't know better would think they were together.

Sarah slipped away from Derek. She went to the bar to get another drink and found herself face to face with Dimples.

"Hi," he said.

"Hello," Sarah replied.

"I'm Christian." He flashed her another smile and she felt her cheeks get hot.

"Nice to meet you. I'm Sarah," she answered.

"Hey, here you are." Derek came up and put an arm around her. He swayed a bit in his overexuberance.

"Hi, I'm Christian. Didn't mean to steal your girl away." Christian smiled and held his hand out to Derek.

"No problem, man," Derek said, shaking Christian's hand. "Nice to meet ya."

"Um, we're not together," Sarah said.

"Sure we are," Derek put his arm around her again. "We came together. You can't leave me for another man."

"First of all, we aren't together," Sarah said firmly. She gently removed Derek's arm. "And second, I'm probably nearly old enough to be your mom, and I'll be damned if I'm going to have some young punk tell me who I can and cannot speak to."

Sarah pushed through the crowd, away from Derek and his youthful arrogance, and went to the other side of the room, where a large glass wall gave a beautiful view of the Vegas lights. She leaned her head against the glass.

"I love a girl who knows what she wants," a voice said from behind her. She turned and Christian was standing there, smiling. "You sure told him what's what."

Sarah rolled her eyes. "Seriously. How ridiculous." She laughed. "What did he do when I walked away?"

"He went to the bathroom. I think he had to puke." Christian laughed. His smile was delicious.

"Do you need me to get you out of here?" he asked.

"Oh, look, I'm..." Sarah wasn't sure what to say.

"Are you married?" he asked.

"No. I'm separated. Have been for nearly a year. It's not that. I've been through a lot and am trying to be very cautious."

"I promise to be a perfect gentleman. No strings attached. Let's just go gamble, or see the night life or do something, anything," Christian said. He made it sound so adventurous.

"How can I resist?" Sarah said, laughing. "OK. I'm here with my friend Jenny. I need to find her."

"Awesome. Bring her along. It'll be fun," Christian said.

Jenny was dancing with some of Derek's friends. She reluctantly went with Sarah until she saw Christian. Then she perked up.

The rest of their night was a whirlwind. Christian had a town car with a driver, which made it easy to spend the next several hours hitting the clubs, casinos, and parties on the strip. Sarah found Christian extremely easy to talk to and, as he promised, he was a perfect gentleman. Sarah didn't drink much—she wanted to keep in control. Jenny, however, was extremely inebriated, and she got louder as the night wore on.

Christian seemed amused by Jenny, and by the time they ended up back at the hotel, Sarah and Christian had to support Jenny to get her up to the room. Sarah took off Jenny's shoes after she flopped, passed out, onto the bed.

"Well, that was some night," Christian said, ever smiling.

"Yes, it was. Thank you so much," Sarah said. "What a great time."

"What are you ladies up to tomorrow?"

"Getting our tan on by the pool," Sarah said. "Relaxing."

"I have a golf tournament in the morning, but if you ladies are free for dinner, I'd like to spend more time with you."

"That would be fabulous," Sarah said. She couldn't help but stare at his lips. They formed the best smile, and he had the kind of face she'd never tire of staring at.

"I'll text you when I'm done golfing. Goodnight, Sarah."

Even with Jenny moving in slow motion, they managed to don their bikinis and hit the pool by eleven. Jenny and Sarah's banter skimmed the surface of their lives. Nothing went any deeper than the kind of stuff you'd find on Facebook. Drivel. Crumbs of conversation, without ever getting to the meat. That was OK with Sarah. Jenny had no idea what Sarah had been through at the end of the last year, and where would she even begin to describe the pain and torment?

The closest Jenny ventured to their previous place of intimacy of friendship was when Jenny asked Sarah, "Are you and Alex still separated?"

"Yes, we are."

"You doing OK?" Jenny asked.

"I'm fine. It's been rough, but I'm trying to save enough money to live on my own with the kids."

"Won't he pay you child support?"

"He won't move out of the house," Sarah said. "He won't agree to enough support that I can find a place big enough for me and the five kids."

"Sorry to hear that. Hey—how was Nationals last year? I can't believe I didn't even ask you. You must think I'm the worst friend ever."

Sarah smiled. "I came in fifth."

"Congratulations!" Jenny exclaimed. "Way to go, girl. That calls for another mojito."

Sarah watched her friend walk to the bar. For the hundredth time she played through in her head how to tell her what happened the last time they were in Vegas. She still didn't see any way it could end in anything but pain.

At four o'clock they went upstairs to shower. Christian picked them up at five-thirty. It was Super Bowl Sunday, and their first stop was a party where Sarah found herself rubbing elbows with ex-NFLers and other sports stars.

"What exactly do you do for a living?" she asked Christian as she looked at all the muscles around her.

"I run a sports marketing company," he answered casually.

"So that's how you know all of these famous people," Sarah said. "Impressive."

Christian shrugged. "Not really. It's business. With a lot of great perks."

The game was still in the first quarter when Christian leaned over to Sarah and said, "Come on, let's go get dinner."

"And leave the game?" Sarah asked.

"Sure. Unless you really care who wins." Christian smiled at her.

"What game?" she said.

Christian treated them to another amazing evening. Dinner at TWIST, zip lining over Fremont Street, drinks at Minus 5. Being with Christian felt like hanging out with a best friend. A few times Jenny flirted and grabbed at Christian. He was so smooth as he gently discouraged her behavior. Sarah was impressed at how respectfully he treated them and how he seemed to genuinely enjoy their company.

They ended up back in the bar at Sarah and Jenny's hotel, comfortably seated in lounge chairs and sipping merlot. There the conversation turned to personal matters.

"Let's play a game," Jenny suggested. "A get-to-know-you game. Christian, we can ask you any three questions, then you get to do the same for us."

Christian looked at Sarah and smiled. Jenny amused him like a little sister who was hard to get rid of. "OK, I'll play along."

"Are you married?" Jenny asked.

"No. I am divorced."

"Do you have children?" Sarah asked.

"Yes. I have triplets. Girls."

"Oooh!" both Jenny and Sarah laughed at that thought.

"You are in trouble when they hit their teenage years," Sarah said.

"Yes, I know," he said, laughing. "I have four more years till that happens. One more question."

Jenny gave him a seductive smile. "What are you looking for in your next woman?"

"Interesting question. I want a woman who is confident. Who runs her own business maybe. Who loves kids. She has to have a lot of energy and a great sense of humor. And I have to find her easy to talk to." Christian's eyes did not waver from Sarah's as he gave his description. Sarah felt her cheeks flush yet again as she watched his mouth form the words.

"Now, it's my turn," he said. "Sarah, what do you look for in a man?"

Sarah didn't have to even think about her answer. "My next man will be someone who understands what it is like to be divorced. Ideally he will have his own children, otherwise he won't understand my lifestyle. He'll be someone who is my best friend. He will know how to be a gentleman. I can be a bit goofy, so he will be someone who likes to laugh and knows how to make me smile."

"Good answer," Christian said. "I knew when I heard you put down that young punk yesterday that you were a woman who knows what she wants. I know you'll get it, too."

"I won't settle," Sarah said.

They chatted a bit more, and then Christian said he had to go. "I've got an early flight out tomorrow, but I'll have Marcus, my driver, come for you girls around eleven if you'd like. He'll be at your disposal. Wherever you want to go, use him. OK?"

"Oh Christian, that is so sweet." Jenny hugged him tightly. Too tightly. She tried to linger on his neck, but he easily moved away from her. He turned to Sarah.

"I enjoyed getting to know you," he said. "I hope I was a gentleman."

"Perfectly," Sarah said.

"Could I call you sometime?" Christian asked.

"Definitely." She smiled at him, and he gave her a warm hug.

"You are a beautiful woman, Sarah," he said. "I hope to see you smile a lot more."

TWENTY-EIGHT

Sarah and Jenny let Marcus take them shopping in the morning, then they lolled by the pool, sipping and soaking until mid-afternoon. Christian texted Sarah when he got back to Los Angeles, thanking her again for the time spent together. Marcus returned at seven to chauffeur their evening activities.

Sarah stopped drinking after they left the second nightclub, when she realized Jenny was nearly completely wasted.

"Saaaarah," Jenny said. "I want to find a guy tonight."

"Oh sweetie, I don't think that would be a great idea," Sarah said. "Why don't we switch to water and see if we can grab a late-night snack."

"Don't be a party pooper," Jenny said. "I want to go dancing. I want to get laid. We've got a driver and everything!"

Jenny insisted that Marcus take them to VooDoo, where the dancing was a storm of steamy bodies, sweating in unison as hips rotated and arms flowed to the beat.

Sarah loved dancing and for a long time enjoyed the grind and bounce among the crowd. When she felt sufficiently worked out, she retrieved a glass of water from the bar. She went to the upper level for a higher vantage point to catch a glimpse of Jenny.

She scrutinized the dancers, searching for a flash of Jenny's silver-sequined top. Nothing. She turned her gaze to the tables around the perimeter. Along one of the walls she spotted Jenny, lips locked with a handsome someone.

"Oh Jenny," Sarah said to herself. She abandoned her water and pressed through the crowd.

"Hey you," Sarah said as she sat down across the booth from where Jenny and her new friend were groping one another.

Jenny peeled herself off of him. "Sarah. This is my new friend—um, what's your name, friend?"

"Adam," the guy said. He gave a nod of his head to Sarah. "How's it going?"

"Wonderful," Sarah said. "I think we should go, Jen. I'm getting tired, and we have an early flight out tomorrow."

"Sa-raaah. I'm not finished here with Adam. We've got more stu-uff to dooo." Jenny straddled Adam's lap and grabbed the sides of his face with her hands. She slid her tongue into his mouth. His hands crept underneath Jenny's shirt as he let them roam along her back.

Sarah sat there for a moment, not sure what to do. "Jenny," Sarah said.

"Mm-hmm," Jenny responded without removing her mouth from Adam's.

"Don't leave without me, OK?" Sarah said.

"I won't," came a muffled reply.

Sarah stepped onto the balcony for air and to soak in the view. They fit a lot of fun into this weekend and, although she hadn't had the opportunity for an unreserved conversation with Jenny, she did feel like she and Las Vegas set aside their hostilities and enjoyed one another's company again. Meeting Christian gave her an inkling of hope that perhaps, maybe, there were decent men in the world who didn't see her as a sex object but as a woman with positive qualities to be appreciated.

She contemplated Christian as she viewed the city below. His dimples and smile were beautiful, a word she didn't often use to describe a man. Yet, that's exactly what he was, a beautiful person from whom kindness and joy radiated. She wondered what his daughters were like, and imagined that he probably took great pleasure in spending time with them. She knew that whatever man she dated would have to enjoy and appreciate kids. Men who couldn't be around children were selfish and narcissistic, qualities Sarah had enough of in her life.

The night became chilly, and Sarah went to retrieve Jenny. The table where she last saw her friend was now occupied by someone else.

"Shit," Sarah said. She frantically began to look around the club. She had about given up hope, when she saw Jenny stumble from the bathroom. She rushed to her.

"Jenny! Oh thank God," Sarah said, putting her arm around her friend.

"Jeez, I was just in the bathroom, Warden," Jenny said angrily.

"Jenny, I was worried I'd lost you."

"Well, you don't have to worry about me! I'm just fine," Jenny said.

"Come on, let's get out of here," Sarah began to propel her toward the door.

"Where's Allen?" Jenny said.

"Adam," Sarah corrected.

"Oh what the fuck ever. Where is he?" Jenny pulled away from Sarah and began to look around. Adam wasn't in view. "Adam!" Jenny called out. "Aaaaadaaam!"

Sarah took her arm and began to lead her out of the club. "Maybe he went outside to get a cab. Why don't we go see if we can find him."

"Oh, good idea. Sarah, you're so smart," Jenny said, taking Sarah's hand. "We're gonna find Adam, then I'm going to get laid."

Sarah hoped that Adam would not be anywhere to be seen. They rode the elevator to the lobby of the Rio, and Sarah sat Jenny in a chair while she texted Marcus that they were ready. He texted back: *five minutes.*

Sarah sat next to Jenny. "Do you want some water?"

"No, Warden, I don't want no stupid water," Jenny said. Sarah forgot that sometimes Jenny turned into a mean drunk.

"OK, hun," Sarah said lightly. "Our ride will be here soon."

"Is it Aman? I mean, Adam?" Jenny asked.

"I don't know who will be in the car," Sarah lied. "We'll see if we can find him on the way back to our hotel."

"Yes, Warden," Jenny said.

Sarah saw Marcus pull up outside, and she managed to guide Jenny to the car. Jenny climbed in and let Sarah buckle her seat belt. They pulled away before Jenny realized no one else was in the car but them.

"Hey! Where is he?" Jenny asked.

"I guess he left," Sarah said. "I'm sorry, Jenny."

"You did this on purpose!" Jenny yelled. "You don't want me to have any fun!"

"Aw sweetie, I just don't want you to do anything you'll regret." The last thing Sarah would wish on someone was to be used and treated like trash, the way Ricky and Jenny's own husband had made her feel.

Jenny pouted the whole way back to the hotel, occasionally slinging pot shots at Sarah. Sarah thanked Marcus profusely and once again steered her overindulged friend to their room.

A mere three hours of sleep flew by before they had to get up, pack, and leave for the airport. Jenny's trip home was quite miserable, but Sarah was proud of herself for making her own choices that weekend. Her independence and self-confidence were boosted, and she told Dianne as much in their next meeting.

"That was a big step for you," Dianne said. "Congratulations."

"Thank you. It felt so good to enjoy myself without pressures or demands from anyone else. Even hanging around with Christian felt comfortable and normal. I haven't felt normal around a man in a while."

"Yes, I can imagine not," Dianne said, smiling. "You haven't been around normal men in a while. Which leads me to wonder, how are things at home?"

"Alex was in a rotten mood the day I got home from Vegas. He always is when I go away. It's like he has to punish me for being gone."

"How is your plan to move out coming along?"

"I've got about ten thousand dollars saved," Sarah said. "It's not bad, but I'm not sure what to do next."

"Sarah, I don't often give outright advice," Dianne said. "I ask you questions to guide you to making your own choices. However, in this case, I need to say something."

"OK."

"If you ever plan to have a life of normalcy, you must not continue to live under the same roof with that man.

Sarah, he pretended to be someone else to get you to have phone sex with him. Then he blackmailed you into continuing the relationship, even pressuring you to have sex with someone you had just met. He pushed you to your breaking point, then stood back and watched you crumble. It's not right."

"I know it isn't right," Sarah justified. "Part of me can't really believe he is Ricky. Is that wrong?"

Dianne shook her head. "No, it isn't wrong. Sometimes our brains have a hard time accepting that someone we are close with can do monstrous things to our hearts. You can't live in denial. Even if he really wasn't Ricky, and there is another explanation for the phone bills, he has personality disorders that make him dangerous for you. Promise me that this week you'll think about what next step you can take at home to be free."

Sarah nodded. "I promise."

The next day she got a text message from Christian.

Christian: Hey Sarah! How are you?
Sarah: I'm well. How are u? Still smiling?
Christian: Always. Can I call you sometime?
Sarah: Yes, of course. I'd like that.

He didn't like to text; he wanted to hear her voice. She learned all about his girls, and he asked about her children, too. He remembered their names and wondered about their sports and their interests. There were no sexual innuendos, inappropriate remarks, or anything that made her feel anything other than that he had an interest in getting to know her.

He suggested that they go on a date.

"How are we going to pull that off?" she asked. "You're in Los Angeles, I'm in Miami."

"If you can get away for a couple of days, let me know and leave the rest to me," he said.

Sarah arranged for her mom to stay with the kids so she could get away without having to ask Alex for any help. Whatever had been occupying his attention lately kept him away from the house and away from her bedroom. Christian e-mailed her an itinerary for a flight to Los Angeles, leaving on a Friday morning and returning Monday. She had a reservation at The London hotel in West Hollywood.

Christian arranged a car to pick her up at LAX and take her to her hotel. On the pillow in her room was a red box adorned with a huge white bow. Taped to its top was a handwritten note:

Sarah ~

Welcome to California ~ I'm looking forward to getting to know you better. Rest up! Slip into this and I'll take you to dinner at 5 pm. See you soon!

~ Christian

Inside the box was a white cotton sundress. It had thin spaghetti straps. The V-neck and bustier top enhanced her figure, and she twirled in front of the mirror in awe at how perfectly it fit.

"How did he know my size?" As quickly as the thought came into her head, she felt a shockwave of horror. *Was he in cahoots with Alex? Or Ricky?*

"Stop it, Sarah," she chided herself. "Don't let your mind go where it shouldn't."

Sarah opened a small bottle of Cabernet from the mini-bar. As she poured it into the wine glass, she glanced up and laughed out loud when she saw her reflection in the mirror. *Why do all these mini-bars have mirrors above them?* she wondered. She imagined all the mini-bar mirrors she'd encountered over the years. Precaution, confusion, disgust—side by side, like she was reading a newspaper comic strip, she could remember the look on her face in each of those mini-bar mirrors, and the emotion that bubbled inside of her each time.

What did she feel this time? She stared herself in the eyes and considered herself. Confidence.

She took her glass out to the balcony, reflecting on the path she traveled that brought her to this place. For the first time in a while, thinking about the past didn't bring feelings of shame. She could analyze her actions separate from the intensity of the emotions that accompanied them. This realization made her wonder what had changed inside of her to abate the pain.

She pulled her iPad from her bag. Dianne had encouraged her to keep a journal, and she could see no more perfect place to start than right there. She stared at the blank notepad for a moment, unsure at what point in her sordid story to begin. She began with, *I met Ricky Jameson* and let her fingers take over. Emancipating the words from the prison she had locked them into was like releasing wild dogs into a jungle. They ripped free and didn't stop until she had filled ten pages in her journaling app.

When she paused, her head swam with the recognition that although she was exhausted, she definitely felt liberated; free, free, free from the bondage Ricky and Alex held her in. The sun was rising, it was going to chase away the darkness. This time, there was nothing Alex could do about it.

When Christian arrived she looked and felt beautiful. He noticed right away that she had a peace about her that he hadn't seen in Las Vegas. They hugged warmly, and he took her hand as he led her to the lobby restaurant for dinner.

"I'm so glad you are here," he said. "You look radiant."

"Me too. This place is absolutely gorgeous. Thank you for taking care of everything. Thank you for this dress."

"You take my breath away. I don't want you to feel pressured for anything. I really want to get to know you and give you a relaxing, amazing time. You don't have to take care of your drunk friend, your kids, worry about your ex, or anything this weekend."

They shared caramelized sea scallops, followed up with Maine lobster and a praline chocolate crunch for desert at Gordon Ramsay's restaurant in the hotel. The wine was so elegant and aromatic, it was heaven on her palate.

As the dessert plates were cleared, Christian ordered another bottle of wine and said something privately to the waiter, who nodded and walked away. Christian stood and held out his hand to Sarah.

"Come, I have a surprise for you," he said.

She took his hand and he led her back through the hotel lobby to the elevators. They rode to the top of the hotel, where they were met by a maître 'd for The Rooftop Restaurant. He guided them to a love seat in front of a lit fireplace, where a bottle of wine was chilled and a tray of chocolate cherries waited on a small glass table. A thick fleece blanket invited them to snuggle beneath. Sarah curled her legs underneath her and leaned into Christian's shoulder. The waiter poured and handed them each a glass of wine and left them to bask in the glow of the fire and indulge on the cherries.

They sat, eyes reflecting the light of the fire for a while, sipping wine and lost in their thoughts. Sarah couldn't imagine anywhere she'd rather be.

At long last, Christian turned and kissed the top of Sarah's head.

"Comfortable?" he asked.

"Mmm. Very," Sarah replied. "I've not been this comfortable in a long time."

"Good. I don't know what all you've been through, but I sense it has been really rough for you. I don't want to know the details, but I do want you to know I very much enjoy your company. From the second you walked into that party in Vegas, there was something I found fascinating about you, and I just want to get to know you better."

Her eyes dampened with the purity of how he spoke. "I'm not ready to be hurt again," she said, "but I want to get to know you, too."

He kissed the top of her head again and she turned her face to look up at him. He set his wine glass down and took her cheeks in his hands. He gently kissed the tip of her nose, then he kissed each of her cheeks before placing his lips perfectly on hers. The softness of his lips took her breath away, and it was a moment before she could respond. They kissed, tasting one another and letting their mouths explore one another gently, as if there were nothing else in the world to do but sit on that love seat and kiss for all eternity. Sarah was taken by the passion that flowed from such delicate kissing and got the impression that he would be satisfied to sit there forever with her.

They paused and looked at one another. "You look like an angel in the moonlight," he said. She felt her cheeks blush, the way they did when their eyes had met in Las Vegas. His lips were beautiful, and she couldn't help it— she reached out and stroked his bottom lip with her thumb.

"Thank you," she said. "You've made me feel like an angel."

She snuggled into him again and they sat, sipping wine and talking about everything from favorite books to desired travel destinations to their childhood to secret fears. When the wine bottle was gone, the maître 'd brought another. When that was nearly gone, the stars had long been out and Sarah was feeling tired. She tried unsuccessfully to stifle a yawn.

"Want to go back to your room?" Christian asked.

"No, I want to stay here forever," Sarah said truthfully, "but I'm getting sleepy."

"Come on." He stood, and she followed. As she started to walk toward the elevators, her foot missed a small step. She fell, landing flat on her butt, with her wine glass held high—not a drop spilled. They looked at one another and laughed.

"Impressive!" he said. "Way to protect the wine. You must be an angel."

"I have many talents," she said, standing and not feeling even the slightest bit of embarrassment. This surprised her. Ordinarily she would have wanted to crawl away and hide. That wasn't the case with Christian. He smiled at her like she was the most precious thing on earth, and he proudly took her hand and led her back to her room.

At the door they paused. She used her key to open it, then turned to him. "Would you like to come in?"

"I very much would like to come in," he said, "but you know that isn't why I invited you to L.A."

"I know. And I also know if I said, 'Not tonight,' that you would be a gentleman and would leave."

"I would. And I would come get you for breakfast and we'd have a fabulous day tomorrow," he said, smiling.

"How about if you come in, we have an amazing night tonight, and still have a fabulous day tomorrow?" she suggested. She held the door for him to enter her room.

The rest of their weekend was spent making love. Sarah was ensconced in his arms, safely trusting that there was nothing ulterior behind his caresses and affection. It was an effortless love story that she didn't want to see end.

The morning of her flight home, they took a bubble bath together. They faced one another from opposite ends of the oversized tub, legs entwined, sipping mimosas.

"I don't want to leave," Sarah said.

"You'll see me again soon," Christian answered.

"Will I?"

"Of course, angel. This is only the beginning," he promised. He stared at her face and his eyes glimmered.

"What is it?" she asked.

"You. You looked so beautiful when we went out to dinner last night, but right here, this, is how I love you best. No makeup, hair in a ponytail."

"You're crazy," she said, and she pushed a stray hair behind her ear. "I look awful."

"No. You're perfect like this. You look so pretty and innocent."

She laughed. "I don't know about that."

"Sarah, you need to know, I care about you," he said. "We have a fresh start here together."

Their hug at the airport lasted a solid five minutes. Each time she tried to let go, she couldn't. Finally, reluctantly, they peeled themselves apart.

"Don't fret," he said. "You will see me again."

Words choked in her throat, and she couldn't even speak. She picked up her carry-on bag and wordlessly turned and walked away. The woman who stood in front of her in the security line noticed a lone tear trickle down Sarah's cheek.

"Love?" she asked Sarah.

"At first sight," Sarah replied with a small smile.

TWENTY-NINE

On the flight back to Miami, Sarah recalled Dianne's admonishment to move forward with the separation with Alex. Separated and living under the same roof wasn't working; anyone could see that. She had seen it for months and now needed to act on it. Burying her fear of not having enough money would be difficult, but she knew it could no longer be an excuse for her. There had to be something she could do.

Tanya was there to greet Sarah's plane.

"You look different," she said as they cruised the highway to South Beach.

"Do I? I feel different," Sarah said.

"How so?" Tanya asked.

"I'm beginning a new chapter," Sarah said. "This is Day One. I need to move forward with my life, not tangled in the web of deception and lies that Alex continually spins all around me. I've tasted normal, and I am not going back."

"So the guy was good?" Tanya asked.

"You know, it isn't even about him," Sarah said. "Yes, he was amazing. A perfect gentleman. We had the sweetest weekend. Nice, caring men exist. And I deserve one."

"Yes, you do," Tanya said. "Absolutely."

"I'm going to tell Alex we need to push forward from separation to divorce."

Tanya was at a stoplight, and she turned to look at Sarah. "Oh shit. He's gonna flip."

"I don't care," Sarah said. "We shouldn't be living in the same house. I can't be afraid to go up against him in this. He'll take care of the kids. I know he will. He also knows they belong with me. No judge would argue that. The lifestyle Alex leads is not suitable for raising children."

"When are you going to tell him?"

"As soon as possible."

Turns out, Alex was away on a trip until Thursday of that week. On Friday, at dinner, he let her know he was leaving Saturday morning for a trade show related to the gym.

After dinner, Sarah excused the kids and told Alex they needed to talk.

"I have to go to Jugar," he said. "Gotta make sure Javier has everything he needs for the weekend."

"This will only take a minute," Sarah said. She turned on the record feature of her iPhone underneath the table. She looked him in the eyes as she spoke, unwavering in her resolve. She practiced what she wanted to say all week and was more than ready to present the words to him.

"Alex, we have been separated for nearly a year. So much has happened in this past year, I can't even keep up with it all. One thing is certain—you and I have a dysfunctional relationship. We don't get along. You keep coming to me for sex—and you hold it over my head for things like grocery money and spending for the kids. It isn't right. We're separated. You shouldn't come anywhere near me."

He narrowed his eyes at her. She kept composure and pressed on. "It is time we take the next steps. You need to move out. I've spoken with a lawyer about beginning divorce procedures. I don't know what you meant the other day when you said you've put plans in place so I won't get any support from you; but I can confidently say there are laws that require you to provide for your kids. I know you'll do right by them."

"I told you, I'm not leaving," Alex said.

"Yes, I know, but according to my attorney, I can request to have you forcibly removed if it seems detrimental to my well-being. Your sexual attacks and constantly showing up in my bedroom are more than adequate circumstances to qualify. I don't want to have to do that. I'd rather you go peacefully."

The silence that followed made her tingle. She pressed her nails into the palms of her hands to remain calm. Finally, he spoke.

"So who did you really meet with last weekend?" he asked. "Because I am guessing it isn't the girl from Nationals, Stephanie, you told me you were going to visit."

"Doesn't matter who I met. This has nothing to do with that. It is time to move forward. I've got the whole Ricky/Gabe thing behind me. I feel recovered from the shock of the horrors of last year. It's time. I can't imagine you're very happy here, either."

He stood up. "Don't tell me what I am." He left.

She sighed to herself. "That went well."

Alex left for his trip without another word to Sarah. Relieved to have the weekend to herself, she spent Saturday with the kids. Bowling, pizza, and ice cream left them feeling reconnected and full of life. They watched a pay-per-view movie at home, and Sarah found herself joyfully in bed by ten-thirty. She started reading a new book she downloaded to her iPad when her cell phone rang, showing Alex's number.

"Hello?" she answered.

"What do you think you're doing to me?" Alex said.

"Alex, what do you mean? I'm not doing anything."

"Like hell you're not. You're trying to take away my family."

"No, I'm not. The kids will always be your kids. You know that."

A long period of silence made her wonder if he was still there. Then she heard him breathing.

"I'm standing on the edge of the pier in Atlantic City. I'm going to jump," he said.

"Alex, threatening to kill yourself isn't going to change a damn thing. You know what I'm saying is true. We are over. We have been for months." Sarah felt an odd calm about this. Sadly, she realized, she almost hoped he would jump. It would make things much easier.

"I'll do it, Sarah. I will. Then you can live with the guilt knowing what you drove me to."

She thought about the phone bills she found, about his forcing himself on her on her birthday, and every cruel word he ever said. "Go ahead," she offered. "Do it." She hung up.

The next day she had no word from him, or anyone else. She knew her friend Tracy was at the same trade show and that if anything had happened to Alex, Tracy would have called. She called Dianne.

"Sarah, you cannot let him manipulate you," Dianne assured her. "If he chooses to jump off the pier, or whatever, those are his choices. Not yours to own. He wants you to feel responsible, so he has a sense of control over you."

She resisted the urge to call him. He strolled through the door Sunday evening as if nothing had happened and went directly to his man cave. Monday morning, however, he cornered her in the kitchen.

"You don't even care if I live or die?" he asked.

"You're the father of my kids. Of course I care."

"I can't believe you didn't call to check on me," he said. "I checked on you when you had your breakdown in Los Angeles."

"I knew you were fine," she said.

"You've changed," Alex said. "I want to know why."

"There's nothing to know. I'm tired of everyone pushing me around."

He shook his head and left the house. She didn't see him for the next two days.

Sarah and Christian talked on the phone every couple of days. She didn't feel worried or panicked if she didn't hear from him, and each time they hung up she felt better about herself than she had at the beginning of the call. They planned their next getaway.

"Meet me in Barbados next weekend," Christian said.

"That would be lovely," she said. "Let me make sure my mom can watch the kids and I'll be there."

Barbados was a fairy tale. Christian rented a small house on the beach, and Sarah lost count of the laughs they shared and the number of sweet caresses he gave her as they lay together in the warm breeze. They found a small restaurant owned by a romantic couple in their seventies, where they ate and sat talking for hours.

Leaving Christian at the airport on Monday morning was easier this time—not because she liked him any less, but because she felt they had a connection that was not going to be broken. As she kissed him goodbye, she let her eyes stare for a moment on his lips.

"What are you looking at?" he asked her.

"Your perfect lips," she said, "I want to remember every detail of your face when we're apart."

He smiled at her and she had a flashback to the lips on the man in her dreams. "Is it you?" she wondered.

"What?" he asked.

"Several months ago, I dreamed of kissing a man with flawless lips. I was just wondering if you are that man," she said with a smile.

He hugged her tightly and said, "I love you, Angel."

"I love you too." The words flowed easily from her mouth.

When Sarah arrived in Miami, she checked her cell phone messages and her blood ran cold when she heard what had come through over the weekend:

"Sarah Ruiz, this is Detective Carolyn Lancaster of the Las Vegas Police Department. It is imperative that we speak to you as soon as possible. I'll try calling again on Monday, so if you could please try and make yourself available to talk to me then, we'd appreciate it."

Sarah stared at her phone, wondering what to do. There was no number that came in; it was a blocked call, so she couldn't return it. She wondered how the blocked call came through—after Ricky's last contact she had changed her phone settings to not accept blocked calls at all.

She considered calling Alex but restrained the impulse recognizing that she needed more information. It didn't take long before the detective called back.

"Hello," Sarah answered.

"Sarah Ruiz?" a woman's voice asked.

"Yes."

"This is Detective Lancaster. Las Vegas Police. We have a problem we need to discuss with you."

"Um, sure," Sarah said tentatively. "How can I help?"

"It isn't really your help we need. We need to tell you that there are some serious things going on here that involve you. Do you know a man named Ricky Jameson?"

"Well, I've never met him personally, but I've talked to him on the phone," Sarah said. She had to swallow the bile that was beginning to rise in her throat.

"Ma'am, we know you've done more than talk to him. He has been arrested here in Las Vegas and as we searched his computer and home, we found an unusually high number of pornographic materials that involved you. Are you aware of these items' existence?"

Sarah could barely choke out the word. "Yes."

"Although pornography is not a crime, the things Ricky has been arrested for are crimes. And, they involve some of the materials we found in his home. Until we know the status of your involvement with him, we need to advise you not to leave the country and to avail yourself to our questioning. We may require you to come to Las Vegas for questioning. Do you understand?"

"Not really. What did Ricky do?" Sarah asked in a small voice.

"I can't discuss the details of his arrest with you. All I can say is, don't disappear anywhere, Mrs. Ruiz. We are trying to round up his accomplices and get a clear picture of who is part of his crimes."

"I hear what you're saying," Sarah said, "but I have to tell you, I really don't know anything."

The detective replied, "I hope not ma'am, but we'll see. Maybe you should have someone ready to watch your kids, in case we call you away suddenly."

Sarah's heart was in her sneakers. She would have to tell Alex what was going on. She dialed his phone but had to leave a message. Her hands shook so much she could barely keep a grip on the steering wheel, but she managed to make it home. Lila was in the kitchen peeling vegetables for dinner.

"Lila, have you seen Alex?" Sarah asked.

"Señor Ruiz told me yesterday he was going to another trade show. He left this morning," Lila answered. "Is everything all right?"

Sarah shook her head. "It's always something, Lila. I can hardly keep it all straight."

"You are a strong woman, Señora. Whatever it is, you'll figure it out." Lila smiled at Sarah, who took her by surprise by throwing her arms around Lila's neck and hugging her tightly.

"Thank you, Lila. For everything," Sarah said with a squeeze.

Alex returned her call later that day. Sarah's mind had played tricks on her all afternoon. If the Las Vegas police were involved, it would mean that Alex wasn't Ricky. She couldn't decide which gripped her with more fear: her husband masquerading as another man to blackmail and mentally torment her, or an unknown figure following her moves, fixated on making her life a living hell. Was there a lesser of those two evils?

"I received a call from a detective with the Las Vegas Police Department. She said that Ricky has been arrested and they found my pictures and audio sex files at his home. I don't know what he was arrested for, but they are investigating me. They said I can't leave the country and might be needed for questioning. What the hell should I do?"

"Just leave it to me," he said. "I'll look into this."

"Alex, what if Ricky has implicated me in something illegal? I can't go to jail for that asshole."

"You won't have to. I'll get to the bottom of it." Alex hung up.

Sarah looked out over the pool as she sat in her favorite chair, thinking about what could be happening to Ricky. She wished the detective had given her more information. She looked up the Las Vegas Metropolitan Police website. There were eight command centers listed. She chose the downtown location to call first.

"Officer Parkes, badge 777 speaking, how can I direct your call?" a woman answered the phone.

"Hi, I had a call from Detective Lancaster today and I need to speak with her again. I'm not sure if this is the police station she works from, but I was wondering if you could help me?"

"Do you know which department she works in?" the officer asked.

"She called about someone who was arrested for sexual crimes."

"Hm. Well, Detective Lancaster does not operate from this station, but let me put you through to our sex crimes department. David Allen is the detective on duty. Those guys all work together, so it's likely they will know where to find her."

"Thank you," Sarah said. She scribbled *Parkes, badge 777* on a slip of paper.

A moment later a man answered the transferred call. "Detective Allen here."

Sarah told him about Detective Lancaster's call and asked if he could help her locate the detective. He took down all of the information and said he would call Sarah back.

"If she calls you back, ask her for her badge number. That will help tremendously," Detective Allen said. "In the meantime, I will do some looking into this for you."

She didn't hear from the LVPD or from Alex the rest of that day. The next morning, however, Alex sent her a text message.

Alex: I got a hold of the detective. She is going to call me back later.
Sarah: I think you should ask for her badge number when she calls.
Alex: If she calls you, just be cooperative. Don't want to piss them off.

Sarah began to type that she had contacted the police department herself as well, but stopped, instead deciding to hold onto that information. Something felt off, and she couldn't place what.

Detective Lancaster did call Sarah back later that day.

"Mrs. Ruiz, Detective Lancaster here."

"Hello," Sarah said.

"Mrs. Ruiz, did you ever have physical contact with Ricky Jameson?"

"Do you mean, have I met him face to face? That answer is no," Sarah said.

"So you never actually had sexual intercourse with Ricky Jameson," the detective asked clearly.

"No, ma'am, I haven't," Sarah answered. "I should tell you though, Ricky blackmailed me for weeks."

"Blackmail? Interesting," Detective Lancaster said. "And what did he blackmail you with?"

"He had photos and information on me that would ruin not only my life, but the lives of close friends," Sarah said, choking back a sob, "and he said if I didn't let him listen while I had sex he would send the photos to my husband and to my friend's husband."

"So you did what he asked?" the detective asked her. Sarah's intuition gave her a kick in the pants.

"Um, detective, before I forget, what is your badge number?" Sarah asked.

"Four-one-four-six," Detective Lancaster answered. "Why?"

"Thank you," Sarah said, ignoring the *why* question. "Look, I have to go pick my son up from school. They just called that he is sick. Can I give you a call back?"

"I'll call you back, Mrs. Ruiz," Detective Lancaster said. "But remember, you need to take our calls."

"OK, thanks." Sarah hung up. She immediately dialed Detective Allen, who took her call.

"There are a few things I see wrong with this," Detective Allen said after Sarah conveyed the recent call from Detective Lancaster. "I have to tell you, red lights went off for me the other day when I heard your story. I wanted to do some research before saying anything. There is not a Ricky Jameson or Detective Lancaster in the LVPD system. You need to understand, we would never discuss something like that with you over the phone. If you were being considered as a suspect in a crime, we wouldn't give you the heads-up. We would simply conduct our investigation."

"So what are you saying?" Sarah asked.

"I'm saying someone is impersonating a detective to frighten you. Badge number four-one-four-six belongs to a desk officer who answers the main phone line at our South Central Command Center, and I can assure you he has nothing to do with any sex crimes case."

"I'll be damned," Sarah said.

"Impersonating an officer is a crime. She is imposing fake authority to get you to divulge information and who knows what other motive she has. You need to be careful. I would contact your local police in Miami and advise them of your situation," Detective Allen warned her. "And don't, under any circumstance, agree to meet with whoever this is. If someone shows up at your door, call your local police and ask them to dispatch someone to your home. Do you understand?"

"Yes, sir. Wow, I am partly relieved, but also a bit scared."

"You might have reason to be. Promise you'll contact your local police," he said.

"I will," Sarah said.

Sarah's wheels were turning. *What was Ricky doing now?* She noticed the slip of paper on which she'd written *Parkes, badge 777* the day before. Something wasn't right. Then it clicked. She didn't tell Alex the detective's name. There was no way he could have found her.

She heard Dianne's words ring around her mind. *He needs to control you.*

"I went running right to him for help," she realized. "Again."

She began to dial his number. It rang once, then she hung up. *Do I tell him I know?* she wondered. Part of her said no. The other part wanted to punch his smug face in. Her phone rang back. Alex's number.

"Hello," she said.

"You called?"

"Have you heard anything else from the detective?" she asked him.

"She said the same thing I'm sure she told you. That they are investigating his case and because of all of your photos and calls they need to know what you've done, too."

"Did she tell you what they are charging him with?"

"They said he raped someone," Alex said, "and while investigating the rape they came across a prostitution scam and some other things."

"You're kidding." She feigned shock.

"Can you believe it? I'm sure it'll all be all right for you. We need to ride this out."

"Thank you for your help," Sarah said dryly.

"Good thing I know people. Without me, you'd probably be behind bars," Alex said before he hung up.

She sat and shook her head. *Unbelievable.* It was almost laughable. Almost. If he was Ricky, which she was nearly one hundred percent sure now that he was, he was going through a lot of trouble to get her to depend on him. How much farther would he go? Thinking about what he put her through angered her.

Her phone rang again. It was a blocked call. She could only imagine it was from whoever Alex hired to play his game. Her blood suddenly boiled hot for revenge.

"Yes?" she said into the phone.

"Mrs. Ruiz, Detective Lancaster here. Do you have time to talk now? You know how important it is to be available to us, don't you?"

"Detective, I contacted the Las Vegas Police. They advised me not to talk on the telephone any more about this. Hopefully you understand, I've been through a lot over the past few months and have had several people pretend to be someone who they aren't over the phone. You are welcome to come here and I'll have someone from the Miami police department here as well, but I am finished talking on the phone to you. Goodbye." She hung up smiling. *Damn that felt good.*

The air surrounding Alex was heavy when he got home. The frustration that surrounded him was so thick Sarah thought she could reach out and touch it. She figured it was because his latest scam was up, but she didn't say a word. Sensing the heaviness in the air, the kids ate their dinners quickly and scurried off to the safety of their rooms.

Sarah did the same, but Alex barged into her bedroom anyway.

"I know you've gone away with someone," he said.

"We're separated. I can see whomever I want," Sarah said.

"Does Christian know you pimped yourself out for a cover shoot with a magazine?"

"Excuse me?" Sarah said. She picked up a vase and held it over her head. "Go ahead, say that again."

"You don't scare me," Alex said. "I know everything. How you met him in Vegas, your weekends away. I know it all. Maybe he'd like to know the side of you he doesn't get to see."

"Stay away from him," Sarah warned. "He's more of a man than you'll ever be. He's good and kind and he doesn't hide behind false identities to get people to do what he wants."

"What do you mean by that?" Alex asked.

"Just leave him alone," Sarah said, "or I'll fucking kill you. How did you find out who he was? Still bugging my phone?"

"If I say 'yes' will you run out and get another phone again?" he said, laughing. "I'm one step ahead of you, Sarah. I called Jenny and asked her who you met in Las Vegas. She told me everything. In exchange, I treated her to some information she didn't know, either."

"What do you mean?" Sarah asked, her eyes wide with fearful anticipation of what he was going to say next.

"I mean, I told her you had sex with her husband," Alex said, pleased with himself.

The vase released from Sarah's hands and smashed into the wall next to where Alex stood laughing.

"You bastard! How did you know that? I only told Ricky. You *are* him. I knew it!" she screamed.

"Me? Ricky? I don't think so," Alex said. "The recording of you telling him was in the information he sent."

"Then you know what happened. It wasn't like I was a willing participant," Sarah said.

"Ah, but I can't really know that, now can I?" Alex said. "Jenny was quite upset."

Sarah picked up the alarm clock from her nightstand and chucked it at Alex. He turned, and it hit him on his side. She punched some numbers on her phone.

"Officer, my ex-husband is in my bedroom threatening to attack me. Can you send a car over to one-two-seven-seven-one Mayfield Drive?

"You bitch," he said. "This isn't over." He left her room and left the house.

THIRTY

Sarah called her mom. Through desperate sobs she managed to communicate the parts of the story that mattered. Her mom was there within the hour. In that time, Sarah's phone had rang twice—both times Jenny's number. Sarah didn't answer the calls.

Sarah's mom already knew much of what had gone on, but Sarah hadn't yet had time to tell her about the Las Vegas Police impersonation. Her mom was furious.

When Jenny's number showed up again, Sarah's mom answered.

"Hello," she said.

"Sarah?" Jenny asked.

"No, Jenny, this is Kimberly, Sarah's mom," Kimberly said.

"Oh, can I talk to Sarah, please?" Jenny asked.

"I'm sorry, darlin'. Sarah is not feeling well right now."

"It's very important."

Kimberly looked at Sarah, who shook her head. "No, Jenny. Sarah is not going to come to the phone right now." She hung up.

Sarah sobbed into her pillow for the next half hour. Her phone rang again. Kimberly looked at it. "Christian calling."

Sarah took the call. "Hello?" She tried to sound normal.

"Angel, what's going on?" Christian said.

"What do you mean?" she asked.

"I got the weirdest call from Jenny. She said you slept with her husband and now you won't talk to her. She asked if I could make you talk to her."

"She told you *what*?" Sarah screamed into the phone. "That bitch. That's not what happened. Last summer her husband raped me. Alex found out about it and called and told her lies."

"Calm down, Sarah," Christian's voice was gentle. "Whatever happened, you need to talk to her and explain. Just make it right."

Sarah lowered her voice, "Christian, it wasn't like that. How do you tell someone that her husband is a horrible person?"

"I know, Angel," he said, "but you have to face her sometime. Get it over with. I'm so sorry that happened to you. I'm not going anywhere though, OK? The week after next we're still going to meet in New Orleans, right?"

"Definitely," Sarah said. "I'll call her."

Jenny came over and they sat out back by the pool. For a long time, neither woman spoke. Sarah knew she had to go first.

"I'm sorry," Sarah said. "I should have told you sooner, but I didn't know how."

"You slept with Ty?" Jenny said.

"It wasn't like that," Sarah said. "It happened that night you went back to the room and I texted you to come get your husband. He was all over me, Jenny. I tried to push him away. I told him to go find you. Then he gave me this drink and it was as if I had no control over my arms and legs. He took me to my room, he used my key to get me in there, and I can't even recall what happened."

"Are you saying it's his fault?" Jenny asked with more than a hint of incredulity.

"Jenny, I couldn't get him off of me. You've told me before Ty can be very forceful at times. Surely you know what I'm talking about."

Jenny shook her head and looked off into the night sky.

Sarah continued, "*And* you told me to give him a blow job. That wasn't exactly helpful or respectful."

Jenny looked back at Sarah. "So now it's *my* fault?"

Sarah said, "I don't know what went wrong that night, but you have to know that I did not want that to happen. I didn't know how to tell you. I couldn't."

Jenny stood. "Well, now I know." She left.

Sarah sent Christian a text message.

Sarah: I talked to her. She's furious, but at least I did it.
Christian: Good girl. I'll call you in the morning. Get some rest.

Sarah figured Alex wouldn't come home that night, and he didn't. Her mom slept over and helped Sarah get the kids to school. While they sipped their morning coffee, Sarah's phone rang. It was Christian.

"Hello?" Sarah answered.

"Sarah, your ex just called me," he said.

"What?" Sarah couldn't believe what she was hearing.

"Not my cell phone number, either. He called my office. He spoke to my secretary. She put him through to me. He asked how I liked fucking his wife. He told me your relationship isn't over."

"Oh, no," she said. "Christian, I'm so sorry."

"Sarah, this is my business. He asked if my clients would like to know what kind of man I am. I can't have him threatening to call my clients. This is my *business.*"

Sarah felt panic. She had no idea what to do. She knew Alex would contact his clients without a moment's hesitation. She didn't want to lose Christian.

"Christian, let me talk to him. I'm so sorry," she said.

"Please do. Call me later."

"I will. I promise I'll take care of it," she said, knowing full well she was once again unable to control what Alex did.

Alex didn't answer when she called him. Later that day, Christian didn't answer his phone, either. Sarah sent each of them a text message, stating she had to talk right away. Her phone was silent. No incoming messages the next day, either. Her brain wouldn't shut off, and she considered taking a flight to L.A. to see Christian face to face. She felt desperate for connection with him.

She dialed Christian's number the minute she woke up the next morning.

"Hello?" he answered.

"Oh thank God," Sarah said. "How are you? Did you get my texts and my messages?"

"Sarah, something's happened." Christian's voice was weak. Shaky.

"What is it?" The chill in Sarah's bones forewarned of something terrible.

"My brother was killed in a car accident yesterday morning. A drunk driver ran him off the road." He wept as he said it.

"Oh, sweetheart, I'm so sorry," Sarah said. "Want me to come there? I can be on the next plane."

"I'll let you know. I've got all kinds of family coming in and stuff. I'll talk to you later." He hung up before she could say goodbye.

Sarah's hands began to shake again, as they did the night she broke down in Los Angeles. She felt she was about to lose it. She called Dianne.

"I need you," Sarah said.

"Can you drive?" Dianne asked.

"No."

"I'll be right there."

Sarah was sitting on the floor of her kitchen when Dianne arrived. Knees tucked into her chest, arms folded protectively around them, gently rocking back and forth. Kimberly sat next to her and rubbed her back.

Dianne sat in front of Sarah and placed her hands on Sarah's arms. Kimberly told Dianne what had gone on the past seventy-two hours, and even Dianne's eyes got moist.

"Sarah, will you let me contact the police and begin the process to have him forcibly removed from here? When a couple is separated, one spouse does not have the right to interfere with the other spouse carrying on life. He crossed the line of interfering long ago and is downright destructive. You have to do something."

Sarah looked at her mom, who said, "She's right, honey. It's time."

"What do I do?"

At that moment, Alex burst into the house. He took one look at the three women on the kitchen floor and laughed.

"What's going on here? A Tupperware party?"

Dianne stood. "My name is Dianne Murray. I am a psychologist who has been working with Sarah to help her over the traumatic events that have happened over the past few months. You must be Alex."

He looked away. "Yeah. What's the matter with her?" He nodded his head in Sarah's direction.

Sarah unleashed on him. "Christian's brother was killed in an accident yesterday. I don't suppose you know anything about that, do you?"

"That's terrible," Alex said. "We should send a card. Or flowers."

Dianne said, "Alex, you and Sarah are separated. You shouldn't do anything except allow her to live her life peacefully."

Alex looked at Dianne with hatred. "So you're the one trying to get me out of here?"

Sarah found her strength and stood. "No, Alex, it's my decision. I've filed a restraining order on you and will have you forcibly removed by the Sheriff's office if you are not out of here by six p.m. today. Christian filed a restraining order, too. You are not to have any contact with me or with Christian. You may not call his office or harass him in any way shape or form or you will be brought up on charges." She was bluffing but hoped he wouldn't call her on it. Alex feared the police, and she didn't think he'd take the chance that she was telling the truth.

Alex's eyes traveled back and forth between Sarah and Dianne three times before he said, "I'll go, but this is far from over. You can't keep me from my kids and my house."

He went upstairs. Dianne hugged Sarah. "Well done. Now, let's get you down to the police station to file that report. When your friend gets past the next couple of days, have him file a restraining order, too."

"I will," Sarah said.

Alex packed a bag and left the house. Sarah sent Christian a text message to let him know she was thinking about him. The next two days went by with no word or contact from either Alex or Christian.

The restraining order prohibited Alex from ever coming into Sarah's bedroom. He was allowed in the house, as long as it was to visit with the kids, and he had two weeks to move his things from the house and establish residency somewhere else. When she got word from the Sheriff that the restraining order was delivered to Alex at the club, Sarah felt the relief in her shoulders and her lower back. Finally.

THIRTY-ONE

Days continued to tick by with dead air from Christian, and Sarah was beside herself throughout the day. She was at the point where she texted him every four hours, pleading with him for a sentence, a word, *any*thing to let her know he was out there. The void was unbearable.

The weekend of their New Orleans trip came and went. She spent the weekend drinking wine, in her bedroom, and watching chick flicks on Lifetime. Finally, on the Tuesday after they were supposed to have been away together, she received a phone call. She was sitting on the weight bench in her gym, having finished up with a client, when she saw his number come in.

"Hello?" her voice shook as she answered.

"Hey, how are you doing?" he asked.

"I'm awful," she said, unable to control the emotion. "Where have you been?"

"I'm sorry. Things have not been good around here, you know?"

"Because of your brother?" she asked.

"There was that. Last week was a nightmare. My wife and I are having problems with custody over the girls," he said.

"I thought you were divorced," Sarah said. "Isn't that all settled?"

"It is and it isn't. Custody has been an ongoing problem, and I need to be very careful that I don't run into any issues. I'm trying not to lose my kids. You can understand that, right?"

"Your voice sounds different," she said. "What's going on?"

"I wrote you a long e-mail, explaining everything. I'm going to send it to you. Read it over and we can talk about it later."

"OK," she said, feeling anything but OK.

"I'll talk to you later. Bye, Angel." He hung up.

She took her iPad into the house and curled up on the couch. She stared at it, waiting for the message to arrive in her inbox. Finally, it appeared. When she saw the subject of the e-mail, she didn't want to go any further. It simply said, *Good-Bye.* She forced herself to read on.

Dear Sarah:

The last couple of weeks have been really hard and I am going to try and explain why. When I first met you, I thought you were a single woman, free from any ties. I knew you had children, but I didn't realize your husband was still so closely in the picture.

I'm going through my own issues here at home. Over the last while my wife and I have been trying to find a way to make things work for the girls' sake. I'm not ready to throw in the towel and give up. This is what I would encourage to you, too.

You have a chance to make things work with your husband, so you should take that chance while it is there. Your kids deserve two parents to be together. I'm not prepared at this time in my life to have someone else involved in raising my kids and you shouldn't be either.

Just kiss and hug him in front of your kids and you'll see their faces light up. That will be the motivation you need.

It's not healthy for me to be in an outside relationship with you right now. The past weeks haven't been reality. You and I have different realities and it is time to wake up. You alone hold the keys to making your life there work. I know you'll do the right thing. Please don't contact me again after this. No more texts, emails, or phone calls. It is time for us both to move on. I will always be happy that our paths have crossed.

- C

Sarah couldn't speak. She couldn't breathe. She couldn't blink. Any movement at all would indicate she was alive and, at the moment, she didn't want to be. She read the e-mail again. Then again. None of it made sense.

She had confided to him the degrading way Alex acted, not only toward her, but toward all women. Christian had been disgusted at Alex's sexually twisted fantasies. How could he suggest she stay with such a monster? The only person who thought Sarah should stay with Alex was... *Alex.*

Her eyes widened in horror. *He got to him.*

In a frenzy, she typed an e-mail to Christian:

Christian,

These words don't sound like you at all. Either you have lied to me from the beginning or someone else has convinced you to send this. You know the pain I've been through here and you know how terrible my life here has become. I know you wouldn't suggest, even for a minute, that I stay with Alex.

If you and your wife are truly trying to work things out, then call it like it is. But don't suggest you have some special insight that I should remain with my ex. He is not my husband. He is my ex. He will never be my husband again. My children would think I was crazy if I hugged or kissed him. They have seen him spit in my face and have seen him hit me. It is not a healthy environment.

I don't know what this is about, but don't worry. I won't bother you anymore. I'm tired of people pushing me around and I suggest you don't let anyone push you around either. It isn't a fun way to live your life. I bet money that Alex is behind this. In the end, the truth always comes out. I truly believe our paths will cross again, because it feels like our destinies are intertwined. Until then, take care of yourself.

- S

After she sent the message, for the thousandth time in the past year, she cried. Another love lost to Alex. She was sure he played a hand in Christian's goodbye. With the impeccable timing he always has, Alex came into the house at that moment with Eric and Antonio, dropping them off after spending some time at the gym lifting weights.

Alex looked at her crying on the couch, smiled, and left.

"What's wrong, Mom?" Eric asked. He sat next to her on the couch. She closed her laptop and put her arm around him.

"Eric, do you think you can watch the rest of the kids for a while? I have to go run some errands."

"Of course. Is Lila here?"

"Yes. She'll take care of dinner. I just need you to help keep the peace and don't go anywhere till I get back."

"No problem, Mom. I love you," Eric said, hugging his Mom tightly.

"Thanks, buddy. You're a good kid," she said, squeezing him back.

Sarah called Tanya after Eric left the room.

"Wanted you to know, I'm going back over to Jugar and breaking into his office. I need to see what else he has in there. He fucked with Christian, and now Christian ended things. I'd love to get that gun and shoot him, but I'll settle for something I can maybe take to the cops. I need him out of my life for good."

"You want company?" Tanya asked.

"That's why I'm calling," Sarah said. "You in?"

"I'll pick you up in ten. We'll take my car."

Sarah spewed every venomous thing she had built up inside of her to Tanya while they sped to Jugar.

"I know you want to kill him, but be very careful, Sarah. Remember, he is still certifiably insane. He wouldn't hesitate to hurt you," Tanya warned. "What if he's there?"

"He shouldn't be. He left the house after working out at the gym with the boys. My guess is he went to his condo to shower and eat and won't hit the clubs till later. I don't give a shit if Javier or anyone sees me. I'm done with the crap."

They pulled up at Jugar. Sarah used her key to unlock the door. The alarm wasn't set, and she realized Javier's office door was open. They walked down the hall and she poked her head into Javier's as they went past.

"Hi, Javier," Sarah said casually.

"Hola, Sarah," Javier said. "Cómo estás?"

"Muy bien. Listen, I need to get some of my stuff from Alex's office. I'll only be a couple of minutes."

"Bueno," Javier said with a wave.

Sarah went right to the safe and opened it. It had obviously been rearranged since the last time they were there. The cash bundles now totaled forty-five thousand dollars, and many of the documents and phone bills were missing.

"Tanya, the phone bills are gone," Sarah said.

"Oh, really? That's weird," Tanya said. "So what's he got in there?"

Sarah pulled out an envelope. It was addressed to Alex at the club. Inside were photos of her and Christian in Barbados. Walking hand in hand on the beach. Sitting in the restaurant, laughing with the owners. Going into their beach house.

She handed them to Tanya.

"Woah. This is intense. Who the hell takes hard-copy pictures anymore?" Tanya asked.

"He probably didn't want electronic records of them," Sarah said. "I can't believe this."

She tucked the pictures into her purse. The other item of interest in the safe was a diagram of The Port of Miami's Cargo Shipping Terminals. Some of the bays were circled with dates and times handwritten on the page. Sarah took a picture of it with her camera.

"What do you think he is tracking at the docks?" Sarah asked Tanya.

"Maybe he's smuggling stuff," Tanya replied. "Secret shit."

"You think? Hey look, this one that's circled has today's date on it and five forty-five p.m. That's in forty-five minutes. We should see what's happening." She took the map with them. It was much easier to see than the photo on her phone.

Sarah pulled open the desk drawer again which contained the same items as before, with one new addition: A small black box that had a headphone plugged into it. The box had a dial and a couple of switches on it. TVC-919 was imprinted on the side. It was a voice changer.

She shook her head and closed the drawer.

"Let's go," Tanya said.

They parked the car and walked through the shipping yard, carefully watching for signs of Alex. As they neared the terminal that was highlighted on the page, strong arms suddenly grabbed them from behind. Before they could scream, they were face to face with two large men who each had a hand clamped over their mouths.

The men were wearing FBI jackets.

"I'm going to remove my hand," said the man holding Sarah, whose jacket said *Lucas*. "Don't scream. We're FBI."

The girls nodded, and the men removed their hands.

"Who are you and why are you here?" the other man asked. His jacket had the name *Frank* on it.

"I'm Sarah. I found this map in my husband's office. I have suspected that he is up to something, and when I saw this date and time with this location circled, my friend and I came here to see what he is up to. He's a bastard of a guy and I have five kids to care for at home."

The two FBI agents looked at one another. "Sarah Ruiz?" Lucas said.

Sarah nodded.

"Look, Sarah, your husband is into some serious shit here. This is no place for you. We are going to bring him down tonight, and we can't have you interfere."

Sarah's eyes widened. "No problem. You can have him. I have nothing to do with his shit."

"We know," Lucas said. "We also know about your restraining order. It would probably be best for you to get out of here. Now."

"Do you want this?" Sarah asked, handing him the shipping docs diagram. Frank took it and as he began to fold it, Sarah noticed an e-mail address scribbled on the back of the page.

"Wait," she said. She took the paper from him and examined it. It was the same Gmail address that came from the e-mail she originally received from Marion, Alex's cousin. She had completely forgotten until that moment that it was Marion's e-mail that first introduced Gabe into her life. Sarah bit her lip and handed the paper back to the agent.

"Walk out that way," he said, pointing, "and just go. You won't be seeing him for a long time after tonight. After the information we found out about him, I am guessing you won't mind that too much."

Sarah laughed nervously. "Not at all."

She and Tanya walked quickly back to the car. Tanya was about to start it up when Sarah said, "No, wait. Let's sit here for a minute and see what happens."

They waited thirty minutes. Nothing. Sarah got out of the car to see if she could hear anything, and at that very second, two dozen FBI agents came out from inside the shipyard, leading eight handcuffed men. Sarah picked Alex out of the crowd immediately. Unfortunately, he looked her way at the same moment.

Their eyes met. Even at the distance that separated them, she could see shock in his black, hollow gaze.

She got back in the car. "Quick, go back to Jugar," she told Tanya.

"The cash?" Tanya asked. Sarah nodded.

Sarah and her mom stayed up late into the night trying to determine what Sarah should do. There was no phone call, no contact at all from Alex. Sarah watched the news, looking for word of a bust at the shipyards, but there was nothing. She decided not to tell the children anything until she knew what to tell them.

A week went by. Dianne finally suggested she call the local FBI office and ask them what was happening.

"My name is Sarah Ruiz. I know my husband was arrested last week and I was wondering if I could talk to Agent Lucas or Frank." The operator passed the call.

"Frank here," he said.

"Agent Frank, this is Sarah Ruiz," she began, "remember we met last week at the shipyard when you arrested my ex husband, Alex?"

"Yes, ma'am," he said. "What can I do for you?"

"Well, I'm wondering, what do I do now?" she asked. "I've had no word from him, I don't know where he is or what's going on. If I hadn't been there I wouldn't even know anything. No one has called me."

"There's nothing to tell. We're holding him. He does have an attorney. Serious charges are pending," Agent Frank said. "You have no involvement in any of this. We had checked you out thoroughly before the arrest. You can go about your life, Sarah. We aren't freezing your personal bank accounts or anything at this point, so I would suggest you do what you have to do to establish yourself."

"What happens to his businesses?" she asked.

"That's a different story," Agent Frank said. "He doesn't have your name on anything except the gym and the apartment building. Those businesses are clean from this nonsense. If he is incarcerated, you gain control over what happens to the gym and the building and can do what you please."

"Will he be let out on bail?" she asked.

"He is being held without bail until the judge sees him next week," Agent Frank said.

"Oh," Sarah said. "Thank you."

She hung up the phone feeling a combination of nervous and ecstatic. *He might be gone for good.* Her mom had an excellent idea.

"Why don't you get away for a couple of weeks? Just you. Relax, sit on a beach, read a book—heck, you could write a book about all of this," Kimberly said. "I'll watch the kids, and maybe after you've had some time to yourself we'll come out and join you."

"Oh, Mom, I love that idea," Sarah said, hugging Kimberly, "I know just where I'll go."

THIRTY-TWO

Christian arrived at the office earlier than usual. He had a meeting with a young golf protégé and wanted to go over the final details of the contract alone, before everyone else arrived. He opened his e-mail and forgot all about his golfer when he saw the note from Sarah.

Christian ~

I have spent the past week on my own, in a place you and I both fell in love with. I have done a lot of soul-searching. I've replayed the events of the last year of my life over and over, analyzing the details and trying to discern the lessons I needed to learn so I can move into this next phase of my life stronger.

One thing I am certain is that your good-bye was not from your heart. Those words were not yours. I would like to extend one more chance for the happiness you and I were destined to have. We almost made it to that next level. I think "almost" love hurts even more than love that's come and gone.

If you want the chance for the almost love we created, meet me next Saturday at 6:00 pm. I'll be in a little restaurant, talking with an elderly couple, at our table, waiting for you. I'm sure you'll recognize me. I'll have my hair in a pony tail and will be wearing my white sundress.

I'll be counting the minutes, hoping to see your dimples one more time.

Love, Sarah

Christian leaned back in his chair, considering the words. His Google Alerts for the day also arrived in his inbox. He had set an alert to catch any web-based information that had Alex Ruiz's name in it. An article from *The New York Times* gave him pause.

Miami, FL—Alex Ruiz, who was arrested last month by the FBI in Miami on charges of human and gun trafficking, was released from federal custody today. A judge in Miami ruled that one of the FBI's wire taps be thrown out of evidence, contaminating further evidence that was keeping Ruiz in custody.

FBI Agent Tom Lucas said, "This is but a small setback in this case. We do have enough evidence to put Ruiz away for a long time and will refile our charges in the near future."

Ruiz declined to comment.

Christian buzzed his secretary on his way out the door. "Krystina, cancel my appointments today. I have had an emergency come up."

THIRTY-THREE

5:45 p.m. Saturday. Barbados. Sarah's pulse raced as she waited in the cozy beachfront restaurant. She watched the sweat drip from her glass of iced tea, her mind scripting her hello to the man she loved. She traced a heart on the side of her glass. The anticipation of seeing Christian made her want to jump out of her skin. She had received a reply to the e-mail she sent to him, but she was puzzled because the return message had no text in it. It was as if Christian hit "reply" and "send" all together. *Was that a code? Did he want me to know he had read it and was unable to say more? Or was it accidental?* The possibilities and mystery surrounding his empty e-mail made her mind swim. She desperately wanted to see him and ached to know what he thought.

For the hundredth time Sarah imagined his gorgeous face walking through the door, smiling at her. The thought that his perfect lips might soon once again be pressed to her own made her tingle with longing.

"Not here yet?" Greta, one of the owners, said to her.

Sarah shook her head. "Not yet, but I am hopeful that he will be."

"I learned a long time ago that true love cannot be stopped. It has a destiny all its own, and when two people are meant to have a future together, nothing will stand in the way. It is uncontrollable." Greta picked up Sarah's glass, wrecking the heart she drew, and poured more tea into it from a plastic pitcher. She set it down, smiled at Sarah, and walked away.

"Uncontrollable," Sarah said aloud. She liked that thought. She caught the reflection of a man's face in the glass window of the restaurant. The intake of her own breath was so loud she jumped, and time stopped around her. It wasn't her sweet Christian entering the restaurant. It was Alex.

CPSIA information can be obtained at www.ICGtesting.com
Printed in the USA
LVOW060727290313

326560LV00007B/58/P